Life is a Promise

By Anne Marshall Bunney

First Edition

**Biographical Publishing Company
Prospect, Connecticut**

Life is a Promise
First Edition

Published by:

**Biographical Publishing Company
35 Clark Hill Road
Prospect, CT 06712-1011**
Phone: 203-758-3661 Fax: 208-247-1493
e-mail: biopub@aol.com

All rights reserved. No part of this book may be reproduced or transmitted in any form or by any means, electronic or mechanical, including photocopying, recording, or by any information storage or retrieval system without the written permission of the author, except for the inclusion of brief quotations in a review.

Copyright © 2001 by Anne Marshall Bunney
First Printing 2001

PRINTED IN THE UNITED STATES OF AMERICA

Publisher's Cataloging-in-Publication Data

Bunney, Anne Marshall,
 Life is a Promise / by Anne Marshall Bunney.-- 1st ed.
    p. cm.
 ISBN 1-929882-23-8
  1. Bunney, Anne Marshall,-- Fiction. 2. Life in Canada. 3. Life in United States (California). 4. Psychology. 5. Love. 6. Religion. 7.Politics.
  I. Title.
  Dewy Decimal classification: 813
  Library of Congress Control Number: 2001097844

This book is dedicated to my sons

Bill and Jim

with love, respect and gratitude.

Table of Contents

Preface		5
One	Childhood	7
Two	Adolescence	48
Three	Glimmer of success . . . money, values and young love	74
Four	Love, agony, loss and tears	95
Five	Romantic love and disillusionment	110
Six	Joy, illusions, betrayal and death	125
Seven	Choosing life, reflections on yesterday, today and tomorrow	149
Eight	Embracing the essence of life	157
Nine	New beginnings . . . destiny and a lover's call	169
Ten	We are coming to America	176
Eleven	Spiritual soulmates, courage and the power of love	182
Twelve	Madness, chaos . . . survival	202
Thirteen	Mirrors of our souls . . . clients in treatment	217
Fourteen	Struggling with devastating sorrow and tragedy	232
Fifteen	More trauma . . . family changes	248
Sixteen	The lonely heart	256
Seventeen	New song of love and happiness . . . and tears	262
Eighteen	Memories and a miracle	280
Nineteen	Thoughts of life . . . hopes for the future	285
Epilogue		297
Bibliography		298

PREFACE

The walrus said "the time has come to speak of many things." It is also time for me to speak. I will do so by recounting a woman's life that is filled with moments of pure happiness, incredible sorrow and the courageous struggle to triumph when her loving spirit is set free to heal her soul. Her life's journey commences in Canada and continues in the United States.

There are many exceptional self-help books written by professional writers. While I hope my literary efforts may help others, it is not my intent to provide specific guidelines or recommendations on how someone should live their life. Instead, I hope that by sharing this woman's experiences, perceptions, reactions, thoughts and feelings that have created the mosaic of her life, I may provide some comfort and hope to others.

Characters, situations and philosophies are either the product of the author's imagination or, if real, have been used fictitiously without any intent to describe or portray their actual conduct. Any resemblance to actual events or persons, living or dead, is entirely coincidental.

A loving force compels me to write about the authentic power within us all that transcends traumas, hardships and pain. The shaping of whom we are has been influenced by our life's experiences. In his book "Seat of the Soul " Gary Zukow states "The lifetime of your personality is one of a myriad of experiences of your soul." A truth well spoken. I believe perhaps the authentic power we each possess may also be identified as the soul.

This book is written with much respect and gratitude to my family, friends and all the fellow humans I have met in my lifetime. Many of these people have overcome deep sorrow that brought dissolution to their soul . . . today they are triumphant leading productive, happy lives. Their unfailing courage to be, in spite of the many challenges they faced due to life's events, will hopefully be an inspiration to those who struggle.

The following written by Goethe is quoted by many. I know his words to be true.

> *Until one is committed, there is hesitancy the chance to draw back, always ineffectiveness. Concerning all acts of initiative (and creation), there is one elementary truth the ignorance of which kills countless ideas and splendid plans:*
>
> *That the moment one definitely commits oneself, then Providence moves too.*
>
> *All sorts of things occur to help one that would never otherwise have occurred. A whole stream of events issues from the decision, raising in one's favor all manner of unforeseen incidents and meetings and material assistance, which no man could have dreamed would have come his way.*
>
> *Whatever you can do, or dream you can, begin it. Boldness has genius, power and magic in it. Begin it now.*
>
> Goethe

I thank God for his eternal love as he guides me to live more fully in peace, harmony and joy. I hope you will celebrate with me the power of the loving human spirit.

The luminous journey continues and I reflect upon the words of the Jesuit Paleontologist Teilhard de Chardin "We are one, after all, you and I. Together we suffer, together exist, and forever will recreate each other."

Chapter One

Childhood

The things which the child loves remain in the domain of the heart until old age. The most beautiful thing in life is that our souls remain hovering over the places where we once enjoyed ourselves.

Kahlil Gibran

To what extent are we shaped by genetics, the environment plus our critical period of development that indicates the specific time when an experience or interaction will have the greatest impact on development?

Whispery remembrances of yesteryears.

My memories of childhood at the age of three seem mystical. I am running happily towards my father's outstretched arms. He is smiling and saying "little Anuska . . . come, come." He lifts me way up high. I laugh with sheer delight and so does he. I feel safe. I am very happy. I vividly remember his deep blue eyes. I wonder if maybe someday my brown eyes will turn blue like my Daddy's.

"Let me out, let me out" I scream hysterically among my sobs and tears.

We are at the dentist because my older sister, Maria, who is eleven years old, has been suffering with a bad toothache for several days. Going to the dentist is not a common occurrence in our family since there is little money for such things. My mother is uncomfortable about our visit primarily because she is self conscious about not being able to speak English and she must rely upon my sister to communicate for her. It is fair to say we are all somewhat nervous and anxious.

The three of us wait patiently, not speaking, in the dentist's reception room for my sister's turn to see the dentist. I have no recollection whether it was curiosity or boredom that suddenly prompted my desire to go to the bathroom or if it was indeed a sincere call from nature. Since I am a big girl . . . I was three and a half at the time . . . I well remember telling my mother with much pride I will go by myself. My mother agrees it's all right since the door to the bathroom is off the reception area and visible to her. I am very pleased with myself as I lock the door so no one will come in. My self satisfaction will be short lived.

Several minutes later when I try to open the bathroom door; it won't open. I raise my voice and shout "Mama, mama, the door won't open." My mother calmly tells me "it will open, just unlock the door." I try again. It still doesn't open. I rattle the door knob. It doesn't help. "Mama, mama, help me."

My sister gets involved "just do what you did to lock it but the other way around." I don't understand. I am confused and frightened. My heart is pounding so hard it just may burst. Now I can't see the lock because of the tears in my eyes.

"It won't open." The lock won't move. I hear many voices talking on the other side.

Someone says "the poor little girl is locked in the bathroom . . . how will they get her out of there?"

"Maybe they can open the window and she can crawl out." Don't they realize I can't do that . . . there is no window.

The tears keep rolling down my face. "There's no window, no

window. Please let me out."

The dentist hears the commotion and comes into the vestibule. He is immediately bombarded with inputs from everyone. He confidently assures the people he will solve the problem. He speaks firmly and slowly, a long pause between each word, his mouth close to the door "little girl, just turn the lock; it will open, unless you broke it."

For a few meager moments my childish thoughts stray from being locked in to "what if you broke the lock." I continue sobbing. What if the lock is broken and I broke it. Too quickly reality is back. I'm locked in. My body slides down the door and I sit on the cold tiled floor awaiting my fate.

I hear the dentist finally stating in an irritated voice, the voice adults use when they feel children have been naughty, that he will have to call a locksmith. He says there is no other way to get me out. I am not aware my tears are making small puddles on the tiles where my face is touching them since I am now lying on the floor.

The locksmith has a difficult time opening the door. He concludes the lock is not broken but really jammed. After he succeeds in opening the door and I rush past him to my mother's side, he tells the dentist "The lock must be deficient; there's no way this little girl could have jammed it without there being a problem. I strongly recommend you get a new lock or this may happen again."

Maria translates for my mother what the locksmith is saying. My mother looks relieved when she hears the news but still appears mortified. I can tell by the scowl on Maria's face she is angry at me. "Why did you lock the door?" I ignore Maria and cling to my mother trying to hide my face in the side of her body. I just want to go home.

A lady manages to pat me on the head saying "sweet child, it wasn't your fault" then smiles at Maria gently saying "she's just a little girl, not a big girl like you."

It seems I was locked in the bathroom for about two hours, crying uncontrollably in the beginning graduating to sobbing more softly the rest of my confinement time. I thought no one would ever get me out?

To my relief, I heard my mother say "we are leaving" followed by "we will find a new dentist for Maria." I knew I had embarrassed my mother and Maria. I hoped in time everyone would forget I had done so. In the weeks that followed, Maria did not bring up this incident and I believe the kind lady's remarks had something to do with my reprieve.

This incident seems to have had an indelible impression on me. I more often than not still check to see how a bathroom lock works before I lock the door. Years later, as an adult, I remember being in an airport bathroom when the lock got stuck and wouldn't budge. I became somewhat anxious. Fortunately, it was one of those airport bathroom doors with space beneath it. I crawled out on my hands and knees to the shock of the other people using the facilities. Was I relieved? Very!

Less intense and less abstract is my memory of Miss Cairns, my first grade teacher. She looked like Mrs. Santa Claus with snow white hair and round steel rimmed spectacles perched on the middle of her nose. I was five years old, minus two months when I went into first grade. There were no kindergartens in our neighborhood and most children stayed home until they turned six years old. Since I wished to emulate my older sister, Maria, I desperately wanted to go to school. On the first day of school, my dad brought me to school and convinced Miss Cairns to let me stay for the day. She agreed, believing as my Dad did, I would want to go home after a short period of time.

Months went by before it dawned on Miss Cairns that her star pupil, Anna, was underage. Only then did she reflect upon the circumstances that had brought me to her class. She was very fond of me and always took pride in my achievements. Due to her support and intervention I remained in school to be promoted with honors to grade two.

One day I overheard some of the teachers talking about my family. Though I listened attentively, I didn't understand when they said my father spoke fairly good broken English considering he had no formal training in this country. What did that mean? Everyone who knew my father knew he could fix anything that was broken.

For the first time, I also heard that my parents were immigrants. Miss Cairns asked the other teachers she was talking to "How do these immigrants manage to instill such ambition in their children? Little Anna works so hard and just loves to learn. She is pleased to be in school."

I asked my parents what ambition meant. They didn't know. My father promised to find out though he was sure it was a good thing to have.

I also meant to ask them what it meant to be immigrants but only remembered ambition because I had repeated it over and over again which wasn't easy since that was the day Johnnie decided to chase me all the way home.

Before I proceed with other memories of significant childhood friends, I believe it is important to describe the backdrop of my childhood environment that greatly influenced the shaping of my character.

Most of the homes I remember living in were duplexes made of brick, usually red, that had a wrought iron staircase on the outside. The staircase rails were made of cast iron and were sometimes curved or sometimes linear. All had wooden steps. These staircases were typical for duplex or triplex housing in

Montreal and considered by many as distinctive and endearing Montreal characteristics or features. I do not recall ever living in a triplex though my mother told me I was born on the third floor of a triplex. We had access to backyards, sheds and the back lane that was often a social gathering place for me and my friends.

In the front of our houses, sometimes there were patches of green grass that included dandelions and weeds. Heavy foot traffic helped control the weeds somewhat but it also helped eliminate much of the grass. Some streets had maple trees, oak trees and birch trees. The birch trees often looked too fragile to endure our winter weather. The maple trees were most memorable particularly in the autumn when the leaves turned red, orange, yellow. I would gently collect the leaves and carefully press them into hot wax. I would place them in my school books and on bitter cold winter days they would remind me this season would pass and others would follow before too long.

Our sidewalks were used for hopscotch, skipping and marbles. You were considered fortunate if the sidewalk in front of your home was flat and not misshapen by tree roots. We claimed ownership when that was the case. Not always an easy task. Today, I can still close my eyes and see myself skipping doubles, or playing hopscotch with my friends. I should mention, I grew up not knowing anyone that lived in a single family home until I went to high school where I met students from middle class families.

Even when we were renting, my mother and father spent a lot of time and effort making our home attractive and pleasant to live in. My father always freshly painted our new home after he had patched up any cracks or holes in the plaster walls. Our windows were enhanced with colorful curtains that my mother sewed by hand to hide the usually, worn out, pull-down shades. Our home always had a few plants growing that my mother proudly displayed on shelves my father built for this purpose.

Plants thrived in our home. Over the years, tiny cuttings from peoples gardens blossomed year round.

Red geraniums as big as apples, the smell of herbs wafting through our kitchen and of course, the tiny rubber plant that grew to be a giant created a warm atmosphere wherever we lived. What a conversation piece our rubber plant became! People would ask my mother many questions.
"Do you have a special formula? Some people feed rubber plants milk. Is that your secret?"

"Do you use manure in the earth? Can't smell it if you do."

After many years, my father gave the rubber plant to the local funeral parlor because we no longer had room for it. I recall on a walk with my father we visited our rubber plant. I thought the reception area looked more cheerful because of our plant. From my child's perspective, I was pleased it looked happy and well. My dad made me feel even better about the whole situation when he said "Anuska, our plant is probably cheering people up at a difficult time in their lives. Perhaps they feel less sad when they see it." I believed it was so.

I well remember one of our landlords telling my father he would lower his rent if my father didn't move away. "You are such good tenants I don't want you to leave." My father refused his offer as he had just bought our first home, a duplex.

It was an old house that my father lovingly renovated from top to bottom. It had beautiful embossed tin ceilings throughout and incredible old wood floors that were laboriously refinished and polished by my mother and father. The unique lighting fixtures were polished and repolished until they finally embodied the grace and beauty of each room in the house. Many years later, my father sold our first home at a good profit when he was ready to build a new home.

Our next door neighbors were the Pasquali family. While I had no grandparents, this family had two sets of grandparents along with the couple who had three children, and a daughter who had a baby. I was curious about the Pasquali grandparents who were friendly to our family. What were grandparents like even if they weren't mine? I wanted to know them better. I really liked the one grandfather who had planted grapes that he brought from Italy over an arbor, in front of their house. There was a little bench that he sat on and eventually I often joined him. I liked sitting under the grapes . . . it felt surreal . . . there was no need to talk and we seldom did . . . it also felt cool when it was extremely hot outside.

Our backyard was filled with lush, old trees and bushes and we had a vegetable garden that flourished all summer long. We had an abundant supply of rhubarb, peppers, squash, tomatoes and string beans every year. I truly loved that house and the garden and I was very sad when we moved. I felt our newly built home lacked the traditional beauty and character our very first owned home had not to mention it didn't have the Pasqualis as neighbors. I refrained from mentioning how I felt to my parents knowing both of them had achieved a lifelong goal . . . they now owned a brand-new duplex. The rent from the two upstairs units would help my parents financially for the rest of their lives.

The day we moved in, Mrs. Pasquali . . . we never knew which one . . . there were so many . . . sent Dominic over with some Italian food. A few weeks later my mother sent some Czech food over to their home. As a result, sharing ethnic dishes became a custom that we all enjoyed for many years. I have never tasted better Italian food than that which came from the Pasquali kitchen . . . it was unbelievably delicious.

Occasionally, in the summertime, my father would join the Italian men for a glass of home made wine in the backyard. My father could speak Italian quite well. He learned some of the language due to necessity during the First World War when he was a prisoner in Italy. His knowledge of the Italian language really impressed the Pasquali men.

The first time our family heard loud yelling and what sounded like screaming next door, we became alarmed. Fortunately, it was shortly followed by much laughter and we knew that whatever was going on was all right. Over time, we realized that the Pasquali family were extremely expressive, emotional people. They all spoke in strong, loud voices . . . yelled when they were angry . . . laughed a lot when they were happy . . . and had warm, generous hearts. Gina, their daughter apologized to us more than once for being such noisy neighbors after a particularly boisterous afternoon. We listened to their Italian operas and learned to sing along with them in our own home unbeknownst to them. We felt fortunate to have such wonderful neighbors who enriched our lives. We accepted and enjoyed the Pasquali family as they were . . . delightful and fun-loving.

I would be remiss if I did not mention that the Pasquali family's faith in God and the Roman Catholic Church sustained them through many ordeals. Briefly, we learned about their shame and pain when their daughter Gina had a child out of wedlock. Dominic told us with tears in his eyes that his young son, Anthony, died in a tragic bus accident when he was eighteen years old.

"His spirit is always with us. We do not question God."

Gina told my sister Maria that she knew God had forgiven her. "When God finally forgave me, my family forgave me. My parents love their grandson, Vincent. You know it's really strange. He looks just like Anthony and when he smiles, I see Anthony and remember his smiles."

Our family witnessed and felt the depth of the Pasquali family's true compassion, empathy and love for each other. Though I was only a young child, I somehow knew the Pasquali family's unwavering faith in God, no matter what befell them, was the strong foundation in their lives.

But now I will hark back to some of my earliest memories that are recalled in a home that was filled with boarders from the old country that my sister and I called uncles and aunts.

As previously stated, I never had any grandparents. Perhaps better stated, I never knew any of my grandparents. Most of my biological relatives were living in Czechoslovakia. My mother regularly showed me their pictures, told me their names and how I was related to these people. I listened attentively but for me they were only pictures in an album. The loving, animated look on my mother's face when she spoke of her family in the old country showed me these pictures meant a great deal to her. Perhaps it was fortunate that I understood how hurtful it would be to my mother if I tried to explain why I felt the way I did. I chose to be a silent listener that never betrayed my lukewarm interest in relatives I would never meet.

I was a precocious child who enjoyed the companionship of people. Consequently, early on I shared some of my memorable school experiences with my adopted Canadian uncles and aunts . . . the people I loved. Though people came into our lives for different periods of time, I always felt and knew there was a permanent atmosphere of ongoing loyalty and love that nourished our lives.

I was a fortunate little girl in many ways. How many young girls had two giants in their life? I had Uncle Boris and Uncle Vanja, two brothers from Russia. They towered over everybody, justifiably so, since both of them were six feet three inches tall. They worked in the woods far, far away, somewhere up north, cutting down huge trees, returning to our home every three months with big black beards that they shaved off shortly after their arrival. They had exceptionally white teeth more pronounced when they had their black beards as well as broad, powerful shoulders. Under a thatch of curly black hair, I remember dark brown sparkling eyes that I thought were always smiling at you.

Aunt Sofie told my mother "Your Russian boarders are handsome men and so good natured as well. If they weren't working in the forests all the time, they'd be married by now."

My mother answered Aunt Sofie "Yes, they are handsome . . . and Sofie, they also love children and will be good fathers someday."

I never thought of Uncle Boris and Uncle Vanja as boarders in our home. They behaved like generous, loving uncles to my sister and me. They spent more time with me since I was the youngest and home more often. My parents often affectionately called me Anuska. Before too long, Uncle Boris and Uncle Vanja decided they would too. They always found something to laugh about and made others laugh with them. To my delight and my mother's appreciation, they enjoyed playing games with me for hours on end.

My mother did the laundry for most of our boarders and I know this was one of the most difficult, tiring chores she had to do. It was evident to my Russian uncles, when they were at home, that my mother's labors over her washboard required all the energy she possessed. It was not too long before they laughingly suggested they help her out so they could stay in shape.

At first my mother refused. She was shocked at their suggestion. After all this was woman's work and they were her boarders. A day arrived when my mother was totally exhausted, at which time their jovial persistence prevailed and she allowed them to help her. I still can see my petite mother struggling over the washboard. By the time she was rinsing and wringing out the clothes, there were permanent beads of sweat on her lovely face with a steady flow of perspiration running down her entire body. I cannot forget how red her dainty hands became especially during the winter months when she hung the laundry outside.

My Russian uncles were comfortable helping my mother. They would say "We are strong" while beating their chests playfully. "We will do this laundry quickly. Watch how fast we are." They made it a game.

My mother quickly found the way to reciprocate their generosity was baking a special treat, though she expressed many times it was insufficient thanks for their efforts. She was always grateful for the help they gave her, as was my father who was fully aware how difficult it was for his beloved Helen to do the laundry. "I wish to lower your rent for helping my wife. Some day soon I hope to buy her the machine washer."

Uncle Vanja and Uncle Boris both said in unison "No, No."

Uncle Boris chimed in "Of course not, she rewards us with her special treats. We never get such good food in the bush."

My father was silent. He accepted their gift by shaking hands with both my uncles.

Uncle Boris and Uncle Vanja always seem to notice if we were getting low on certain groceries. They would go for a walk coming back with apples, oranges, bread and milk. When they came to the bottom of the grocery bag they would laugh, look surprised and say "Where did that come from? Candies for Anuska." This was indeed a special treat for me since my parents very seldom bought candies and I understood at an early age the reason why they didn't. Money had to be saved for school clothes and food.

Everyone knew my Russian uncles were exceptionally strong men. They could lift me up with one arm. In spite of their strength and size they were very gentle, kind men. They would wipe away my tears when I bruised my knee singing Russian songs to cheer me up. They told my sister, Maria she would learn to dance when she was discouraged because she didn't know how, but best of all they fixed a robin's broken wing that was lying in our back yard. I can still see Uncle Boris's large hands holding the frightened robin while Uncle Vanja softly speaks to it in a cooing sound. We all cheered when the robin was healed and he flew away. I was always positive he came back to see us every year.

Before my uncles's two weeks in our home was over, and it was nearing time for them to go back in the woods, I knew they would cook a Russian stew. It was now a family tradition. We would have a happy, happy party. We would all sing beautiful songs . . . our family sang Czech. ones, I sang some French ones, my sister sang some English ones and our uncles sang Russian songs. Occasionally we all sang together creating a joyful melody the likes of which I have never heard since and may never hear again. Along with the singing, Uncle Boris played the mandolin and my father played his small accordion. Occasionally Uncle Mike gave a solo performance playing his violin.

While I did not understand all the words in the Russian songs, I could tell my uncles were missing their wonderful Russia and the families they had left behind. Their dark brown eyes sparkled even more because of the nostalgic tears within them. They talked about their dream of going back to Russia someday soon with enough money to build their parents a solid home. They described their life in Russia; how it was much harder than in Canada yet they admitted they missed it anyway.

They came in and out of our lives for about eight years filling our lives with so much joy. Uncle Boris married a Canadian lady and never returned to Russia. Uncle Vanja did return but came back "I missed my brother and it was not the same over there anymore." A generous man, we learned from Uncle Boris that Uncle Vanja left all of his hard earned savings with his parents so they might build the home he had planned for them.

Upon his return from Russia, Uncle Vanja went much further north where he eventually became a partner in a sawmill. He became a very wealthy man that never forgot his humble roots. He valued his family, children and friends and never coveted his wealth. Uncle Vanja was respected by many whose lives he influenced in a positive loving way.

Uncle Boris, the eldest, adored his young brother. He married later in life. Both my Russian uncles had large families. The two brothers remained close friends all the days of their lives.

Our family heard from them sporadically and I was always delighted when they included a special message for "our little Anuska." When I was an adult, I still was their little Anuska.

I attribute much of my positive feelings about men in general to the many good experiences in my early childhood, made possible, in large part, because of Uncle Boris and Uncle Vanja. What fun it was to love them both. Sometimes when I think of them, we are playing hide and seek and I can clearly hear their deep, loud voices saying "Anuska, Anuska, we love you . . . can you hear us Anuska, we love you wherever you are."

Later on I will talk about another dear soul in my life, Uncle Mike. But for now let me share with you more memories of childhood friends that first started in Miss Cairns's class at Evans Protestant Elementary School.

The school building looked like a long warehouse not unlike the warehouses across the street. It was a shabby, grey color peeling more excessively after the bitter winter season. Our building's distinguishing features were nonexistent except for the rows of tall evergreen trees surrounding the school as well as many lilacs and flowering bushes in the spring and summertime.

Every day our janitor, Mr. Sam White, a decorated veteran of the first world war, flew our flag, the Union Jack, with pride reminding us frequently it was the biggest flag in the surrounding area. We were sure it was. Sam kept the lawn in front of the school free of dandelions and weeds in spite of the prolific profusion of dandelions everywhere else.

Sam knew most of the students by name including the names of many parents, particulary those whose children were in the principal's office quite often. He was a soft-spoken man whom the kids seem to talk to when they felt they couldn't talk to anyone else. He patiently listened to them, asked a few questions, then shared his thoughts with them in a non threatening way. Whatever he said or did, often changed a young person's life.

Over the years, he was loved by many former students that maintained contact with him. He earned the respect and undying devotion of several families whose rebellious children had been influenced by his friendship. Our school was home for Sam, the students and teachers, the only family he had. Very few knew the hardships Sam had experienced in his life.

Sam was an orphan from birth and grew up in the Atwater Orphanage for Boys and Girls. Because he was never adopted, he lived in the orphanage until he was sixteen years old, at which time he started his first job working for a local hospital in the maintenance department. When the First World War broke out, he joined the army. He came back to Canada a war hero with high hopes for his future. Having little education but a skill for repairing things, he returned to his job at the hospital.

Sam also started visiting the Atwater Orphanage on a fairly regular basis hoping he might possibly help the young boys; it was the only family he knew. At a joint Christmas party for all the orphans, boys and girls, his gaze fell upon a petite young lady with violet eyes and dark brown hair. He knew very little about ladies, nothing about love but he felt his heart was racing faster than it had ever raced before. He was dumbstruck.

Sam was sure a miracle happened when their eyes met. This vision of beauty broke into a smile, came over and said "you're Sam White, aren't you? I've been looking for you."

Before he could answer her, she said "I wanted to meet you. I recently found out you were going to be here. I learnt you were in this orphanage at the same time I was. Believe it or not, we grew up together and never knew it."

Sam White had fallen in love at first sight with the girl who had violet eyes. He couldn't believe he mustered the courage to court this young lady whose name was Amelia Jenkins. The wonder of it all was Miss Amelia Jenkins, who was so beautiful, loved him too. No one had ever loved him before. Sam felt he was living in a dream. Amelia told him she felt the same way. She reminded Sam how much she had talked when they first met because she was so nervous. He told her he was speechless that she was interested in him. She confessed she was certain they were soulmates the very first day they met. They were married shortly after.

I wish I could say they lived happily ever after for a long time but people's lives are often full of unexpected surprises, twists and turns. It was no different for Sam's life. Sam and Amelia were blissfully happy for one year.

Amelia died in a fire at the orphanage that had been her home trying to rescue several young girls who survived due to her efforts. The Atwater Orphanage for Boys and Girls was completely destroyed and never rebuilt. Walk-up apartments were built on the site.

Sam felt like a lost soul for many years. His healing was an arduous process. He never forgot the love that he and Amelia had for each other. He acknowledged his one year of marriage was the happiest time of his life. It would sustain him for the rest of his life.

With the passage of time, Sam realized he wanted to work with young boys and girls. His mission in life was dedicated to Amelia's memory. He would help young people whenever possible. Strangely, his maintenance job at Evans Elementary School allowed him to do just that. Sam was a natural healer; a true listener who could hear someone's pain. The young people knew Sam was authentic in his compassion, empathy and understanding.

Sam's real home was really my school that had seven classrooms, the grouch's or principal's office, nurse's office, Sam's office that was the size of a cubicle and a middle sized room that served as a teacher's meeting room. Outside the main school building was a big gymnasium that was also used for school assembly.

Each classroom had a black, pot bellied stove, our only source of heat during the cold winter months. Mittens, the type with long strings that went around your shoulders and through your sleeves, were placed around the stove to dry. Coats, parkas and scarves were hung up on wooden pegs along the wall. Beneath all this, we placed our varied assortment of winter boots.

In spite of snow, rain and the dirt, some of which we inevitably tracked into the classroom, the hardwood floors shone with a grand patina due to the many coats of wax and polishing Sam gave them every day. Before class began, the boys enjoyed sliding around in their stocking feet with a few adventurous girls joining in as well. I confess sliding around more than a few times. Occasionally, the so called bad boys did "bum rides" on the waxed floor that possibly increased the high gloss on the floors as well as their backsides.

My mother, an excellent home maker, remarked our school had the cleanest windows and shiniest floors she had ever seen. During recess, I told Sam what my mother said and he smiled, looking very pleased. A week later, I think he demonstrated his appreciation for my mother's kind words by giving me a bunch of lilacs to take home to my family saying "I hope your mother enjoys these."

Spring and summer enhanced our weather-beaten school as we had an abundance of vibrant, colorful flowers blooming everywhere. The flagpole was especially dramatic with a generous display of patriotic flowers in red, white and blue planted by none other than our beloved Sam. To this day I associate the smell of lilacs with early school days. The fragrance from the lilacs wafting through the windows created a perfect atmosphere for daydreaming to the chagrin of our school teachers.

It was a long time before I realized our school was rather old and considered a relic. Though each class contained anywhere from 30 to 35 students, discipline was enforced vigorously by visits to the principal's office where you either got the strap, the ultimate physical discipline, or a hard ruler on the knuckles. School classes commenced with the Lord's Prayer and our national anthem. The few Jewish pupils in our class joined us in prayer.

In my very early school years, I believe little thought, if any, was given to the fact that our school morning prayers and rituals in our classes did not take into consideration there were students who were from different religions. Only when I got to high school did I hear the subject of religion come up basically as follows: there are Protestants and Catholics and Jews and others . . . they all have their places of worship . . . so why worry. The majority of students didn't seem comfortable discussing faith and different beliefs in God, or lack thereof. They preferred leaving the status quo as is.

Today, it would appear our schools reflect a new way of thinking regarding prayer. I believe that we are in a constant state of flux when it comes to religion in the schools. It is interesting that so many years later, though we have eliminated prayer in most schools, the controversy continues.

Over the years, I have learned the positive and negative effects of various disciplines imposed upon me by my schools. I personally never felt my praying in school was an imposition or negative influence. Quite the contrary.

In grade five we all said the Lord's Prayer every morning but it was the situations or dilemmas that I faced that I believe resulted in certain hallmarks of my personality. Miss Wiggins looked disheveled during the entire school year. Her hair was an unruly mass of curls. Her eye glasses were constantly slipping down her nose. One earring was missing by the end of the day while a series of pins, especially in the wintertime, seemed to keep her skirts or dresses less askew. What was really strange, is the pins looked like they were fastened to her body. Given some grooming, Miss Wiggins would have been considered fairly good looking.

The only time the class responded to her feeble attempts for order was when she talked about her travels in India as a young student. We were mesmerized by her descriptions of this far away land, the numerous pictures of the prince and his family who invited her to visit them and the many artifacts she brought to class. She introduced us to Kipling and our imaginations soared. We were silenced by Miss Wiggin's soothing voice as we journeyed with her to India once again. I can hear her reciting:

> *To Love's low voice she lent a careless ear;*
> *Her hand within his rosy fingers lay,*
> *A chilling weight. She would not turn or hear;*
> *But with adverted face went on her way.*
> *But when pale Death, all featureless and grim,*
> *Lifted his bony hand, and beckoning*
> *Held out his cypress-wreath, she followed him,*
> *And Love was left forlorn and wondering,*
> *That she who for his bidding would not stay,*
> *At Death's first whisper rose and went away.*

There were many different opinions in our class as to what Kipling meant when he wrote those words but everyone liked the mystery of it all. Occasionally a student would pretend to lift his bony hand and beckon but nevertheless we remained silent and attentive in spite of these attempts at humor.

When the euphoria ended, we unfortunately reverted back to our raucous selves. While I believe Miss Wiggins had a profound effect on us, the following incident was never to be forgotten and perhaps overshadowed her valuable offerings to all the students.

Miss Wiggins was teaching geography and drawing a map on the blackboard. As she reached up high, her "bloomers" fell to the floor. The quiet was overwhelming possibly due to disbelief at this turn of events. Then one nervous giggle, another and another, finally a chorus of nervous laughter that grew louder and louder. Someone said "Miss Wiggins lost her pants" which then became a repetitious singsong. Miss Wiggins, her back to us, still facing the blackboard, slowly bent down, picked up her pants and without a word left the room.

There was much talking and speculation as to what had happened and why. Had one of Miss Wiggins's many safety pins been holding together the elastic in the bloomer's waistband and it opened causing her bloomers to fall on the floor or had the waist band just snapped? Everyone had an opinion. What would happen next? Our speculations were interrupted a few minutes later when Mr. Saunders, our principal, came to class announcing we were dismissed for the day.

I started feeling sorry for poor Miss Wiggins. She must be so embarrassed. What would she do when she came back? Would she come back? I liked her a lot even though she so often seemed confused.

Miss Wiggins returned to school the very next day and stated in a shaky, but very clear voice "I regret you missed an hour of school yesterday because of what happened." Gilbert, the class bully, started to chant yesterday's sing song. There was a deafening silence. Miss Wiggins looked at Gilbert. We waited. She said nothing. Gilbert didn't stop.

"Gilbert, shut up." I shocked myself and everyone in the classroom when I told him to shut up. This was not the way I usually talked or behaved. Several students followed suit telling Gilbert to "shut up," "be quiet" . . . lo and behold he did perhaps from shock as well.

Miss Wiggins commenced teaching. This class was probably the most attentive class Miss Wiggins ever taught. On my final report card she wrote "Anna is an excellent student but more important, she has a compassionate heart."

My compassionate heart was to be sorely tested the following year. Mrs. Roberts was the complete opposite of Miss Wiggins. Her dark-brown hair that was severely pulled back in a bun was always in perfect order, as was her attire. She either wore a navy blue or grey skirt topped off with a white blouse, buttoned all the way up, black oxford shoes and pearl earrings. During the cold winter months, she wore a navy blue cardigan. Her tortoise horn-rimmed glasses would not have dared slide down her nose and never did. I can't remember ever seeing Mrs. Roberts smile. When she praised a student's work, it usually meant past work would be criticized "John, you did well this time. I can't help wondering why you didn't do well in your last assignment."

Mrs. Roberts believed in rules and discipline. Unlike Miss Wiggins she had no compunction sending a student to the principal's office. I don't think we disliked Mrs. Roberts. Rather, I think she was so formidable, if truth be told we students just wanted to get through the day without gaining her attention. The boys had nicknamed her Mrs. Ramrod because she had such a straight back.

I was falsely accused of giggling in class. My attempts in denying I was not guilty fell on deaf ears. My punishment was the ruler across the knuckles of both hands along with sitting in the hallway in front of the principal's office. The shooting pain in my knuckles was long lasting probably since Mrs. Roberts was proficient at ruler punishment that she often meted out but the hurt I felt, in being falsely accused, was far more painful. I kept my eyes shut so no one would see the tears that kept welling up in my eyes. I was hoping the guilty girl, Carol, would confess and make things right. Perhaps her fear of Mrs. Roberts was too great. She never confessed.

Billy Barton came into my life in grade six. He followed me everywhere. He dipped my blond pigtails into his inkwell. My hair turned green. He always gave me a caramel at recess. Everyone knew Billy was different. The teacher told us to be nice to Billy because he was somewhat retarded. The teacher said "if you make him angry he might hurt you." Billy was very good natured and I couldn't figure out why the teacher said what she did. The only time I saw Billy get angry was when some kids called him retard. He chased them away; then started to cry.

Some of my classmates were afraid of Billy but I never was. When some of the kids teased me because I couldn't skate too well Billy skated near me and the teasing stopped. He was always protective. Together, Billy and I picked wild flowers, mostly dandelions for our mothers.

Billy moved away but I saw him again many years later, a happy chance encounter. I heard him calling my name . . . he came running across the street, smiling from ear to ear, obviously very happy to see me. I introduced him to my neighbor's young son whose name coincidentally was Billy. I will never forget the look on Billy's face when young Billy shook his hand and said "I'm a Billy too, just like you."True to form, Billy reached into his pocket and gave each of us a caramel. I always felt Billy knew he was my special friend.

I know Billy never deserved the label he had been given in school nor the negative comments made about him by our teacher. I was pleased to learn he was married, had a full time job that he liked. Billy ended our conversation with "I'm happy to see you."

As an adult I recognized there was very little understanding of the many challenges Billy faced so bravely on a daily basis. I celebrate that we now view the Billys of the world as gifted children who grow up to be gifted adults.

Later on in life, with a second career in psychology, I was always reluctant to label my clients. So often they surged beyond the limited expectations I saw identified in their folder. I was never quick to judge remaining open minded about their behavior and optimistic about their potential to make positive changes in their lives. I was aware that perhaps in some small measure Billy Barton's early friendship, a genuine gift, had a positive influence on my behavior as a therapist.

The next incident I am about to describe brought me face to face, once again, with ignorance, fear and cruelty. What was particularly shocking, these traits were exhibited by fellow students and casual friends. It had a profound influence on how I would view the world and how I would deal with these major characteristics when I experienced or viewed them in others.

It is a pristine, sunny day that has followed a major snowstorm the day before creating what looks like a magical snow kingdom. The trees are heavily draped in snow, glorious, stalwart, majestic giants that are protecting all they perceive. Birds are chirping, hopefully vigilant since a lone calico cat is ever watchful for an opportunity to stalk one of them.

I approach the school yard and notice a large crowd of students have surrounded something or someone. As I get closer, I realize it is Susan, a classmate. Why is she lying in the snow? There is laughing and yelling.

"Is she having a fit? . . . what a goof-ball." "What did you have for breakfast?"

A teacher arrives on the scene and screams at the top of her lungs "stop it at once . . . John run for the nurse" We are cowed into submission and told to disperse. During class we learn Susan had an epileptic seizure. The class silence is deafening. I notice most of us seem nervous and mystified. I know I am.

A special assembly is held for all classes to discuss epilepsy with the hope that we will better understand what happened to Susan and behave more kindly if we encounter similar circumstances in the future.

Since I was deeply touched by what I learnt at school, in the evening I spoke to my parents telling them everything I now knew about epilepsy. I am taken aback when I learn from my father Aunt Sofie, who is really not my aunt but a good friend of the family, also has epilepsy. I asked my father many questions and knew that I was doing so because I was afraid. Could I get epilepsy? Couldn't people take medicine and make it go away? I was glad I hadn't joined the crowd and said awful things.

That night I decided I was old enough to always think for myself and I promised God I would be kind to all people who had epilepsy or other illnesses I knew nothing about. My father had told me in the past to "always be kind to others . . . remember how difficult it is for some people . . . and how very lucky you are." That night I looked out the window while lying in bed and saw the moon. It was a comfort to know it would always be there. As I lay there, I said a Celtic Child's Prayer:

> *"I see the moon and the moon sees me*
> *God bless the moon and God bless me. Amen"*

Aurora, Myrtle, Lily and Jeannine played major, unique roles in my life starting in my childhood. They reached places in my heart that I treasure and will always remember. I will start with Aurora since my memory of her is distinguished by the overwhelming tragedy she experienced as a young child that affected me deeply. Not knowing what happened to her and the way she was literally plucked out of my life, still rekindles somewhat the sadness and loneliness I experienced at that time.

Aurora lived a block away from our home. Her parents owned a small store filled with wooden barrels, jars full of candy, sacks of flour and sugar that they put in paper bags and weighed on a huge scale. The store was below street level in the basement of a two-storey building where Aurora's family lived when they weren't working in the store.

Aurora was sitting on a small cement block wall along the street level of the building when I first saw her. She was the prettiest girl I had ever seen. She looked like a live doll. Her hair was black and she had brown eyes. She was wearing a yellow dress the color of daffodils. She wore yellow socks that matched her dress. Her shoes had little buttons on the side. She was sorting something in a tin box and looked up when she heard my footsteps. I smiled at her and she smiled back. I asked if I could sit with her. She said nothing but kept smiling at me.

Ours was a brief, unusual friendship since Aurora spoke no English, only Greek yet her impact on my life was long lasting. We managed to communicate without words, sharing coloring books, marbles, cutout dolls . . . all our activities taking place on the little wall outside the store since Aurora was not allowed to go beyond the confines of her home.

Sometimes I would try to talk to her in French because I had more knowledge of French than English. I first learned French because we lived in a predominantly French neighborhood. In turn, Aurora spoke to me in Greek that of course I did not understand. Occasionally, Aurora's grandmother, who was very old, sat on the wall with us speaking to both of us in Greek. I always felt she thought I understood every word she was saying. She often brought treats and I knew that Aurora understood me when I said we were having a picnic. While sitting on our wall, Aurora would say 'picnic' whenever her grandmother put a checkered red and white cloth on the wall. Even her grandmother would say picnic.

My mother was pleased I had a new friend and told me she would be very welcome in our home when her parents decided she could visit us.

My mother said "people in the neighborhood are saying Aurora's mother is as beautiful as a Greek goddess and her father as beautiful as a Greek god."

Was it curiosity that finally prompted my mother to go to their store? When she returned, I asked her if the people were right? "Are they really as beautiful as people say?"

I thought Aurora was pretty and her parents, well I'd never really thought about whether they were or not. I guessed they were since my mother agreed the people were right.

One day there were loud sirens on our street and as I looked out my window, it looked like an ambulance had stopped in front of Aurora's store. A police car arrived as well. What was going on?

"Mama, I have to go over to Aurora's store." My mother insisted I stay at home and not join the crowd that was gathering outside. "We will hear soon enough what is going on."

The next day, my mother's eyes filled with tears as she told me "Aurora and her family have moved away."

"She can't have moved. She's my friend. Did she move away because she was sick and that is why the ambulance was there?"

With tears rolling down her cheeks, my mother went on to say Aurora's father had shot Aurora's mother. He then killed himself. It seems my mother had decided it was best I hear this terrible truth from her rather than from someone else. She accepted it was public knowledge, and I would hear about this tragedy sooner or later.

"I know you and Aurora were good friends. I am so sorry."

I cannot explain how confused and scared I was, I just was. Though I cried for a long time every time I thought of Aurora or passed our picnic wall, it didn't seem to help make this strange feeling inside me go away.

I never saw Aurora again. The neighborhood talked about this tragedy for a long time. With the passage of time, people referred to it as "our neighborhood Greek tragedy."

I often overheard adults saying "They were the perfect couple." "She was just too beautiful . . . they say he was such a jealous man"

"She loved him . . . how could he have done this especially in front of his only child?"

During the many days that followed this event, I wondered where Aurora was. Did most fathers have guns? I knew my father didn't have a gun. Would Aurora ever visit me again? I still had her favorite string of beads from Greece that her father gave her. I knew they were important to her. She had put them next to her heart; then she put them next to my heart. We often shared our possessions returning them a few days later. My mother and father told me not to worry about the beads. They felt wherever Aurora was she knew I would take good care of her beads. We were both six years old when this tragedy happened.

Lily became my best friend in Miss Wiggins' class. She told me she was Jewish. I figured she came from a Jewish immigrant family. The word immigrant was now a familiar word to me. She asked me if I thought she was different? "People often don't like Jews."

"Why" I asked? Lilly said she really didn't know why.

I told her about my father's friend, Mr. Irving who was Jewish. He often played checkers with my father in the park during the summer and in our home during the winter. When my father always beat him at checkers, Mr. Irving decided to teach him how to play chess. I heard Mr. Irving tell my father "and now you are beating me at chess."

He brought cookies for me and Maria. We all liked him and I know he liked us as well.

There were very few Jewish families living in our neighborhood. Apparently many of them lived in an area around Cote de Neiges that was a good distance from where we lived. Lily's father was the local shoemaker and the family lived in the upstairs flat above his shop.

Myrtle was my first black friend. There were only five black students in all seven classes and only one black student, Myrtle, in mine. Myrtle started school in the middle of the year. She arrived in our class with very little fanfare but much visibility. Myrtle was exceptionally quiet, somber and very reluctant to participate in school activities. During recess, I accidentally bumped into her nearly knocking her over. She immediately apologized to me. I said "I knocked into you . . . I'm the one that should be sorry." My talking to her was the beginning of a wonderful friendship.

I remember well the first time Myrtle invited me to her home. I really liked it because it was full of plants, records, books and an old beat up piano that still worked. Myrtle's mother played the piano for us, she taught me how to play chopsticks and eventually the words to many black ballads that I loved.

They also had an old phonograph player that we used a lot. I first heard Billie Holiday sing at Myrtle's house and we couldn't play her records often enough. I met Myrtle's father who worked at the local train station. He told us stories about where the different trains came from and where they were going. Myrtle's brother Milton was the best runner in school. He always said he would be a champion one day. He did become an outstanding professional athlete when he grew up.

I was spending a lot of time at Myrtle's house. I enjoyed listening to the music. Hearing Myrtle's mother sing her "old black ballads" always tugged at my heart. After sometime, my mother insisted we reciprocate and I invite Myrtle to our home.

Myrtle asked "are you sure your mother won't mind?"

"Why would she mind . . . you're my friend, aren't you?" I assured her it was fine. My mother wanted to meet my new friend.

When Myrtle walked in the door, I noticed my mother looked rather startled. We played in my room and Myrtle was so happy when my mother gave us cookies and milk.

Myrtle's father picked her up after work. I could see my mother was flustered when she opened the door to the tall, handsome gentleman who introduced himself as Myrtle's father. He thanked her for having Myrtle over at our house. My mother said "you're welcome" with a smile. I was pleased she was learning a few words in English.

"Anna, you never told me Myrtle was black. You should have told me."

"I didn't . . . I guess I forgot . . . it really doesn't matter" I said.

"Oh but it does, Anna" . . . black people aren't like us.

"Mom, Myrtle is my friend and she's just like me . . . except she has prettier colored skin."

"Anna, we'll talk about it when your father comes home."

Had I deliberately not told my mother Myrtle was black? It was not important to me and certainly it wasn't important to Myrtle either. I already knew that adults or parents felt differently about things. They thought certain things mattered that we kids didn't think really mattered at all.

We never talked about Myrtle being black. Supposedly I was sound asleep when the following conversation took place . . . excerpts only:

My father: "Helen, so Myrtle is black. Anna and Myrtle are good friends. You said Myrtle comes from a nice family so what is the problem?"

"Joe, what will people think? Myrtle is a very sweet little girl, so well mannered but she is black."

"That's true and we're white. Think about it Helen. God created all of us. We are all God's children. Isn't that good enough for you Helen? It is for me."

My mother said no more possibly because she always professed she was a God-fearing woman.

I believe my father's conversation with my mother allowed me to continue my friendship with Myrtle. I think I spent far more time at her house than at mine because of the music. I knew Myrtle enjoyed her visits to my house as she spoke about them quite often. Her favorite story was the day my mother played her old country records, particularly the polkas. She showed Myrtle the dance steps I already knew and I watched with glee as she and Myrtle twirled around the room. My mother looked like a happy, young girl and Myrtle's eyes were shining with joy. There is no doubt in my mind my mother had completely forgotten the color of Myrtle's skin. Myrtle always referred to my mother with affection as "the nicest lady" I know.

Jeannine, a French Canadian, was my one friend who did not attend public school with me. She was a Roman Catholic and the first time we met she told me "I have an older sister and a younger sister . . . I'm in the middle . . . my grandfather lives with us . . . he only has one ear like that famous artist, and two tin legs . . . he lost his ear and his legs in the first world war but will never talk about what happened. My grandfather has many medals . . . people say he is a hero . . . I love him . . . he reads to me a lot . . . if you are my friend you can come over and listen to the stories my grandfather reads . . . and my mother makes the best taffy in the world." Jeannine could talk a blue streak . . . she was full of fun and together we had many mischievous adventures.

Unbeknownst to both sets of parents, Jeannine and I spent many hours in a huge lumber yard where together we moved around planks of wood of various sizes to build dream castles, wonderful walkways and sculptures. We fancied ourselves artists, pioneers, runaway vagabonds . . . whatever we felt like that day. Sometimes we would just lie on boards pretending they were ships while gazing at the enormous, fluffy clouds as we sailed to faraway countries.

Often Jeannine would sail to France with me . . . or we would sail to Czechoslovakia to visit my mother's relatives . . . and every now and then we would sail to Greece where I told Jeannine we would find Aurora and give her back her father's beads. Jeannine was never too keen on our visits to England possibly because she didn't speak English and I did. I taught her some words in the Czech language that she really liked using. Since we both couldn't speak any of the other languages, I knew she felt comfortable visiting these foreign countries.

We had to be careful the watchman never saw us during his periodic inspections of the lumber yard. We figured out he knew we were there because of our lumber creations that we never dismantled before he walked around doing his inspection. For some reason he allowed us to stay. Perhaps because we never met face to face, it was easier for him to just overlook us. I realize how fortunate we were to have escaped serious injury. Where did we find the strength to pick up these heavy planks of lumber? Perhaps we were able to do so because we didn't know we couldn't. Today I still enjoy the smell of lumber that triggers happy memories of the many fantasies and wonders Jeannine and I created so long ago.

Another pastime was cleaning old, discarded glass jars that we then filled with water inserting a piece of colored crepe paper that had been discarded by a local stationary shop. The result was jars filled with water, every color of the rainbow, that we placed on a long bench on my mother's backyard balcony. Eventually we had tiers of colored jars on display. The sun gleamed through the jars creating an array of ribbons of color on the metal roof of my father's shed. It was truly spectacular and beautiful.

Word got around in the neighborhood that Anna and Jeannine could make rainbows in the sky, a slight exaggeration but certainly enticing. So many children showed up to see this phenomenon, we had to get them to form a line in order that they all had a chance to see the colors. It occurred to us that we should charge them a penny to see our exhibit. To our surprise, charging was not a deterrent . . . instead more children showed up. On a good day, we made 30 cents. It was always easier when we made an even number since we were at a loss as to how we would divide that one odd penny.

It was an extremely hot, humid summer day. Jeannine

suggested and decided we would go to her Roman Catholic church to cool off. She said it was always cool in there because the church was built out of stone. We walked in very quietly with deep respect for our holy surroundings.

At the church entrance, where we beheld the church altar, Jeannine and I both genuflected and Jeannine did the ritual sign of the cross with holy water and told me to do the same. She tried to show me how not to take too much holy water. Our hands touched the holy water at the same time creating a splash. We started to giggle and before you knew it, we were splashing each other, oblivious that we were in church.

A strong arm grabbed each one of us by the back of the neck. It was a penguin . . . our nickname for a nun. Reality set in with a bang! We had been splashing each other with holy water and laughing out loud in a church. We were doomed.

"What are your names and where do you live?" asked the nun, in a stern voice.

"Jeannine Gravel and I live on Leduc Street."

"Anna " I gasped and "I live on Leduc Street."

"Anna is not Roman Catholic. She is just my friend," said Jeannine rather bravely.

Our dialogue was in French, the language Jeannine and I always spoke when we were together.

The nun's name was Sister Bernadette. She took both of us to Leduc Street walking so quickly we could barely keep up. Not a word was spoken. All I heard were our footsteps and a swishing sound the slight breeze created in her nun's habit.

She dropped me off first advising Jeannine she not move from the sidewalk until she was through with me. I saw Jeannine's face. She looked worried and was rather pale. What would happen to us?

Sister Bernadette spoke to my mother in French. At first, I was relieved because I realized my mother wouldn't understand a word she said. She said "merci" to Sister Bernadette. Was this the extent of her French? What if my mother knew more French than I thought? My mind was twirling . . . maybe she wouldn't find out . . . what would she do when she found out?

Fortunately or unfortunately, my mother knew immediately that Jeannine and I had done something wrong. How do mothers know these things? My mother demanded the truth. The tone of her voice was such that I confessed my sin to her without delay. I told her everything since God was probably displeased with me too. She never said a word until I had finished my story. She said she was extremely upset with me and I was severely chastised. I knew that misbehaving in church was never acceptable and that Jeannine and I were in serious trouble. I was prohibited from playing with Jeannine . . . it was not clear for how long but I decided it was best under the circumstances not to ask any questions.

Jeannine was reprimanded and also could not play with me for at least a week. She had to say many prayers asking God's forgiveness for her behavior. As we lived across the street from each other, we talked to one another during our punishment period. It became a game that we both enjoyed when our mothers weren't watching us.

Jeannine's aunt, who lived with them, died suddenly. As was the custom in those days, her body was displayed in the living room. Jeannine said I could come over and see the body on a day when there were no afternoon visitors. I was curious to see her aunt since I had never seen a dead person before. I didn't know what to expect. I must confess I was nervous and it felt a little strange standing there with Jeannine looking at her dead aunt.

Jeannine decided to fix her aunt's hair . . . it seemed something was not to her liking. In doing so, it looked to me like her aunt was suddenly getting up. I screamed in terror, running out of the house in record time. Coincidentally, my mother said "you look like you've seen a ghost." Since Jeannine and I had recently been in trouble at the church, I decided not to tell my mother what had happened.

My friendship with Jeannine was filled with many adventures and lots of excitement. We were both inquisitive children who genuinely enjoyed each other's company. Life was never dull when we were together.

Jeannine and I remained friends until her life's journey took an unexpected path the outcome of which surprised us all.

Jeannine didn't date very often but when she met Pierre she fell madly in love astonishing herself, family and friends. She had strongly believed, and advised us accordingly, that she probably would never find someone to love. Nor did she expect to live happily ever after.

"There are too many unhappy, married people."

A complete transformation was taking place before our eyes. Jeannine admitted she was in love. She couldn't stop talking about how much more wonderful life had become since Pierre. She admitted that her life had always been pretty good but loving someone like Pierre and him loving her back was magical . . . a dream come true . . . "it's like you feel totally understood for the first time in your life and you don't have to explain yourself; your lover knows who you are."

The relationship ended quite abruptly with no logical reason for the breakup. Jeannine told me her heart was broken and she would never love again. With every passing day, she became despondent and I was becoming very concerned about her state of mind.

Her caring family suggested she visit relatives in France. The change might help her frame of mind. I also encouraged her to take this trip.

Upon her arrival in France, I had several short letters from her that suggested she was still pondering what her life without Pierre would be like. Then I stopped hearing from her for several years. Eventually I contacted her mother who was surprised I had not heard that Jeannine had become a nun and was working with a strict religious order taking care of terminally ill children in France. She was now Sister Teresa.

I know Jeannine became a loving, compassionate nun and the children she cares for love her as much as I still do.

I received a letter from Jeannine, now Sister Teresa, that she had mailed me two years ago that had been returned to her "address unknown." She had not forgotten me! I was extremely pleased when she expressed her tremendous happiness and joy in her new life. She touched my heart when she said "Anna, your loving friendship played an important role in my past life. Today know that I am truly joyous in doing God's work."

As I reflect on my childhood, I now recognize my family and friends' families only had money for the bare necessities in life. In order to enhance our lives, we learned to be creative, seeing endless possibilities for our creativity in bits of fabric, broken pieces of mirror, stones, wood, and buttons. We discarded very few things and recycled just about everything. Our unfailing appetites as children to experience magic and wonder allowed us to make endless treasures. We openly rejoiced in our accomplishments and generously and enthusiastically shared our riches with family members or friends.

So many children appear to be deprived of the many joys of imagination and the vast opportunities that may evolve if they are not inundated with materialism and allowed the freedom to develop their own ideas and concepts. I realize that my life was enriched in many ways in spite of what some people may have viewed as meager surroundings. I was so fortunate to have experienced these early successes and vividly remember how I was always filled with hope and inspiration that my, or our next artistic project would be even better than the first.

Earlier I mentioned my friend Uncle Mike. On the heels of my description of the antics I shared with my friend Jeannine, and how the commingling of our frolicsome imaginations allowed us to enjoy wondrous fantasies, this is a good time to acknowledge Uncle Mike's contribution to my world of make believe.

Uncle Mike was born in the old country, in the same village as my parents. Like many others, he had been told, back in Czechoslovakia, to look up my parents who would provide him friendly help as they had done for other countrymen upon arriving in Canada. As a result, my parents often had potential boarders knocking at their door. This was not always easy, as my parents had limited income to tide people over until they found employment. Somehow, they usually managed to provide shelter, food and guidance based on their own experiences until their countryman was able to function without their support.

Uncle Mike lived with us for many, many years though he originally only planned to stay for a short time. He was a complete contrast to my Russian uncles. I remember a man of small stature with a thatch of blond hair complemented by deep blue eyes. I always thought he looked like an old boy instead of a man. I recall people saying "he has a young boyish face that never seems to age." Uncle Mike was a shy, quiet man who read a lot and spoke very little. Overtime, he surprised us all when he developed a passion for cowboy movies.

Every Saturday morning, Uncle Mike went to the movies by himself. He saw three movies that were offered for the price of one if you started with the early morning matinee. Before day's end, my father often engaged him in a conversation about the movies he had just seen. I was usually present and I listened attentively to his detailed descriptions of horses, the wild, wild west and the cowboys who always beat the bad guys. Uncle Mike particularly loved the Lone Ranger and Tonto.

My friendship with Uncle Mike began when my father found himself working on a Saturday, not unusual, and my mother was asked to help a country woman in an emergency leaving me without supervision. My sister Maria was unavailable as well. Serendipity . . . Uncle Mike volunteered to take me to the movies to help out. He assured my mother it was no problem and I just might enjoy the experience.

I couldn't believe my good fortune. When we got to the movies, I was totally engrossed in what I saw. I was mesmerized. On the way home, I recall talking a blue streak, similar to Jeannine, and reliving everything in detail that I had seen. Uncle Mike seemed to enjoy my commentaries and observations and, thereafter, invited me quite often to see the Saturday movies with him.

The mutual interest and passion he and I shared in the movies were the beginning of Uncle Mike's participation in other family activities. Though very shy, he gradually developed a strong, loyal friendship with all of us. He had an avid interest in my life. He was very interested in my geography lessons and Canadian history. He attended many of my school concerts on a regular basis and always informed me afterwards "you were exceptionally good tonight." Always a gentle soul, he died very peacefully and quietly in his sleep in his mid sixties not unlike the way he had lived. He had entered our hearts and we all missed him very much when he was gone.

Someone who definitely had a strong influence in my early years was my only sister, Maria, the first born. Seven years later I arrived. I loved my sister but we often went our separate ways because she and her friend's didn't want me tagging along.

I well remember a painful event and major disappointment that involved Maria and two of her best friends, Jennifer and Penelope, known as Jennie and Penny. The three of them were going to see the Wizard of Oz on a Saturday afternoon. My mother insisted that Maria take me to the movie as well. This was the one and only time I ever remember her asking Maria to do this. As a young child, I did not understand why my sister and her friends insisted I walk way behind them to get to the theater ... they also kept scowling at me every time they turned around to look at me.

When we got to the movies, the person at the ticket counter said I was underage according to the provincial laws in Quebec and he couldn't let me in to see the movie. My sister had to leave her friends and take me home. It felt like she ran all the way back to our house that was at least seven blocks away, with me trailing behind her, huffing and panting to keep up.

Maria was very angry and made no bones about telling me how I had messed up her afternoon. Her words only compounded my disappointment in being too young to see The Wizard of Oz.

I never got to see the Wizard of Oz until I was an adult. By then I certainly understood and appreciated Maria's feelings when we were children ... she was frustrated and had to deal with her own disappointment. I believe this childhood incident was the turning point in my separating from Maria, becoming more independent and developing my own set of friends.

I know now that I still tried to emulate Maria, more from a distance, not being aware that the age difference between us was significant and thus affected what I could achieve in comparison to my sister's efforts. I did not consider myself strident in trying to skip rope as well as my sister, or perhaps do math as well as my sister but the underpinning was being established within me to be a super achiever. My need to achieve would not remain dormant forever.

It intrigues me that it never occurred to me that I couldn't do something if I just kept on trying. I acknowledge this attitude was fostered by a loving father as well as a cadre of uncles and aunts who diminished, to a great extent, some of the negatives I had to deal with.

Psychology states various personality traits have been associated with different birth order positions because children are often treated differently as a result of their birth order and, therefore, develop specific personality traits.

It is often stated that the first born child tends to be highly motivated, successful and ambitious, also tending to be cautious and conservative. The last born child is more sociable but sometimes maintains a younger, weaker stance throughout adulthood.

I have always questioned generalizations about birth order and its effect on personality. Later in my life when I became a therapist, I found it astounding how often the birth order helped account for patterns of behavior. I believe when there is a big difference in age between two children as was the case between Maria and myself, children may tend to develop specific personality traits of only children.

I believe I developed a personality more in keeping with a first born child though I never saw myself as being overly cautious or conservative. To my knowledge, Maria was never very ambitious nor highly motivated.

I always felt no matter how close siblings may be in families, it is often difficult to be the first born. Even though young children often say they want a brother or sister, they are obviously not aware of the many significant changes that will take place in them.

I recall a family in therapy whose young daughter was having problems adjusting to her young brother's active presence. She told her parents a simple truth, her feelings at the time "you loved me so much, you went and got another." This precocious child felt she had not been enough for her parents. This particular child did eventually adapt to her new environment and family structure as do the majority of children.

Chapter Two

Adolescence

Identity formation involves "the creation of a sense of sameness, unity of personality now felt by the individual and recognized by others as having consistency in time . . . of being as it were an irreversible historical fact"
                                                                                          Erik Erikson

I felt I was now ready for the many challenges high school would present. I was certain memorable turnings would take place in the next four years that would allow me insight and thus more vision to better know my own connection to the world. All dreams were possible. I liked being a dreamer and an idealist.

I could not count the times, I clearly heard my teachers say "education is the doorway to many opportunities in life." With more education, I hoped to understand the compromises I saw people make and better understand why adults often believed "sometimes dreams don't come true." Yet, I still acknowledged that it is essential to dream in life . . . perhaps make the impossible dream come true. I was a true believer upon entering high school.

Our high school was unique in that you could get a degree by studying the basic high school subjects plus the classics or a degree by studying the aforementioned as well as shorthand and typing. I decided to study both supported by my father who felt shorthand and typing were important working skills. I noticed that most of the English-speaking girls from middle class families did not seem very interested in learning working skills. They planned on going to college for a while, hoped to get married and become homemakers.

Since we all had to wear navy blue tunics with white cotton shirts, the one distinguishing factor among the students, not prohibited in the classroom, was the sweaters we wore. It quickly became apparent the middle class kids wore white sweaters while the working class kids wore black or navy sweaters.

The only person I knew when I first started high school was Myrtle. I was overwhelmed seeing all the new faces but discovered I was not alone in the feelings I was experiencing. I usually made friends easily but for some reason I wanted to wait and see what the kids in this new school were like.

Myrtle heard there was a young man playing the piano in our high school gymnasium during lunch time and suggested we go check it out. Since Myrtle's family had introduced me to blues and jazz that I really liked, I was eager to explore the sounds that were emanating from our gym. As this was a spontaneous opportunity to listen to music, the students had to sit on the gym floor. We sat mesmerized by the music created on the piano by the young man. At best it was an incredible experience and for a short time, I believe our souls were fed and we soared uninhibited to places where dreams come true. Except for the music, it was always so quiet you could hear a pin drop.

We appreciated that the piano player was a gifted, talented young man and his music was phenomenal. Any time he played the piano in our gymnasium, Myrtle and I and many others came to listen enraptured by his music. We both agreed and we were certain whoever he was he would be famous some day. We were right. His name was Oscar Peterson. Many students enjoyed his outstanding performances . . . it was hard to believe he was only practicing on the high school piano.

I became aware I was attracted to Gary, the president of the debating team. He sure was cute, very tall, had dark brown, curly hair that emphasized his deep blue eyes. What I liked most was his infectious smile. Prior to my noticing Gary, I had never paid much attention to boys. I decided to try out for the debating team probably because of Gary, and was very pleased when I made it. Overtime, I came to realize it was also something I enjoyed doing. Only Myrtle knew I had a crush on Gary but I knew my secret was safe with my best friend.

When Gary invited me to our midterm dance, my secret crush was out when I said yes. Wow! I was floating on a cloud.

Gary also told me "I really like you. You're smart, pretty, and have a great personality."

Gee . . . could things get any better? For weeks I was as happy as a magpie. Were magpies really as happy as I? I daydreamed a lot and kept wondering what it will be like going to my very first dance with Gary, my prince charming. We danced so beautifully together in all my daydreams!

Gary called me several days before the dance. He wanted to meet me in the school cafeteria for a coke. I was so happy. I guessed we would be talking about our pending date.

Why is Gary so nervous? I immediately sense something is wrong but I can't imagine what it is. Gary sure looks miserable. I hope he's not sick but he can't be or he wouldn't be at school. He blurts out "Anna, I'm really sorry but I can't take you to the dance."

I am speechless. I certainly didn't expect this. I say absolutely nothing.

"Anna, say something please. You know how much I like you. It's you I want to take to the dance"

I can tell Gary is waiting for me to speak. When I don't he continues "My mother says I have to take Fannie to the dance. She is my mother's best friend's daughter. When Fannie didn't have a date, our mothers, decided I would take Fannie. I told my mother I was already taking you. We argued back and forth. She said I need to go out with Jewish girls. My mother said she was positive you would find a nice Christian boy to take you to the dance and your parents would be happier too. Please, Anna, try to understand, I am so sorry."

I think of Lily. I remember when she first told me she was Jewish back in elementary school. Lily and I are still the best of friends. I don't understand. I hope all Jewish mothers don't think like Gary's mother. Why is my not being Jewish an issue? Now that I think about it, am I somewhat surprised my parents never asked me about Gary? Perhaps knowing that Gary went to my high school and was on the debating team with me was enough for them.

My parents loved Lily and Mr. Irving who played checkers and chess with my Dad. I'm sure if they knew, they wouldn't have cared that Gary was Jewish.

I hear Gary's voice again "Anna can we still be friends?"

I remain silent too disappointed, upset and confused to speak. What could I say to Gary anyway? Under these circumstances, I really don't know whether we can be friends. Without a word, I quickly leave the cafeteria so Gary won't see I am on the verge of tears. I never did drink my coke.

Word gets around that I am not going to the dance with Gary. It seems everyone knows he is taking Fannie. Agnes, the most outspoken girl I ever knew, confronts me in the locker room "What did you expect? You should really stick to your own kind. The Jews killed Jesus Christ. Remember that." I am shocked and walk away as fast as I can.

I decided not go to the dance even though Myrtle said there were many girls going stag and I shouldn't let Gary ruin my life. "You know Anna, Gary's mother's behavior is really strange when you think about it. Usually people pick on the Jews when they're not picking on the blacks. This is kind of unique. Sort of like reverse discrimination."

Myrtle often surprised me with her pearls of wisdom. Maybe she was right.

It took sometime before Gary and I resumed our friendship. My disappointment had not severed the strong bond and liking we had for each other. We mutually agreed after much discussion and to Gary's great sorrow, we would not date. We would remain very good school friends.

My parents were curious why I didn't go out with Gary but did not pry once I made it quite clear I didn't want to talk about him. I knew my father had eventually somehow figured out what had happened no doubt based on tidbits of information he picked up from conversations I had with Myrtle.

At an appropriate time when we were having a heart to heart talk, my wise father said "people sometimes hate because of fear or they have been taught to hate, but whatever the reason, as long as you remember we are all God's children I know you will never buy into racial hatred and prejudice." It sounded so simple but I would unfortunately learn not everyone thought as my father did.

Gradually I resumed being more sociable. I went to a local church dance for young teens. After the dance I walked home with a group of friends that included one young man, Colin, a mulatto, a label frequently used in those days. As the group dispersed, Colin and I walked home together.

The following morning a neighbor telephoned our home asking "do you know Anna came home with a black boy?" Maria who answered the phone, admitted she was dumbfounded by the call particularly since we hardly knew this neighbor except to say hello when we saw her on the street. I could tell my mother was uncomfortable in discussing the "call" perhaps because of our previous conversations regarding Myrtle whom she now genuinely liked.

Though she appeared hesitant, she said "Anna, people will talk about you if you date black boys and it's probably not good for your reputation . . . having a black girlfriend is different."

I told her how it happened Colin walked me the rest of the way home. I explained Colin and I weren't even friends yet. I gently reminded her that Colin's family had recently joined the local church. They were the only black family in our neighborhood. I assured her she didn't have to worry about a thing. My mother looked relieved. I knew she was trying to protect me from harm.

Coming right after my major disappointment with Gary, though I now knew there was prejudice directed at Jews and blacks, interestingly I was discovering it came from both sides. Our neighborhood was white, with many immigrants who practiced different religions. The majority of people were French Roman Catholics followed by English, Scottish and Irish Protestants though the majority of Irish were Roman Catholic. It seemed to me that many people persisted in seeing others "as less than," promoting negative or distorted images of people who came from other ethnic backgrounds and religions.

I believed I was managing not to buy into prejudice and hatred. I could not deny my friends from a variety of ethnic backgrounds and religions in my early years had greatly influenced my thinking and beliefs.

While I certainly remembered the name calling . . . the French and occasionally the English children called us pollacks when they were angry . . . this included Russians, Hungarians,

Ukrainians . . . to them everyone was a pollack.

We in turn called them Frenchies, frogs, pea soupers. The French called the English maudit anglais . . .this included the Scots and Irish.

. . . and the Italians were mostly called wops by all groups.

The Jews were called kikes and other very offensive names from all the groups.

There were so few blacks, as a young child, I personally never heard the "n" word. I unfortunately did hear it in my teens.

The Russians, Hungarians and Ukrainians usually belonged to the Greek Orthodox Church that the Protestants felt resembled the Roman Catholic Church in many ways. Other religions such as the Jehovah Witness were not common in the environment that I grew up in.

Despite the name calling, random fist fights, we were merely children, who when they settled their differences, played together harmoniously completely unaware that some day we would all have to face the profound cultural dilemmas in our country. In some instances, in spite of parental interference life long friendships were formed and intermarriage took place. What is most interesting, it never destroyed the dual identity in Quebec that continues to have European and North American qualities.

A short description of Montreal in a brochure would read as follows:
"There are more French-speaking people in Montreal than in any other city of the world excluding Paris. About two-thirds of the city's inhabitants trace their ancestry to the settlers of New France; some 20% are of British origin, the balance are made up of numerous other nationalities. The predominant religion in all of Quebec and the city of Montreal is Roman

Catholic."

There were many Nuns Orders and I specifically remember the Grey Nuns Order that was founded in Montreal that served the poor and orphaned.

There were Roman Catholic priests and many Jesuits who taught at the Roman Catholic schools. We children did recognize that the majority of children in our neighborhood were both French and Roman Catholic. Ethnic groups tended to live together . . . there was a Polish area that included other Slavic groups such as the Russians . . . an Irish area . . . an Italian area . . . and mixtures thereof but I don't think we ever realized when we were playing that we were so outnumbered by the French.

As children we did not recognize to what extent much of the French population was becoming discontent with their lot in life particularly relating to the language issue. As we got older, we would become aware that this situation had simmered for a long time before aggressive outward action was taken by the French.
In later years, I was deeply saddened when I could no longer ignore that the distrust and prejudice, I and others were experiencing, appeared to be emanating from the adults or parents. I would spend much time in my life exploring why certain children succumbed to the negative thinking their parents had about certain minorities and why others did not.

Charlotte Bronte said "Prejudices, it is well known, are most difficult to eradicate from the heart whose soil has never been loosened or fertilized by education; they grow there, firm as weeds among stones."

Many years later, I would mull over these profound words as the environment that I grew up in became more hostile.

For the time being, I concentrated on my studies, made friends regardless what country they came from and dealt with problems or issues if and when they arose. I was very optimistic since I felt I had made progress in my own life with the various friends I had. For example, no one questioned my friendship with Myrtle or Lily anymore. Progress had been made. Unfortunately I had yet to learn about subtle innuendoes, cruel indifference and isolation of certain ethnic groups, especially blacks and Jews in our society. Had I yet been exposed to blatant hatred? I had little realization I had much to learn.

Was it possible that in my new high school environment my self-concepts would change? Would I resist some of the mindless conformity confronting me and be able to make thoughtful, committed decisions? It seemed appearance was becoming more important and some students were definitely more socially successful than others.

I could see sexuality while not openly discussed, except with true friends, was affecting the way students behaved. Though my mother had never discussed sex with me, she had emphasized over the years the importance of not becoming pregnant until I was married. She had made it clear my life would be ruined, along with my reputation, and our family would be shamed. I believe her greatest fear was that her daughters might get pregnant. I listened to her comments hoping I would learn more about sex but that was the entire extent of our conversation, repeated many times.

Alice Novak and Angela Bryson were class students. Alice became pregnant and had, what was then called, a back street abortion. It was public knowledge because she nearly hemorrhaged to death while at school and had to be rushed to the hospital. There was much speculation as to whom the father was and who had paid for the abortion since Alice came from a lower income family. Alice returned to school and was ostracized by the female students but received more than her fair share of attention from the male students. She finished her high school year and never came back.

Angela Bryson who wore white sweaters and came from a middle class family, possibly upper middle class, left school in the middle of the year to stay with a sick aunt two thousand miles away. A year later she returned to high school to resume her studies. While she never acknowledged she had been pregnant, the young father, a student, had confided in a friend when Angela told him she was having his baby. The news spread like wild fire that Angela had given her baby up for adoption.

With the passing of time, I had the opportunity to witness the tremendous effect these experiences had on their lives. Alice moved back to the Hochelaga area, a working class neighborhood after leaving high school. She worked as a cashier in a grocery store, waited on tables and finally worked in a bar where she made most of her money in tips. Unfortunately, Alice got pregnant again and had another abortion. When she became pregnant a third time, she decided to keep the child.

"I can't keep doing this anymore. It's wrong. I'm going to keep my baby and be a good mother." She named her daughter Candy.

Alice was finding it very difficult to support herself and her daughter. She gradually drifted into becoming a prostitute that was very easy for her to do in her working environment. She was ashamed at what she had become but she was always quick to say, she only did it part time, earning just enough money for the two of them. Alice loved Candy and was determined that eventually she would change her life before Candy got too old to understand what her mother did.

Alice had been physically and verbally abused since she could remember going back to the age of four. She was the oldest of six children and often had to take care of her younger brothers and sisters when her parents got drunk which was often since they were both alcoholics.

There was never enough food or proper clothing for all the children and Alice often went to a local mission for help. Her parents were oblivious of Alice's activities . . . how she was attempting to provide some family stability for her siblings.

Her parents continued to make unrealistic demands upon her. They had completely abdicated their role as parents. They were harsh in their treatment of all the children but Alice was beaten more severely whenever her siblings misbehaved.

Her behavior in high school was not that surprising. She sought acceptance from others . . . her pain was intense . . . she constantly felt unloved and unlovable. Alice believed sex was love . . . by having sex she was being loved.

Dr. Erik Erikson stated "development is not random but, instead, proceeds according to the outline from the plan. Also, development is not automatic but, rather, depends on the interaction between the person and the environment."

The plan Erikson is referring to is his Ground Plan for Psychosocial Growth in which he identifies ages and related bipolar crises at each age. The most salient single theme of personal development during adolescence is identity formation.

That being a given, Erikson's statement "the sense of personal alienation prevents the establishment of a stable core for the personality" is certainly applicable to Alice.

I hark back to Angela who was also ashamed, felt guilty, mistrustful and had become diffused in her identity.

When Alice decided to take Candy to a lake resort far away from home where nobody knew her, she had no idea it would change her entire life. It had taken her a long time to save enough money so she and Candy could have a real vacation.

While at the resort called Morning Glory, that she selected because of the name, Alice unconsciously adopted a new persona. She became free to play with Candy with a sense of joy she had never felt before. Though always a loving mother, in this environment she felt safe. Though she didn't realize it, Alice had let her wounded child come out to play. She felt totally carefree and unafraid.

Her innocent spirit attracted a young man to this delightful scene. For a while he thought they looked more beautiful than the Renoir painting he had recently admired of a mother and child frolicking happily in wild abandonment. As he watched them both, he experienced deep feelings that were totally new to him. He was so moved by his emotions, he boldly ventured forth and introduced himself.

"I'm John Andrews. I hope I'm not intruding but perhaps you will let me join you." He looked at Candy and asked "May I play with you and your mommy?" and was tremendously happy when she smiled and said "yes, you can if mommy says yes too."

That simple introduction was to be the beginning of a loving relationship. John treated Alice as an equal with much respect. Alice responded to his behavior in a manner totally unfamiliar to her. She was attracted to John because she liked his caring ways, enjoyed his humor, conversation and good company. She liked the way he made her feel. And best of all, their being together wasn't just about sex. Her new feelings frightened her yet Alice knew she wanted to continue enjoying John's company as long as possible. Candy and he got on so well she started thinking that perhaps Candy missed having a father in her life.

When their vacations ended, Alice and John could not deny a strong mutual attraction existed between them.

"Alice, may I write you and phone as well? I want to see you and Candy. Hopefully we'll see each other before too long."

John was thinking how he must not lose this beautiful, wonderful, kind woman with a generous heart.

Alice agreed "I would like that. We had such a wonderful time together, the three of us, didn't we?"

She felt it would be all right to stay in touch with John since he lived far enough away thus he would never find out about her life. She couldn't help thinking how sad it was that she would never love this man. He was so kind and so good.

What happened next may be an inspiration to others who have suffered major physical and verbal abuse and may have abandoned all hope for a happy, productive life.

John was in love with Alice. After numerous letters and phone calls, he proposed marriage. Alice was both surprised and terrified. Everything felt like a dream. She kept thinking she would wake up only to find her dream would never come true because John now knew who Alice really was.

John was a decent man with a good heart unlike the men she had known in the past. As Alice agonized over John's love for her, convinced he had never known anyone with a past like hers, Alice realized she loved him as well. She finally felt a sense of peace when she decided she would tell him the truth. John surely did not know who he had fallen in love with. Alice would make it easier for John to end the relationship and say goodbye. He deserved the best in life and certainly a lot better than her.

John, the incurable romantic invited Alice back to the resort so he could propose to her again in person. Because Alice felt it would be kinder to tell him about herself face to face, she owed him that much, she agreed to come. She told him she needed to talk to him about whom she was. In her mind, she was trying to set the stage for their inevitable, final farewell. She was determined to be honest and not manipulative. She loved John. There was no alternative. She must let him go.

John swept Alice into his arms with a warm embrace and a deep loving kiss completely unaware of Alice's initial hesitancy in responding to his affection.

"John, please I must talk to you right away."

"All right, Alice. I can see now that you are agitated. I'm sorry. I was just overwhelmed when I first saw you. You can't imagine how happy I am to see you."

John listened to Alice who did not spare herself in any way. She told him about her family but did not blame them or try to justify her behavior. She told him she had been working part time as a prostitute for the last two years. She told John he was the most wonderful man she had ever met.

"I will never forget how kind you have been to Candy and me. We laughed a lot and had so much fun. The time we spent together has been the happiest time of my life. I will always remember you."

There was a long silence as John waited to ensure Alice had completed telling him about her life. He had suspected that Alice had a troubled past. Upon hearing the details of her life, he was filled with compassion for her suffering.

John saw Alice as a courageous, brave woman who as a child valiantly tried to bring up her brothers and sisters in the most difficult circumstances while enduring both physical and verbal abuse. He saw her tremendous love for Candy and her frantic attempts to provide a loving home for her, trying to give her the material things she had never had in her life.

John looked deep into Alice's heart and saw the goodness and generosity it possessed.

John said clearly in a strong, but gentle voice "I don't care about your past. We are now in the present that is loving and good. We have a great future to look forward to. I love you Alice. I love Candy. Marry me."

Upon hearing John's words, Alice was overcome with emotion and disbelief that John loved her in spite of her past. As she looked at his face, filled with strength and goodness, though not a religious person, at that moment she felt God had forgiven her for all her past sins. She bowed her head and silently gave thanks to the Lord who had not forsaken her. It took Alice several weeks before she agreed to marry John who patiently reassured her she was a wonderful person worthy to be loved and cherished.

It is not surprising that after marrying John, Alice still struggled with major issues particularly low self esteem. With professional help, Alice learned the past must be dealt with sooner or later. John's steadfast, unconditional love was also extremely important in helping Alice get to a place where she saw herself as a different person.

Alice had contact with some of her siblings who unfortunately had not fared too well in life. However, their love for each other had survived in spite of their many traumas and Alice remained the shining beacon in all their lives. Overtime, she managed to help two of her siblings greatly improve their life styles that further helped her well being. It was not an easy task, but with much love and support, Alice succeeded in reinventing herself to be the person she truly wanted to be finally acknowledging within herself she was lovable.

John's parents were unpretentious, kind, generous people who had not been corrupted by their good fortune and ensuing wealth. John's family willingly opened their hearts to Alice and

Candy. They had never seen their son, John, this happy before. This loving family environment was such a dramatic contrast to the abusive, alcoholic parents she knew, needless to say it took some time for Alice to completely accept their love for her and Candy.

Prior to meeting Alice, John had been pursued by many females who were primarily attracted by his wealth and prestigious family. When Alice accepted John's marriage proposal, he knew Alice's love was genuine and had nothing to do with his social status. All she knew about him, when he proposed marriage, was that he worked in a small factory doing administrative type work. She didn't know he was a wealthy man, the president of a factory that delivered goods all over the world.

A few years later, Alice gave birth to a girl that they named Glory. As a family, they often returned to Morning Glory where Candy would recount to Glory "this is where my mommy met my daddy" . . . .and they lived happily ever after.

Angela who by society's standards came from a 'good family,' was not immediately as fortunate as Alice. It will become evident later on, Angela's family members had repressed emotions and there were many imbalances in the family relationships that were compounded by Angela's pregnancy. The parents believed an awkward situation had been taken care of when Angela's baby was given up for adoption. All that mattered was the family's image was untarnished.

Angela became promiscuous, drank excessively but somehow managed to graduate from high school. She went on to college but dropped out. Shortly after, she was diagnosed with severe depression. Her ability to become a productive human being was being severely hampered by her inability to deal with the loss of her child. Angela spent much time in and out of mental institutions often returning to her parents who maintained they could not understand why Angela wasn't feeling well when she had the best of everything life could provide.

R. D. Laing spoke of "mystification" that is a process of distorting a child's experiences by denying or relabeling it. Angela's parents were classic examples that could be used to demonstrate the process Dr. Laing refers to.

Shocking to all the students in our high school was when Lindsey got a venereal disease from her steady boyfriend, John. While we had all seen the film in elementary school about these diseases, we couldn't help but wonder where John got the disease in the first place. We remembered that a separate presentation was arranged for the boys and girls in grade five which showed the differences between the female and male anatomy, and the various effects of the different diseases. I particularly recall most of the kids said it was "gross" and the boys came from their presentation snickering and laughing nervously.

Several of Lindsey's friends were interviewed by the school nurse, after which the subject was no longer discussed. It was taboo. All the girls refrained from using the bathroom Lindsey used. Lindsey became a social outcast . . . she had been exiled. I never really knew what fate John suffered as his family moved right after this incident.

I was becoming less naive about people's behavior and entertained the idea that there were different reasons for popularity, and it was not based on personality. There were young ladies who were never lacking for male company but were known as sluts, easy makes and whores. It was obvious that the male students did not respect them. I felt sorry for these girls especially when they got pregnant and had to leave school.

My mother regularly told my sister and me it was not a good thing to get pregnant unless you were married. I advised her she had nothing to worry about since I was not sexually active, far from it. Since Gary, I had even become gun shy about liking boys though I was aware of their existence.

I would graduate with honors. Mr. Smiley, my chemistry and science teacher and Miss Fuller, my literature and English teacher, strongly encouraged me to go on to university since I was an above average student. With pride I prepared to explore the universities in our city. I realized I would need to minimize all university costs and expenses as much as possible knowing that my parents would need me to do so.

My father congratulated me on my outstanding achievements in school also telling me "I am very proud of you, Anuska" while the look on his face told me something was askew.

"Anuska, your mother and I have talked this over many times. We don't have the money to send you to university. We know how much you want to go and you should. Your teachers are right you should go but there is no money left over once we pay our regular bills. Your mother and I are pleased you graduated high school with honors.

Look at your sister, she left high school after grade 10 and is making an excellent wage as a secretary. Before too long you will get married. Your mother says girls don't need as much schooling. I know you think differently. I'm truly sorry. If I could help you, I would."

My parents had known for a long time my dream was to work in the summers to save money for college. My father had often proudly stated "you'll be the first one in our family to graduate from a university." I felt it was very difficult for my father to have this conversation with me particularly since we had often discussed my hopes for the future. Though his head was bent, I could still see how his blue eyes were full of sadness.

To say I was very disappointed is an understatement. I also couldn't help but wonder what my mother would have said in these circumstances if I had been a boy. Why had my Dad brought up my sister's situation since I felt it had nothing to do with me? Everything was different. My sister had never been overly interested in school even though she always had exceptionally high marks in all her subjects. It was always my understanding that Maria made the decision to continue working because she liked her job and the money was exceptionally good.

As I pondered my current lot in life, rightly or wrongly, I acknowledged I had often felt a lack of encouragement from my mother particularly regarding my hopes to go to university. I usually excused her lack of interest in some of my dreams due to the overwhelming demands of our family situation. There was the need to take in boarders for extra income and as a result, my mother had excessive laundry, cooking and cleaning to do. Given these circumstances, perhaps at times she had little time and energy to listen to my daydreams. I concluded, most of the time, my mother loved me but just didn't have much time to show it. This awareness had come early in my life as I compensated for these feelings by finding loving support from my loving uncles and aunts.

This morass prompted me to remember this unhappy childhood memory. I wanted to bake a cake to please my mother. It was bound to be easy since it was a cake mix and all you had to do was add an egg and water. I had watched my sister do it many times. My initial efforts were halted with "Anna, let your sister bake the cake . . . you'll make a mess." I was crushed. While she was probably right, I so wanted to bake that cake for her and just maybe, I wouldn't have made a mess.

In all fairness to my mother, she occasionally let me help her when she was baking but I felt it wasn't the same as doing it myself. "Anna, why don't you watch. You can do this when you're older. Let your sister do it" were words I heard too often.

It is interesting indeed, all the experiences that shape us to become the people we are. I know many things I did in my life were to prove to myself that I could do them.

When Maria and I discuss early childhood events, she is always amazed at how differently we describe our perceptions of the same situation. She believes she was never my mother's favorite daughter and is surprised when I recollect certain events to substantiate my claim.

I believe my personality was greatly influenced by the tremendous pain and sorrow I experienced, that was prompted by my mother's angry outburst, supposedly, because I had not done a household chore. My mother's explosive anger took me by surprise. I was taken aback and incredibly shocked when she blurted out "your father was really disappointed when you were born, he wanted a son." I couldn't believe what I was hearing. I was devastated.

Where was this coming from and why? Was it really true?

I ran into my room in tears totally devastated by this turn of events. Several hours later, after reflecting on my fairly short life, I concluded I would speak to my father when he got home about what my mother had said. Surely it wasn't true.

My father saved money for our Sunday walks with his family so he could buy Anuska, a double coned, three scoop ice cream that he enjoyed watching me eat.

My father built a wooden high chair for my one and only porcelain doll and surprised me on Christmas day with this special gift. He worked on this project in the evenings, late at night, after I was asleep, dead tired often after working twelve hours a day. He surely wanted me.

No matter how tired my Daddy was, he would tell me my favorite story of Ali Baba and the Forty Thieves. It always sounded best in the Czech language.

My father looked so sad when I told him what my mother said I wondered if I had done the right thing.

"Anuska, before you were born I once mentioned to your mother it would be nice to have a son. Anuska, I loved you from the moment I laid eyes on you. Maria has her place in my heart and you Anuska have your very special place in my heart. I could never want you to be anyone but who you are."

My father's eyes looked very shinny from the tears that were close to falling down his cheeks and I felt somewhere inside he was feeling my pain.

"Anna, I don't know why your mother said what she did . . . just believe what I am telling you." I believed my father.

My mother never said another word about this matter. She acted as if nothing happened. In time, I accepted she would not apologize and I must learn to behave as if nothing had happened.

Whenever I felt sad about my mother's words . . . it hurt so much . . . I would ask my Dad to tell me about his adventures and how it came about that we are all living in Montreal. Only when I got much older, did I truly realize the tremendous risks he had taken and the extreme challenges that he faced to create a new life for himself and his family. I will recount his story as best I can. Many of the words are my own since he told his story in his native language.

"There were many immigrants on the big ship that crossed the ocean to come to Canada to start a new life. Your mother and Maria, who was a baby, were still in the old country . . . they would join me when I earned enough money to pay for their ship's fare. You, Anuska, were born in Canada years later.

The authorities had given us labels with our names on them as well as our final destination in Canada. Your father was destined to go to Saskatchewan to work as a farmer. Since my family had never been farmers, they were all craftsmen, I felt the authorities had made a big mistake. I didn't speak English except for a few words that I learned on the ship. I made friends with a Hungarian man on the ship because I spoke Hungarian. I was a prisoner in the First World War . . . that's how I learned the language . . . but that dear Anuska is another story for another time.

When I discussed my problem with my new Hungarian friend, he said he too was scheduled to go to western Canada but was not planning to do so. His cousin had written him a letter, before he sailed for Canada, telling him that when the train slowed down, you could jump off . . . and then you could work your way back to Montreal and no one would be the wiser.

My father said then and there, I made up my mind that I would be successful in jumping off the train to live in the city where I would find a good job. I was optimistic . . . your mother and Maria would not have to wait a long time to join me in our new life. There were so many immigrants, the name tags were often wrong or got lost, I was certain the authorities would not spend time looking for one or two men.

The train slowed down, my heart was beating very fast, it was time . . . I jumped, rolling my body down the hill. When I came to a stop, I was lying on my back in the middle of nowhere. I felt my arms and legs and realized that I hadn't broken any bones. I gingerly stood up and walked around in a circle because that's all I could do . . . there were so many trees around. I recognized how lucky I was that I didn't hit a tree . . . it probably would have killed me. Instead, I had rolled into some bushes that had broken my fall.

I looked to see if my suitcase, that I had thrown ahead of me before I jumped, was anywhere in sight. It took some time but I found it. The miracle was that the suitcase had not opened up because of the strong cords I had tied around it. I started wondering if my Hungarian friend had jumped as well. I didn't think so . . . perhaps he did so later on at another stop.

It took over a week to get to Montreal and I quickly discovered that most of the people spoke French; in fact, some of them spoke less English than I had learned on the ship. I finally got in touch with a Michael Romanski, someone from the old country, that would supposedly help me get started in my new country. This too took time since he had changed his name to Michael Roman.

I learned Michael's help was not real help. I came to realize he was taking advantage of his countrymen . . . exploiting them . . . and I swore, someday, to help others in a positive way. You must remember, Anuska, your father didn't know the difference between a nickel, dime or quarter. In the beginning, when I bought a loaf of bread and some milk, I would let people take the right amount of change out of my hand. I relied on people not to cheat me.

Your father met some good people and I became a boarder with a nice family where I lived for a year and a half, after which time, I had enough money to bring your mother and Maria to Canada. I usually worked eighteen hours a day, seven days a week since that was the only way to bring my family to Canada as soon as possible.

From the beginning of my life in Montreal, I knew it was important that my children learn to speak French but it was more important that they learn English since all the major businesses were English speaking. Anuska, that is why we live in a French neighborhood and you go to an English school."

My father was a very bright man who was probably way ahead of his time in much of his thinking regarding the language you needed to speak in order to prosper in Canada.

I am my father's wanted, beloved daughter. In the midst of my pain and anguish, I am trying to deal with the disappointment that my parents cannot assist me financially to go to university. I am determined to find a way and decide to talk to my strongest supporters at the school. Is there scholarship money?

The answer is no. Mr. Smiley, a sentimental man in the best of times, has tears streaming down his cheeks. "Anna we must find a way. It would be a crying shame."

I think of how ironic his words are given his current state.

Graduation day is coming quickly but I am not absorbed by the details apart from buying the material for my graduation gown that my mother will be making for me. I am still trying to figure out a way to go to university.

Lily and Myrtle both have dates to the prom. It occurs to me I don't have a date. Well I can always go with good old Jerry who lives down the block . . . I know he would be happy to take me.

At the last minute I get an invitation from George, one of the handsomest boys in the school. He is very popular so I am somewhat curious why he already didn't have a date. I also wonder why he waited until the last minute to ask me? Then I decide whatever the reason, I am delighted he asked me. I think Lily is more excited than I am when I tell her I'm going to my graduation with George.

"Gosh, Anna, aren't you excited? He's so cute . . . always surrounded by the ladies . . . you sure are lucky" said Lily.

"I'm pleased . . . lucky I don't know."

I really appreciate my gown that is really lovely thanks to my mother's exceptional sewing skills. I get a beautiful gardenia corsage from George. I am embarrassed when my mother and father say we look great together. It is fun driving to the graduation dance in George's father's Studebaker.

I admit I am slightly surprised George and I have such a wonderful time especially with Myrtle, Lily and their dates given that parts of me are feeling sad for many reasons. Momentarily, I wonder will any of us be this young and carefree again?

I will miss some of my teachers and friends. I know we will go our different ways. What sustains me is that some of the intimacies we shared together will be memories to treasure. I feel nostalgia. I recognize a part of me is longing to cling to my early hopes and expectations that I had when I first came to this high school four years ago. I know this longing is unrealistic. I have changed and so have my perceptions and expectations.

To commemorate our pending graduation, three months prior to my graduation, as Editor-in-Chief of our high school paper, I wrote the following:

"The other day I realized, after looking over my old anthology, which I have kept ever since my public school days, that the poems within were all the hopes and wishes of different individuals, written in various ways, and I came to the conclusion that life is almost entirely centered on one's hopes and desires. Perhaps I have exaggerated, somewhat, but just think of the many times you wish this or that would happen. Yes, you honestly can say that it occurs, though unconsciously, at least once a day.

A poet once wrote,
If there were dreams to sell,
What would you buy?

If you were the fortunate owner of Aladdin's Lamp, what would be your foremost desire? At first thought you might mention some immaterial items you might want but after seriously debating the question over in your mind, perhaps you would still find yourself perplexed and floundering in the dark.

Think! What really is the most important desire in your life?

We are all bound to dream some time or other, many of us when we're unhappy, and others because we are natural dreamers. Try and remember far back when you were only about five or six . . . remember how you wanted that new toy for Christmas . . . then when you were twelve, how you built castles in the sky, or often imagined yourself on that bicycle, which Dad thought was too dangerous for you to ride . . . and now at age sixteen or seventeen you have new dreams. I believe, like me, you are dreaming of the day when in a long white gown you will walk up to the platform to receive your high school diploma.

Some of us make these dreams realities, others continuously go on wishing day after day, until we know that we are merely drifters reaching no definite goal.

Today we are in our 'Green Years' and our emotions are unsettled. Thus when we are advised by our elders and school teachers who are experienced, we sometimes doubt them. This seems to be natural; we have curiosity and it's part of growing up, but we should not act without considering the stable advice given to us by them.

If you wish to realize your dreams, you must be a good worker, an honest thinker, and a true believer in the task you are doing. At times it is a difficult job, but the road it leads to means happiness and success."

The balance of the editorial dealt with thanking all school staff and others for helping in the publication of our newspaper.

My prototype in the newspaper was "Starry-eyed dreamer."

Chapter Three

Glimmer of success . . .
money, values and young love

Whatever task you undertake, do it with all your heart and soul. Always be courteous, never be discouraged. Beware of him who promises something for nothing. Do not blame anybody for your mistakes and failures. Do not look for approval except the consciousness of doing your best.

Bernard M. Baruch

I work all summer as a typist. It is clear to me that for the time being I must set aside my academic goals. I will work hard and be the best typist in my company. I can hear my father's words "if it's worth doing, do it well." My parents believe I have adjusted to my work environment as I do not complain about my job. Knowing that only a handful of students went on to university is no consolation to me and does not assuage my inner pain.

My immediate work environment consists of Mr. O'Malley, vice-president of sales and marketing, Joanne Turner, his secretary, Mrs. Hattie Enders, senior secretary and Chris Holmes, chief administrator. I am hired to work for Chris. Mr. O'Malley is always exuberant and cheerful when his sales numbers are up at which time we all appreciate and enjoy his generous contributions of donuts, chocolates and candy. We have also all learned when Mr. O'Malley's sales figures are not up to par, it is best to keep a low profile and stay out of his way to avoid becoming the recipient of his volatile outbursts.

Joanne, Mr. O'Malley's secretary, is a tall, willowy blonde who wears elegant business suits that men in the office say "makes her more enticing than she already is." She isn't married but I learn from the young girls in the filing department "she is off limits to all the young men in our company." Being the innocent, I ask "why?" The response is a lot of giggling and "you'll find out soon enough."

Hattie Enders's husband did business with Mr. O'Malley's family. When Mr. Enders died suddenly, Hattie was astonished to learn from her attorneys that she was in a financial crisis and not well to do as she had believed. Her married life style had been one of wealth and privilege. Her husband had handled all their finances and never denied her anything she ever wanted. Mr. O'Malley, a compassionate man, heard about Hattie's financial predicament and hired her as a secretary. He felt an obligation to help Hattie due to the long history their families had shared.

Hattie was completely lost in her new environment. She had never worked in an office before. She typed with two fingers when someone gave her a small task just to make her feel she was a contributing member of our group. Since the achieved outcome took so long and was often not satisfactory, Hattie found herself with little work and much time on her hands. She called friends and family, and spent most of her time just puttering around or talking to Mr. O'Malley in his office when things were going well for him.

Chris did the bulk of the work required to keep this department going. He came to work first and always left last. He ate his lunch at his desk working while he was eating. He called his wife twice a day, once in the morning and once in the afternoon. These were very brief calls to ask how the twin baby boys were doing . . . and to tell her that he loved her.

The office quickly discovered I was the fastest typist they had ever had. They were also surprised to learn that I listened well when I was given a typing assignment and the results were excellent. Chris was delighted to finally get some help that he said was "really help" compared to the past typists he had endured. We spoke very little but were comfortable with each other in the mutuality of the work we shared.

Hattie sought my help in the few assignments she received when things were hectic at the office and, in despair, someone gave Hattie something to do. I quickly did her assignment for her and soon learned she was taking credit for the work I had done. Of course no one believed her and they gradually figured out what was going on.

I decided Hattie wasn't a bad soul. She was just totally unprepared for the unexpected turn in her life. Hattie had been a socialite. Being in a business office as an employee had never been part of her life's plan. Poor Hattie. Her social conditioning had not required working skills and it was obvious she was overwhelmed by her current life situation.

I knew I would never confront Hattie about her behavior. Most of the time I felt sorry for her. I also felt Hattie saw me as an ally. She started confiding in me during lunch time, telling me about her past life, the gala dinners and balls she had attended, the extravagant parties she had given and the trips around the world she had taken. She told me she was from a prominent family. She was pleased that she had influenced her children in marrying well as she had. Hattie completely ignored the fact her deceased husband had left her in dire straits. Hattie said she very seldom heard from her children and rarely saw them since their father's death. She accepted their absence in her life stating she knew how busy they all were.

I was often curious that Hattie never once asked about my life but came to realize I was merely a sounding board she needed when Mr. O'Malley didn't have time to listen. The only personal comment she ever said to me during our business relationship was when I resigned my job "I will miss talking to you. People don't want to listen. You listen." I was sixteen. Hattie was sixty-three.

Eventually, I accidentally discovered the mystery regarding Jean. Jean was Mr. O'Malley's mistress. Mr. O'Malley was supposedly happily married to his Irish childhood sweetheart. They had four boys and were staunch Roman Catholics. It was clear to everyone that knew about his affair with Jean, now going on five years, that Mr. O'Malley would never leave his wife. Rumor had it, only Jean believed she had a future with Mr. O'Malley when his boys were older at which time, she was convinced Mr. O'Malley would do the right thing.

Jean always treated me well. Whenever I did some typing for her, she always told Mr. O'Malley, in my presence, "Anna did this document for you. There were no errors, perfect as usual and in record time." I appreciated her praise since my boss, Chris, said very little besides thank you.

I thought about love and how complicated it all seemed to be for some people. Jean could have had her pick of the eligible men in our company yet she fell in love with Mr. O'Malley who definitely was not eligible. Do you have a choice who you fall in love with?

I wondered if Mr. O'Malley confessed his sins on a regular basis. I thought of Jeannine who told me how good she felt after her confessions. "God has forgiven all my sins. Now I can start all over again." During the past five years, did Mr. O'Malley ever regret his feelings for Jean? How about Mrs. O'Malley; did she suspect anything?

I was glad I didn't have to figure it out but couldn't help thinking how things might turn out. I did not judge them. I liked them all in their own way. I was sure when I fell in love my prince charming would be mine only . . . and holding hands, together we would walk into the sunset. When I daydreamed about love, it always ended this way.

A friend who shared her romantic fantasies and day dreams with me was Leda Burne.

I met Leda just before I graduated from high school. She was different from all my other friends. She wore spectacular, colorful clothes, with exquisite embroidery that she said represented her Hungarian heritage. She had many real cousins, uncles and aunts that we would sometimes visit together.

I met Whitey, a friend of a cousin, in a group setting. He was tall, handsome in a rugged way and had fairly long curly brown hair and dark brown eyes. He said very little to anyone but appeared to be enjoying himself. I thought he might be much older than the rest of us. Leda said he was twenty, was an electrician who had recently returned from working on a major project somewhere up north. He had very few friends since he had been away for over two years.

Whitey and I became friends in this group setting. I was flattered he spent so much time with me particularly since he was more mature than all the other boys. My parents said I could have a birthday party when I turned sixteen. I surprised them and myself by saying okay. I invited Whitey to the party since Leda was invited too. Whitey gave me a phonograph player that he knew I wanted and didn't have. I was amazed since this was too extravagant a gift to accept and responded accordingly. Whitey said he had the money . . . he was working unlike the other boys, so please would I think about accepting his birthday gift . . . "I really want you to have it." I told Whitey I would discuss this matter with my parents after the party and let him know what they said. Whitey asked if he could talk to me about a private matter after the party had ended.

After the party ended, Whitey and I sat in our garden swing so he could talk to me. Whitey asked me to marry him. I was speechless. He went on to say he knew I was very young but we could grow older together. He said he would be a good provider, he would always love me and take care of me. He would talk to my father since we needed his permission to marry. Whitey had no family and wanted my family to be his.

Once I recovered from the shock, I told Whitey I couldn't marry him. I was only sixteen and while I liked him a lot, I didn't love him. Whitey asked if maybe I wouldn't change my mind?

Shortly after this conversation, Whitey accepted another out-of-town assignment. I wondered if he would have taken me with him if we had married or would he have left me behind. Then I realized it didn't really matter.

My parents insisted I give back the phonograph player. I tried to reach Whitey but he had disappeared and the phonograph player was never picked up. A year later, Leda said Whitey was married and they were expecting their first child. I never told Leda or anyone else about Whitey's proposal. I also never saw Whitey again.

Myrtle and I occasionally went bicycling on a Saturday afternoon. We would sit on the banks of the St. Lawrence River to get caught up on our latest activities. "Have you heard the rumors about your gorgeous date, George? My brother heard from the guys that he's queer." Another surprise right after Whitey.

"Are you sure? You do mean he likes boys instead of girls? Come to think of it, the only time I ever went out with him was to the prom. But Myrtle, he's always been so popular with the girls. When I didn't hear from him again, I figured after the prom, he found a steady girlfriend. He sure didn't act gay . . . he even kissed me goodnight. Gosh, Myrtle you would think I at least would have suspected something was different, don't you?"

"Well, Anna, maybe it's not true. He is a handsome guy. My brother said he was only repeating what he had heard."

"Yea, he was one of the best looking guys at the prom . . . a nice guy but not my type."

"For sure Irene is a lesbian . . . that is definitely not a rumor" said Myrtle emphatically

"I didn't know. Where did you hear that? I played basketball with Irene. What gives all of a sudden? You're full of surprises today."

Myrtle says "I met Irene at Jerry's Ice Cream Parlour when I was buying some ice cream to take home for my mother. She said she was waiting for a friend. She asked me to talk to her for a while while she waited. One thing led to another and she just told me. I'm not really surprised though. Think about it, Anna, she's never had an interest in boys and unlike George who has always been surrounded by girls, have you ever seen Irene with a guy? Irene says she doesn't want everyone to know yet but I told her she is going to have a problem keeping it a secret if she is talking about it. I told her you're telling me, knowing I'll be telling Anna . . . but assured her it would go no further from us."

"Myrtle, this is getting too complicated. I must be awfully innocent but then what do I know about sex? Let's talk about your boyfriend instead . . . if he is still your boyfriend. I know you say you like him but you're not crazy about him."

We chat for a long time about anything and everything and then bicycle back home along the river road enjoying the spring time beauty of nature. The maple trees, birch trees and evergreens are glorious and we also spot many blooming wild flowers along the way. People's lives seem to be more complex than I ever thought but at the moment I am content with my lot in life.

The tango was the rage. Everyone was trying to learn this new dance. Leda, a gifted dancer, was superb at it. She volunteered to teach me the tango but admitted she was not being altruistic in that she needed a dance partner to practice with. Painstakingly she taught me the steps that I finally mastered. She always warned me when she was planning to dip me but nevertheless in my early stages of learning we would both land up on the floor. I loved the tango music and the dance itself. I realized that it was touching a part of me that had never expressed itself before. I was dancing just for the sheer joy of it. It felt completely different than when I had danced in Slovak concerts though they had been fun.

Leda said we were ready for the big time. We decided to go to a local dance. During the entire evening no one played the tango. It was jitterbugging only. Were we like two fish out of water? We had high expectations that would definitely not be met at this dance. Leda said we had to do our homework and find out where people went to dance the tango. In the meantime, we jitterbugged with a few boys, pleased we were not wall flowers for the evening. I met Charlie for the first time who said he would call me. Charlie did call and the tango went on the back burner for a while.

Charlie took me on long walks, told me about his family, his friends, his hopes, his desires . . . I think Charlie told me everything about Charlie there was to know. He was like a big puppy dog that wanted to be liked . . . and I did like him. Charlie taught me how to kiss. I can honestly say, Charlie knew how to kiss better than anyone I ever kissed. I can't put into words why he got this claim to fame, he just was the greatest. I felt special, loved and treated with the utmost respect. He ambled into my life when I needed his puppy dog love and he instinctively knew when it was time to amble out of my life. Whenever I bumped into him, he was always pleasant, happy to see me and still comfortable in sharing what was going on in his life. I always felt Charlie was not a complicated person . . . he was who he was and that was just great.

Myrtle was going steady with a handsome black man but stated emphatically no one was going to deter her from achieving her goals. She was getting more interested in black women's issues and was actively exploring areas where she felt she might make a difference. During a long conversation, Myrtle said I had inherited my mother's charm and the opposite sex was easily attracted to me even though I seemed indifferent to them in many cases. I was genuinely surprised since I believed I was completely different from my mother.

While Myrtle was going steady, I on the other hand felt I had never really gone steady with anybody. I went out with boys on a regular basis but maintained my independence. The longest relationship I had was with Eddy who I believed would always be my friend. Eddy Johnson was the sweetest, kindest boy I ever knew. We went to the movies, concerts, his mother's house for dinner . . . she liked meeting Eddy's friends . . . the ice cream parlour to have banana splits, roller skating, bowling, ice skating, card playing . . . we did it all . . . and we always enjoyed ourselves. I liked Eddy a lot and I thought of Eddy as the brother I never had. When I met Russell, I recognized Eddy and I would be seeing less of each other. I told Eddy about Russell and he said "if you ever need a friend, you know where I am . . . I'll always be here for you." It was the first time Eddy also told me he loved me.

Russell was my first crush after Gary. He came from a large Irish family where everyone always seemed happy. I thought Russell was so cool . . . easy on the eyes . . . dark black curly hair, green eyes, dimples . . . you could say he was tall and handsome. Russell and I saw each other nearly every day for three months. He told me I was the most fascinating girl he had ever dated . . . the smartest too.

We talked about astrology, the planets, religion and sometimes the political situation that continued to brew between the English and the French. Russell talked about his Catholicism and I talked about the Greek Orthodox and Baptist religions.

We talked about our jobs, our hopes and our dreams.

Russell stated I was his girl and he was my guy. While I didn't respond to his statement, I was feeling more receptive to the idea of being exclusive in my relationship with him. I was still a virgin. I got the sense that I must be careful with Russell. He had not been forceful in his attentions to me but had verbally stated he had deep feelings . . . he claimed it was becoming more difficult for him. I knew what he meant. I was experiencing emotions I never felt before. Could this be love?

Russell breaks our Saturday night date due to a family obligation. I assure him it's just fine . . . I will probably go somewhere with my friend Leda, maybe a dance just to keep her company. Fate intervenes. Leda and I go to a dance in her community. What a small world it is. Russell is there with a girl. They dance together . . . they kiss . . . he has his arm around her when they leave the dance floor . . . I think back "this is my guy?" Our eyes meet across the room . . . he has now seen me. He rushes over leaving the girl behind "it's not what it looks like."
"It's not" I say. My head held up high, I leave the dance. Leda follows me "what a jerk, you're better off without him." I start crying. Leda tries to comfort me to no avail.

Russell tries in vain to convince me that he only cares about me. I refuse to go out with him again. I feel betrayed. Russell was dishonest. My intuition tells me he is intimate with this other girl. Eventually I learn from a friend of his my intuition is right. Russell has been seeing his new friend for a couple of weeks, primarily because they are having sex. His friend tries to reassure me that Russell likes me, not the other girl. I think he sure has a strange way of showing it. All I know is I don't trust Russell anymore. I will move on. Obviously, Russell is not my prince charming.

Eddy and I resume seeing each other again, as friends only, what we have always been. He tells me he dated a couple of girls while I was with Russell. What am I feeling when he tells me this? I know Eddy deserves the best because he is the best. I know I love him but not the way he wants to be loved. I swallow hard, then tell him "Eddy I hope you find the girl of your dreams." Perhaps it is just my imagination but it seems to me that Eddy smiles rather sadly when he says "maybe I already have."

The rain is coming down in torrents surrounded by an angry wind. I press my face against the window pane as I did when I was a young child. I like the feel of the smooth glass protecting me against the forceful drops of rain. I am back with my mother at Mrs. Schwartz's house, so many years ago, with my face against the window pane watching the rain drops fall in a staccato that I find mesmerizing.

Apart from the boarders we had, to supplement our family income and meet my parents' goal of saving enough money to buy a house, when I was at school, my mother also occasionally cleaned wealthy people's homes. I believe she was called a charwoman. I had a sore throat on the day Mrs. Schwartz's house was scheduled to be cleaned and since the nurse had sent me home the day before because I was ill, my mother felt she had no recourse but to bundle me up and take me with her. She explained how I would have to be very quiet while she was working and not bother Mrs. Schwartz. I could bring some of my favorite books to keep me company.

Mrs. Schwartz was agitated when she saw me immediately asking my mother "how will you get the house cleaned with your daughter underfoot?" Since my mother's English was limited, she just told Mrs. Schwartz "it will be okay" after which she proceeded to place me in a safe corner in a room telling me under no circumstances was I to touch anything. I wouldn't have dared. I had never seen such a lavish home before. It was so big I guessed Mrs. Schwartz had a huge family. I later learned she had only one daughter.

The heavy rainfall encouraged me to leave my corner of the room, to press my face against the window to play my special game. How many bubbles in the puddle can you count? What shapes in the puddles can you see? If you counted 25 bubbles in one puddle, you made a magic wish. I wished I had a magic carpet to fly to Greece and see Aurora. This was my favorite wish. I wished my parents had enough money to buy me a bike. I would pretend the wish came true and I often drove my make-believe bike, that was always a bright red, to wondrous places. My imagination let me create whatever I wanted.

Mrs. Schwartz spent all her time talking on the telephone. I heard her tell friends that the cleaning woman had brought her child but the child was so well behaved and not the problem she had anticipated. "My Debbie is probably the same age. A terror compared to this child. I must see how she keeps herself amused." I quickly left the window and sat with my books as my mother had advised me to do. Mrs. Schwartz asked my name and then she disappeared.

When I was eating lunch with my mother, Mrs. Schwartz gave me a glass of milk and two cookies. I ate one cookie and asked her if I could take the other cookie home if I didn't eat it. Mrs. Schwartz said yes, in fact she had a surprise for me because I was such a good little girl. She gave me two of Debbie's dresses that no longer fit her. They were so beautiful every time I wore them I felt like a princess. One dress was a pale yellow crepe with smocking on the front and on the sleeves. The other one was royal blue with umbrella pleats in white. They were the best dresses I ever had.

I had to wear my sister's clothes when they no longer fit her but I had grown enough so they fit me. I wanted new things once in awhile but knew my parents couldn't afford them very often. Mrs. Schwartz's dresses were my favorites along with another dress that my parents bought me for my birthday when I was ten. I remember it was a lovely rose color and had white lace around the neck and sleeves.

Mrs. Schwartz said it was too bad Debbie wasn't here to meet me. "She might have learned a few manners from you."

My mother had cleaned this large house only to come home to more work. She cooked our evening meal consisting of meat, potatoes and vegetables plus dessert. She cleaned up afterwards and then made sure everything was set out for tomorrow morning so that her husband and daughters could leave the house in an orderly fashion. My sister and I helped clean up whenever possible but homework was our main priority.

Will my life be like my mother's when I marry? Aunt Jennie never married. Everyone calls her an old maid but she's the happiest lady I know. Everyone overlooks the fact that Aunt Jennie lives with Gustaf. They both laugh a lot and are very much in love. I don't think she is an old maid.

Every time Aunt Jennie sees me she pinches my cheek, which I don't like, hugs me which I do like, then gives me a treat. Gustaf is married but his wife has been in a mental institution most of her life.

Aunt Jennie and my mother were talking about marriage and Aunt Jennie said "Gustaf and I believe we are married." My mother did not respond to Aunt Jennie which was her way. Later that night, she was talking to my father about her conversation with Aunt Jennie "but Joe in the eyes of God they are not married." My dad playfully said "Helen we are . . . let God sort out Jennie and Gustaf." I heard a soft laugh coming from my mother. I stopped listening knowing they were making love.

Let me describe my mother and father as best I can. My mother was the youngest of five children. Her parents were farmers and every child, regardless of their age, had chores to do on a daily basis. My mother told me she was only five years old when her job was to bring the cows back to the barn every evening. She said there were so many cows it was a very difficult job especially when it was raining or it had rained. The ground would turn to mud and she would be sliding all over the place along with the cows. She was often afraid they would run her over since they were much bigger than she. She remembered often holding on to the tail of the last cow who would drag her back to the barn. On muddy days she got back to the barn covered in mud from head to toe.

She learned to milk the cows early on in her life and that too was one of her major chores. Because there were so many cows, she spent many hours in the barn. She had a pet cow that seemed happy to see her. My mother said she was very sad when the cow was sold.

What I could never understand was when my mother told me her family slept above the stove . . . and they had a big comforter filled with goose feathers . . . "it was wonderful and you stayed warm all night." She would describe where they slept as something like a loft above the stove but I had a problem imagining it. How could you sleep above a stove? Many times, I heard the people from the old country reminiscing about their old beds. I concluded everyone knew what my mother was talking about except me.

The story about my grandmother frightened me but it also made me feel good because it had a happy ending. My mother would show me a picture of my grandmother, who I never knew. With much feeling she would tell me the following:

"Your grandmother was not a pretty woman. She was a beautiful woman. When she was still young, and I, your mother, was a very little girl, the Russian soldiers came to our farm to confiscate some horses. Your grandfather heard the horses galloping towards the farm and was very fearful for your grandmother. The villagers knew that the soldiers sometimes raped the local women.

Your grandfather hid your grandmother in a huge haystack and told her, under any circumstances, she was not to say a word or cry out since that would reveal where she was.

The soldiers asked "where is your wife?"

My grandfather answered "she is visiting sick relatives in another village."

The soldiers took some pitch forks and started prodding the very haystack your grandmother was hiding in. Your grandfather said he prayed with all his heart that the soldiers would miss your grandmother's body. He also prayed that we children would not say a word as he had advised us before the soldiers came. I think we were speechless because we were terrified. God answered your grandfather's prayers.

The soldiers stopped poking in the haystack and went to look at my grandfather's horses. At first it looked like they planned on taking all the horses but your grandfather bravely said "surely you will leave me some horses to plow my land." A soldier kicked your grandfather to the ground. He was doubled up in pain but was very relieved when he saw they only took three of his best horses then quickly galloped away.

My mother was also a very beautiful, intelligent woman and looked very much like my grandmother in Czechoslovakia. She was feminine, demure and men were both fascinated and captivated by her. A widow in her elder years, she still attracted the opposite sex and I recall when I told her that, she laughingly stated she would never love again. Occasionally she continued to enjoy a good conversation with one of my dad's friends.

Though she had women friends, I felt many ladies were jealous of her though I can honestly say I never saw her behave in a way that warranted their jealousy. I believe there may have been some resentment because women knew men were attracted to my mother.

Sometimes I think she felt left out of women's groups. Yet in spite of all the extra work she had to do because of our boarders, I believe she sublimated some of her energies in creating a gracious, charming home, along with cultivating a beautiful garden and designing lovely clothes for me and my sister. She always dressed simply which only enhanced her slender body and good looks.

I was about eight years old when I accidentally overheard four ladies from the old country, who occasionally visited our home, gossiping about my mother. I was playing in the park and they were totally unaware of my presence. I quietly sat behind a huge maple tree and some bushes and listened when I first heard my mother's name mentioned.

"I guess some men find her pretty but I don't think she is. True, she has a good figure but overall I can't say she's anything special."

"Well you must admit she does have beautiful eyes and no matter what she does to her hair whether it's tied in a bun, or she let's it hang loose, it always looks great . . . but yes, maybe you're right she isn't all that pretty."

"Those simple dresses of hers . . . ."

At first I felt bad and then the more I listened, the angrier I got. I startled them all, when I suddenly appeared in front of them, while they were still talking, and said "my mother is very pretty and you are all jealous because none of you are."

When they recovered from the shock, the most outspoken one said "you are a bad little girl to talk to us that way . . . we will tell your mother . . . go home right away." I cried all the way home.

I knew I had been very impolite; you never spoke back to your elders but worst of all, I had probably embarrassed my family. I immediately confessed to my mother what I had said to the ladies and why. She wiped my tears and said "you are not a bad little girl but you do know you may not speak to adults that way." I nodded my head in agreement.

Things worked out better than I expected. My mother gave me some cookies and milk along with a kiss and a hug. I promised her I wouldn't act this way again and I told her I was sorry. I kept waiting for the ladies to come over and tell my mother what a bad girl I had been. They never did.

As time went on, I noticed all the ladies in the park acted as if nothing had ever happened and my mother was always friendly and polite to them whenever she saw them. I thought big people sure acted strange sometimes.

My mother taught Maria and me how to embroider, sew, string beads and sing delightful Czech songs . . . all the things her mother had taught her to do in the old country. She created much beauty with her delicate hands.

With the passage of time, my mother suffered major disappointments in how her daughters were evolving. It was clear, we were not meeting her expectations. As our horizons expanded, we identified some of our needs and hopes for the future. Our hopes often conflicted with her hopes for us. Quite often she lamented "what will become of you" followed by the expression I heard too often "what will people say." As I got older and was less timorous, I would ask her "who are these people you worry about? . . . why do you care what they think?"

My want was not to hurt her and eventually for the sake of peace, I learned not to respond to her more frequent outbursts. My sister, being older and wiser, very seldom responded to my mother's statements.

My mother changed significantly when she became a

grandmother. Baba, as her loving grandchildren called her, seemed ignited with a new zest for living. She was less fearful, happier and adventurous in her thoughts. She appeared to be actually enjoying her new experiences. The children loved her and she never tired from playing with them.

It became apparent, my mother was feeling less responsible for whom I was. At times, I sensed she relished hearing about certain aspects of my life that were so completely different from hers.

I have always been grateful for this turn of events. I believe this strong woman, who had crossed a vast ocean to create a better life for herself and her family somehow recognized the need for resilience. Innately she knew in accepting that her daughters' lives were different . . . old country ways did not work . . . she acknowledged that she must make some changes in her attitude and subsequent behavior.

How did she have this personal breakthrough? Endless questions arise. My father's example of unconditional love was probably the major catalyst in her life. It was as if the true meaning of life had been revealed to my mother. She was aware of the many gifts of love she could give as well as receive.

Above all, I admired her steadfast loyalty and devotion to her husband and family, this in spite of difficult events and circumstances in her life that often tested her mettle.

When I think of my Dad in the early and adolescent years of my life, I first recall his deep blue eyes, broad shoulders and large hands that I knew were very, very strong. He was not very tall, only medium height but he had the aura of strength one might attribute to a much taller, physically larger man. He was quiet, kind, nonjudgmental of others and was respected and liked by many of his countrymen and fellow workers.

I was aware that the people who knew my Dad felt he was

exceptionally intelligent, competent and very reliable . . . "Joe never let's you down . . . when Joe makes a commitment, he keeps his word . . . Joe does excellent work . . . he is a true friend . . . he is always there when you need him" . . . were words I heard about my father as a child.

My father taught me many valuable lessons that have remained with me all of my life. He supported his words and beliefs by his behavior and actions that he said "are proof of the words you speak."

My father taught me the value of money . . . how not to waste it but also to not let it control your life. I remember him saying "never measure the success of a man by the dollars he has accumulated." Again most of these lessons were taught by example.

The only time my father ever bought anything on credit was when he purchased a three-piece, burgundy velvet sofa set with chrome arms for our living room that my mother wanted so badly. Every Saturday afternoon, Mom, Dad and myself walked to Brophy's Furniture Store. Maria was usually with her friends. My Dad would take out a small record book that Brophy's had given him . . . to me it looked like a bank book . . . make his installment payment, watch carefully as the passbook was stamped by Brophy's indicating the amount he had just paid, then show my mother the outstanding balance still due. I knew my father was proud of the fact that he never missed a payment and was always on time. Mr. Brophy himself shook my father's and mother's hand when the furniture was fully paid for within the allotted twelve-month period. My mother received a complimentary glass juice set with little red flowers that made this day even more memorable.

Since my Dad cared about people, and was generous with his support whenever possible, many countrymen sought his counsel and financial help when they were getting started in this new country. This was difficult for both my parents since they certainly did not have money to spare. Somehow, they always prevailed in helping in some small measure those that needed help.

My Dad kept a record of the monies he lent to friends, no interest charged, in his little black book. I heard him say more than once "you'll pay me when you can" and his words of encouragement "you're on your way . . . I know things will go well . . . don't worry . . . you'll pay me as soon as you can."

One man whom we called Uncle Stanley borrowed money from my father. Uncle Stanley became prosperous and well established. My father waited a long time before asking Uncle Stanley on two different occasions when he planned on paying him back. Usually my father never had to ask people when they planned on paying him back. Uncle Stanley waffled and never gave my father a straight answer.

My parents had words regarding Uncle Stanley's outstanding account. My mother couldn't understand why the man wouldn't pay . . . everyone knew he now had lots of money. My Dad said quite firmly "That's enough. This man will have to live with himself. I won't ask him again. We won't talk about this anymore."

I think of the contrast between my father's last days on earth . . . while he was dying he was surrounded by his loving wife, daughters with husbands, all the grandchildren and many friends who at one time had been in my Dad's little black book . . . while Uncle Stanley had died without friends or family, completely alone.

Apart from Uncle Stanley, everyone in the little black book paid back my father.

My Dad also taught me about loyalty and true love. When he was terminally ill and his days were truly numbered but he still could function with our help, the hospital allowed my Dad one final trip home. Our entire family gathered together fully aware this would probably be the last time we would do so. My father spent his allotted time back home first hugging his grandsons and granddaughter since he was unable to speak and did the same with the rest of us. He then turned to my mother and together, with her support, they walked through their home one last time.

As long as I live I will remember my Mom and Dad, standing side by side, my Dad's formerly strong hands now weak and fragile, tinkering with buttons on the television, trying to fix something that wasn't working . . . trying to take care of her as he had done all of his life. I witnessed love spoken without words, so profound, just in the telling of it now I joyously relive the beauty of the love my parents had for each other.

Chapter Four

Turning points . . .
Love, agony, loss and tears

Such as thy words are, such will thine affections be esteemed; and such as thine affections, will be thy deeds; and such as thy deeds will be thy life.
Socrates

My sister Maria is engaged to be married to a young man from a Slovak family. My mother is ecstatic. She wants both of us to marry young men from Slovak families. Frank, Maria's future husband, wears tweed jackets and smokes a pipe. My sister is crazy about him. She thinks he is very deep and knows a great deal about philosophy. He was in the air force during the second world war doing gunnery work. Everything else we hear about Frank is all rather vague but we are told by his family he was in the middle of it all during the war. My first impression of Frank is that he is somewhat pretentious. I decide it's not important as long as Maria loves him and I keep my thoughts to myself.

A big wedding is planned to take place in the Greek Orthodox Church where Frank is a member. My father left that particular denomination due to a major disagreement with the parish priest. My father never talks about the disagreement but I have heard it has something to do with the church not supporting its people when they need help.

Our family has become a rather mixed group when it comes to

religion. Once in awhile my father goes to a United Church because he likes that particular minister and his sermons. My sister attends an Anglican Church where she was confirmed and I attend the Presbyterian Church where I was confirmed. My mother still clings to her Greek Orthodox roots though she only attends church on special occasions. She often voices her concern about our various church affiliations.

To complicate matters even further, I enjoy going to Myrtle's Baptist Church that is very lively and has an outstanding choir. Nearly everyone is black but the more I attend, the more comfortable I am. Lily and I have gone to the synagogue together as well. Since I believe there is only one God, we only worship him in different churches, I am never anxious about where I pray or rejoice in his name.

I have several serious conversations with Frank hoping that, since I am a voracious reader and have some knowledge of philosophy, we will have something in common. I am the first to admit I am a novice in this field so I am enthused about talking to someone like Frank. Also, I wish to please my sister by getting to know her future husband. I hope we can be friends. I leave the conversations I have with Frank wondering what is it we talked about? Perhaps I am too inexperienced to have tapped into his wealth of knowledge that my sister claims exist. I refrain from discussing Frank except to say I hope they will be happy.

How well I remember Maria's wedding. I was a bridesmaid. It was a traditional Greek Orthodox wedding ceremony that went on and on and on. At various times, there was so much incense sprinkled around I thought I was going to pass out.

To add to my problems, I was holding a heavy brass holder with a burning candle in one hand and with the other, my flowers plus my sister's bouquet so her hands were free to accept communion and her ring in marriage. Much of the service was conducted in Greek. I wondered what they were chanting. I think the only reason I managed to remain standing was that my mother would never forgive me if I ruined this gala event by passing out. I actually asked God to please give me the strength to complete my duties with grace and dignity.

When Maria and Frank were taking their vows, thunder and lightening came from the skies . . . not once, but many, many times. The wind swirling around the church was loud and sounded angry. I felt the whole situation was surreal. What was my mother thinking since she believed in omens? Was this a bad omen for my sister's future? I came back to the present relieved the marriage service was finally finished.

Three months after her marriage my sister became pregnant. During her pregnancy Frank physically abused her. Maria didn't know what had caused Frank to be so angry. She did not tell my mother and father but she confided in me, her little sister. She said that Frank was really a good man and he promised he would never hurt her again. She lost the baby. Frank was full of remorse and became withdrawn.

Shortly after Maria was pregnant again and had a lovely baby daughter whom they named Jennifer that everyone called Jennie. Their daughter's birth seemed to be a positive catalyst in their marriage . . . they appeared to be happy.

It wasn't too long before I came to realize when my sister stayed away from her family, she and Frank were having problems. I did not want to believe that Frank was beating Maria but I suspected she was hiding her bruises from us. When I found out this was the case, I wanted to help Maria and I decided I would speak to Frank about his behavior. I first informed Maria that I planned on having a conversation with Frank that would be non-confronting over a friendly cup of tea.

I was unprepared for what happened. An ingenue with good intentions was no match for Frank's anger. He became so livid, he lost control and hit me across the face. I fell to the ground at which time he started kicking me before I managed to crawl to the front door and left.

When I got home, I called my sister, fearful for her life . . . she was all right. I told her I intended to tell our parents what happened and that I planned on reporting Frank to the police. She begged me to reconsider. I said I could not since I was also afraid he might hurt my adorable niece, Jennie.

When I told my parents what was going on in Maria's life and what had just happened to me, they were shocked, surprised and grief stricken.

My mother cried hysterically while my father remained calm. My mother was very concerned about Maria. I must confess I also hoped she was not worried about "what will people think?" My father asked if I would give him some time to talk to Maria and Frank before I took any action. Against my better judgment I acceded to his request. Whatever took place between my father, Maria and Frank lead to the request that we all give Frank another chance.

My father also contacted Frank's parents to make them aware of their son's behavior as well as soliciting their support in this difficult situation. At this time, Frank's parents confessed that Frank had stayed in his room close to a year after returning from the second world war. He had many mood swings and sudden outbursts of anger. They thought he was much better particularly after he met Maria and decided to marry. My parents were flabbergasted at what they heard. How could they have kept this a secret? Then as Maria's parents they blamed themselves for not having been aware that Frank had problems.

Two weeks later my sister showed up with the baby. Both her eyes were swollen and practically closed . . . her lip was split . . . she had bruises all over her body . . . she was in acute pain with every breath she took. She made it to my parents' house only because she ran down the street, away from Frank and chanced to be picked up by a taxi driver who saw her plight. My mother gently removed her grand daughter from her daughter's arms. I watched my father, stricken with pain, wash the blood off my sister's face telling her in a soft, soothing voice he was taking her to the hospital. After Maria's examination, my father called the police to file a report.

My father talked privately to Maria several times for long periods of time. My sister told me she was filing for a divorce as she feared for her life.

No one in our family had ever filed for a divorce. Divorces were not common in the fifties and sixties and when they occurred, they created scandals in many families. My father emphasized the importance of supporting Maria in the face of possible censure particularly from the old country aunts and uncles.

My mother surprised us all by firmly announcing we did not have to air our laundry in public. When questioned, we would stand firm and just state that Maria had no other choice . . . and that was it. This was extremely difficult for everyone but extremely difficult for my mother to accept her daughter's dream and her dream for her daughter had been shattered. She displayed much courage and I marveled at how well she handled curious inquiries with firmness full of grace.

For some reason, I thought of Humpty Dumpty had a great fall . . . and no one could put the pieces back together again."

Alfred Adler states "because it is first born, the oldest child lives a favored existence for a time as an 'only child'. It is given central place until another child is born to remove its favored status." He further states the oldest child "trains himself for isolation."

Did Maria ever feel I had removed her favored status in the family? It was obvious she was my mother's favorite daughter.

Would she become isolated because of the divorce? I had so many thoughts and many unanswered questions.

We have all been traumatized and need time to heal. I am not eager to date. Though young, I am smart enough to know not all men have Frank's problems. I know my future will be different from Maria's. Will I surpass Maria? Do I want to surpass Maria?

I was becoming aware that I secretly aspired to be successful in a career.

Alfred Adler says "the second child is the conqueror, using direct and devious means to surpass the pacemaker." (The peacemaker is the oldest child).

I became eager to take on more responsibility to further my career, motivated to earn more money that would enable me to get a university degree by taking evening classes. An advertisement in the local paper for a junior secretary caught my eye. I resigned from my typing job when I was offered the junior secretary position. It was in a small office where I quickly found myself efficiently managing all my assigned responsibilities. I also made significant changes in their administrative procedures. Things were going well. I enjoyed the work until I encountered a major problem.

The elderly gentleman, my boss, that owned the company started making advances . . . in other words, hitting on me. I couldn't believe it. I was certain the problem would resolve itself if I remained professional, efficient and told him I was not interested. For a while, I was able to avoid his uncalled for advances by making sure we were never alone. Unfortunately one day we were. I learned the problem was more serious than I thought.
Today I can see it as a madcap scenario, a comedy scene for a play but at the time, it was devastating. Mr. Thomas chased me around the office . . . when cornered, I threw my files at him

and everything on the desk close by. He retreated. The following day I handed in my resignation.

I had to look for a job and wondered what I would tell a potential employer about my six months at the ABC Company. During job interviews when I told potential employers the truth, it did not serve me well. I came to the conclusion, they responded more favorably to "there was limited opportunity for me to grow so I made the decision not to waste my time." I quickly got a position as a secretary because of the excellent business and personal references I was able to provide. I was rather astounded to hear that Mr. Thomas had also provided outstanding references.

I was now working in the marketing department of a middle sized company and discovered that I had learned quite a lot about this field while typing for Mr. O'Malley and others when I was their typist. I was earning enough money to apply at a university that provided night time classes. I was excited to be on track again . . . the impossible dream was possible . . . it would just take longer than I thought . . . under very different circumstances.

Kenneth Smith came to repair the telephones in our office. There was a physicality about him that I found attractive . . . the way he walked, his broad shoulders, his tousled reddish blond hair and his deep baritone voice that were all embracing when he spoke to me. I accepted his invitation to go out for dinner. I was aware that many of my school friends were getting married and lately I found myself wondering how it would feel being the most important person in someone's life.

My mother was trying to convince me that her friend's son Michael would be a wonderful catch . . . "he would be a good husband." So far I had successfully escaped all her efforts to set me up with Michael as I didn't have the slightest interest in him. My mother was beginning to think I would be an old maid . . . I would never get married. She stated this quite often.

My mother thought I was becoming rebellious. I definitely was questioning the status quo in some instances. I knew my mother was fearful of whom I was becoming; someone she did not understand. I knew she yearned for her birth country whenever she was feeling insecure as a mother.

I make my own choices as to whom I will date, and accept Ken's dinner invitation. Ken and I had a very pleasant first date. My feeling was that we could be good friends and it might be fun to share thoughts and ideas with someone whose interests were so different from mine. Ken liked fast cars, motorcycles and racing. I liked to read philosophy, psychology, literature, history, poetry, etc. Ken liked boxing and hockey. I deplored boxing . . . it was so brutal . . . but I enjoyed hockey.

We exchanged many ideas as well as revealing to each other our secret hopes and wishes. There was a mutual trust and a realization that we were sexually attracted to one another. Our affectionate bonding sustained our relationship though I admit I was truly tempted "to go all the way." Our kisses became more intense and both of us agreed we could not go on like this. Ken respected that I was a virgin. He told me he believed we could have a future together. When I was with Ken, I was sexually aroused. When I was alone, I became ambivalent about whether we might have a future.

I decided to enroll in more night time classes at the university that drastically curtailed my free time. Ken and I dated sporadically and our time together became less dynamic. Since I didn't want to be in a committed relationship, we both agreed we should date other people.

I reflected on our relationship for a long time. I felt somewhat wiser. I had accepted that perhaps I have never been in love . . . infatuated, certainly. I knew that I still entertained the notion that when love comes my way I will be struck by it as though by lightning . . . and yet I wondered if that was realistic. I remember Myrtle saying "you're a dreamer and a realist . . .

tough combination." I also had accepted that you can't will yourself to love someone . . . I thought of Eddy . . . we are still good friends . . . but the passion just isn't there.

In the middle of my exams, my Aunt Sofie died of a sudden heart attack. I was her favorite, her beloved Anuska, the daughter she never had. My parents handled all the details of her funeral. Both of them were extremely saddened by her sudden departure from life. I recall Aunt Sofie's good nature, generous heart and how I never heard her say a bad thing about anyone. She encouraged me to dream saying "Anuska, everyone has a special star in the sky. The more you do in your life, the brighter the star." I loved my Aunt Sofie. In bed at night I recited a childhood prayer to her spirit. She loved to hear me say this prayer when I was little. I knew she would enjoy hearing it.

> *Jesus bids us shine with a clear pure light*
> *Like a burning candle glowing in the night*
> *In this world of darkness*
> *So we must shine, you in your small corner*
> *and I in mine.*

Aunt Sofie left me $1,000.00 and her garnet pin from Czechoslovakia. Her note that accompanied the money said "Anuska, do whatever you wish with this money . . . know that I was happy that I could give it to you. Love, Aunt Sofie." My boss at work played the stock market very successfully. I decided to take half the money and buy some stocks and put the rest in my bank account for emergencies. My action to invest this money felt exciting and something Aunt Sofie would have approved of.

I read in the local paper that Ryan O'Reilly has been arrested for robbing a service station. I am shocked and feel really sorry for Ryan and his family? What happened?

The O'Reilly family had seven sons and two daughters. They were a close-knit, religious family that lived in the Irish part of town. Ryan was at the local skating rink when I met him . . . I was trying very hard not to skate on my ankles as we kids used to say. For the first time in my life I had a new pair of white ice skates and believed this time I would be able to skate properly. I was eleven years old.

I thought Ryan looked younger than my father . . . sort of like an older brother. He was skating around and I guess had been watching me. He said "you're doing okay but I think you're having a problem because your skates are too large for you." "Let's go in the rink cabin and you can borrow my little sister's skates . . . I think they'll fit and you'll see the difference." I was really tired but I went in with Ryan and met his sister Kelly who was ten years old. She was getting warm by the stove . . . said her feet hurt . . . and yes, I could borrow her skates . . . she would watch mine.

Kelly's skates fit more like my shoes. I couldn't believe it.

I knew what it felt like to really skate . . . I was floating around the rink . . . not on my ankles . . . I felt like Sonja Henie, the champion skater. Ryan watched me with a big smile on his face. "See you are a good skater."

I once saw Ryan in town when I was with my father and we both said hello. Ryan said "did your feet grow into those nice white skates?"

"Yes, they have" I answered.

I never forgot the magical day Ryan gave me along with a big boost in my confidence that I too could skate well. I thought he was the kindest person and if I ever had a brother, I wanted him to be like Ryan.

Since Ryan was a local young man, there was much speculation in his Irish community as to what went wrong. The O'Reilly's were known as a respectable, religious family and considered to be honest "as the day is long."

I will always think fondly of Ryan and hope that his life is not completely ruined because of this incident. I think of Kelly, his little sister, and the love I saw in her eyes for her big brother, Ryan. How sad this must be for everyone.

I ask myself why do good people do bad things. Others ask how is it bad people do good things. I guess sometimes it's a matter of perception. Anyone that knew Ryan said he was a great guy who was under too much pressure. I personally believe Ryan is a good guy who made a mistake.

There was a young lady by the name of Joanne Barnes that worked in my new company. We often had lunch together. She was very helpful, being more experienced than I was in the business world and gave me sound advice regarding how best to handle certain work assignments that were given to me. Joanne was easy to like. She was an ordinary looking girl but had incredible green eyes. Everyone said what a delightful person she was and so nice to talk to. I knew she didn't date very often but had a very active life that pleased her.

Joanne met Keith Segal at the local library. He was seated across from her, immersed in many books and papers when she sat down in front of him to research some marketing data for her boss. When their eyes met, Joanne was astounded with the emotions that pulsated through her body. She had never experienced this depth of emotions before. This man was a total stranger yet intuitively, she knew he too was feeling something extraordinary. They sat looking at each other . . . they felt a sense of harmony . . . and joy.

Keith was a handsome man, extroverted and very popular with the ladies. He had many sexual liaisons but there was a loneliness within him that was not assuaged by his conquests.

Lately he felt his life was vacuous. He had recently decided to concentrate on his studies and curtail his sexual activities. It was a game he no longer enjoyed.

He was taken aback by his reaction to the lady with the green eyes. She wasn't his type. He was usually attracted to statuesque blondes with blue eyes. This lady was definitely not statuesque and had brown hair. He was curious why she was having this effect on him. "Excuse me for interrupting you . . . my name is Keith Segal . . . I know this sounds crazy but I'm sure you're feeling what I'm feeling . . . I'm not some lunatic . . . I'm a law student . . . well, maybe that is a lunatic . . . anyway would you have a coffee with me? . . . I would like to talk to you."

Joanne was speechless. She surprised herself when she said yes. Had they fallen in love at first sight? Is that possible? Sceptics may be doubtful and romantics, wishful. Was there a unique chemistry between them when their eyes met that created the opportunity for them to fall in love?

Keith and Joanne immediately knew something special was happening to them. They intuitively felt they belonged together. They openly shared their pasts, marveled at the present and talked about their future. Both of them were filled with tenderness and awe knowing their spiritual union was complete.

Keith experienced the wondrous joy of making love to a woman that he truly loved, a stark contrast to having sex only. Joanne passionately reciprocated his love and delighted in every moment she spent with Keith. Keith proposed marriage . . . Joanne happily said yes.

Keith was Jewish, the eldest, only son of the president of a large clothing manufacturing firm. He was in his third year of law, a brilliant student with a photographic memory who excelled in his studies. His uncle was a senior partner in major law firm and Keith's future had already been planned . . . he would join his uncle's firm . . . and take over from his uncle when his uncle retired.

Joanne was English, the eldest daughter of three children. Her father was an engineer and her mother had been a professional pianist before she became a mother and homemaker. The family attended Trinity Anglican Church on a regular basis.

Keith's announcement to marry Joanne created a tumultuous uproar in the Segal family. Suffice it to say, every effort from numerous family members was employed to convince Keith that he could not marry Joanne.

Joanne's family was less vociferous and believed she would come to her senses. Her father was convinced once she thought about the difficulties in raising a family in a mixed marriage she would change her mind.

Keith and Joanne only knew one thing . . . they loved each other . . . they wished to be together, whatever the cost. They were prepared to choose a new life that they would create together.

Keith's family renounced the relationship and eventually renounced Keith. As far as the Segal family was concerned Keith was now dead. He did not exist.

Joanne's family was overwhelmed with the state of affairs . . . Keith's loss of his family and their support for his education because he loved their daughter . . . Joanne's compassion for Keith's loss . . . her sadness related to her family's rejection of Keith.

The Barnes family sought professional help. They gradually learned that emotions of unresolved guilt and grief over the outcome of events would prevail unless open communication was resumed and all concerned took responsibility for their decisions. This would not be easy . . . many words had been spoken in anger. Joanne's parents were willing to explore why they felt the way they did when they first heard Joanne was planning to marry Keith.

Overtime, they changed and got to the place where they recognized they needed to adapt to the changes that were taking place in their family. They admitted that Keith was a fine young man with excellent prospects for the future. They acknowledged that Keith truly loved Joanne and she loved him.

After much soul searching, the Barnes family decided to accept Keith in their family. They acknowledged Joanne and Keith were both educated adults and as parents they must make a conscious decision not to interfere in how Joanne and Keith would both deal with their different religious beliefs. Overt attempts were begun to strengthen the family and heal the wounds they had inflicted on Keith and Joanne.

Keith graduated from law school by earning money as a law intern. They refused financial help from Joanne's family and lived frugally on her salary. Keith got an excellent offer from a law firm based on his academic achievements. Many years later, Keith had his own law firm that would become well known in the field of international law.

Keith and Joanne lived an extremely happy life. They were aware that when they were together the sun shone more brightly, flowers were more colorful, music shared was more harmonious . . . life had magic in it. They continued to enjoy a passionate, physical love spoken through loving words and actions that touched their souls.

It took a great deal of time and work but they became reconciled to the loss of Keith's family who were not able to accept Keith's decision. It is often strange the twists and turns in life. Keith became the beloved son the Barnes always wanted.

When Joanne was sharing certain aspects of her love for Keith and their life together, I thought of Gary . . . how concerned his mother had been about his taking a Christian girl to the prom. I well remember we were just two young students who had an innocent crush on each other. I would continue exploring the many complexities that people deal with in their lifetime.

I came to the conclusion that love is filled with joy as well as sorrow. I also believed I had not been on a quest for romantic love, the search for my soulmate, but I acknowledged that recently I was experiencing an imaginative longing for the exultation of love. Love may last or it may not. Will I choose to love or not? Is it really my choice?

Marie and her baby daughter, Jennie, are living with us and I recognize this has created disruptions to our family life as well as produced relationship changes within our family. Though Maria takes care of Jennie, parenting responsibilities are sometimes assumed by my mother. My parents are very close to Maria but difficulties arising from this new living arrangement are not discussed or dealt with.

I have disengaged myself from the situation, convinced it is best to do so since I can see my parents and sister are all under a great deal of stress. I was able to rationalize my behavior quite easily. I am busy with my job, night time classes and my social life. Deep down inside, I am concerned that my sister is becoming too dependent on my parents.

I continued to believe my parents were filled with guilt that they weren't able to protect Maria and are often overcompensating by their overly generous actions. My mother and father are struggling and I see no immediate changes occurring that might alleviate some of their pain.

Chapter Five

Romantic love and disillusionment

Love is patient and kind; love is not jealous, or conceited, or proud; love is not ill-mannered, or selfish, or irritable; love does not keep a record of wrongs; love is not happy with evil, but is happy with the truth. Love never gives up: its faith, hope and patience never fail. Love is eternal . . . There are faith, hope and love, these three; but the greatest of these is love.
New Testament; Corinthians 13

I was invited to a football game little knowing it would change my life dramatically. After the game, a group of us went to the canteen waiting for a football player friend to join us. He arrived with a young man that he introduced as Don Watkins, "the best line backer on the team." The best way to describe Don Watkins is to say he looked like Burt Lancaster. Ladies definitely noticed him when he walked into a room. Apart from his good looks, he had a charm about him that people found endearing possibly because he seemed unaware that he was very handsome . . . he also seemed to be very down to earth that was also very appealing.

We had an enjoyable couple of hours together. As our group got bigger and bigger, I noticed Don seemed to get along well with everyone. Several days later I got a call from Don asking me for a date. I never expected to hear from him since he never asked for my phone number the day we met. He told me he got my number from a friend of mine.

Initially, for some reason, I was reluctant to get involved with Don though I was sexually attracted to him. After a few dates, things changed and I found myself thinking about Don, longing to see him and before too long I believed I was in love. Against my better judgment, I put aside my original concerns . . . Don doesn't have a steady job. His dream to become a professional football player seems unrealistic. Don convinced me that since he was playing football on an intermediate team he still had a good chance to make the pros. Am I not the person who believes people can make their dreams come true?

Don swept me off my feet. He was attentive, kind, loving and for the first time I felt I really was the most important person in someone's life. Holding hands, we took romantic walks in Mount Royal Park . . . we fed ducks in the pond . . . we went on picnics . . . to the movies . . . saw friends . . . but best of all, we just enjoyed talking to each other sharing our most private dreams and hopes for the future. Don told me he needed me in his life and in return, I told him I needed him. Don told me he loved me . . . I told him I loved him. Life was wonderful.

I finally understood how Joanne felt about Keith. Don only had to take my hand and I felt transformed by the passion he ignited in me. When he looked at me across the room, I felt his eyes were telling me I am truly loved.

For the first time, on a clear moonlit night, I experienced the ecstacy of sexual love . . . Don had galvanized a passion in me I had never known. Fully aware that I am a virgin, he was caring and gentle. He caressed me with tenderness I never felt before and I was filled with a passionate desire to love him in wild abandonment. After we made love, we committed ourselves to each other and I was filled with joy and expectations for the happy life Don and I would have together.

Unlike past relationships that were only crushes or infatuations, I recognized that I am totally available to Don physically and emotionally. I have fallen deeply in love with my prince charming.

My knowledge of romantic love was gained primarily by reading books and seeing love stories on the screen. I recall reading Roxanne, Forever Amber and Wuthering Heights dreaming of the day when I too would enjoy deep affection and intimacy that the heroines of these books enjoyed. I enjoyed reading poetry and loved Rupert Brooke's beautiful . . .

> *Breathless, we flung us on the windy hill,*
> *Laughed in the sun, and kissed the lovely grass.*
> *You said, "Through glory and ecstasy we pass;*
> *Wind, sun, and earth remain, the birds sing still,*
> *When we are old, are old . . . . . . And when we die*
> *All's over that is ours; and life burns on*
> *Through other lovers, other lips, said I,*
> *"Heart of my heart, our heaven is now, is won!"*

I was very young, a romantic who believed that love would always triumph. I wondered why a working colleague believed "Tis better to have loved and lost, Than never to have loved at all" since she seemed bitter about her breakup with her boyfriend.

Don and I spend a lot of time going to football parties with his friends and their girlfriends. He teaches me about football and I actually learn to enjoy the game.

I meet his sister, Sandra that he is living with along with her husband and three children. They tell me they are "pleased that Don has such a nice girlfriend. Don has had a hard time since their mother died and really needs to settle down."

Sandra tells me all about Don's childhood . . . how he lost his father when he was ten . . . how the doctors saved his life when he was in a serious automobile accident at the age of twelve . . . his long recovery in learning to walk and talk again . . . and how unfortunate it was that their mother died in the middle of his negotiations to play professional football. Though Don had already told me most of what his sister, Sandra, was recounting, she provided more details about his background.

Don has two other married sisters living out of town. It is obvious from Sandra's descriptions of her sisters, they are a close-knit family. I could see how much Don loved his sister and her family. It was obvious she adored him. "Don was the youngest in our family and the only boy . . . I guess everyone spoiled him. He's the apple of our eye . . . we all want him to be happy."

Sandra also told me they came from an upper class family. All the girls graduated from university even though things got tough after their father had a financial setback prior to dying so suddenly. Sandra said it was unfortunate that Don didn't finish his education and hoped maybe some day he would.

Don and I spend most of our time together in a euphoric state. I can't imagine life without him. When Don proposes to me, I happily say yes. I explain to Don that it is a European custom to ask the father for the daughter's hand in marriage. I ask him to honor this custom and though he says it's rather old fashioned, he agrees to do it. I also remind him that I am not of legal age and will need my father's permission to marry. Don gives me an engagement ring with a one-carat diamond . . . it belonged to his mother. I certainly never expected to receive such an extravagant ring and am convinced no one will believe it is a real diamond.

My father is courteous and civil to Don but asks him directly "how do you plan on supporting my daughter?"

Don replies "I am currently looking for a full time job."

"You realize Anna is five years younger than you . . . you also haven't known each other for very long . . . marriage is a very serious commitment and not to be taken lightly."

"I love Anna, and she loves me. I will make her happy and take good care of her."

"You have both made up your mind. I don't wish to stand in the way of your happiness so I will give you my blessing."

I kiss my father, hugging him because I am so happy. I hug my mother, Maria and Jennie and I am delighted that my family is all here to share my joy.

The following day, my father and I have a conversation regarding my engagement. My father states he has nothing against Don but there are things I need to think about. He believes I haven't thought about them because I am so young and when you're in love you sometimes overlook a lot of things.

His concerns are that we come from different cultures and economic backgrounds. He believes that as I mature my needs will change and my wants as well. He says, for example you are still going to university at night, you recently had a promotion in your job and the company plans on sending you to marketing classes since they believe you are gifted in this area. Don's prospects at present are definitely not in keeping with yours.

How will you feel if you have a family in the near future? "Your mother and I know Don is a nice young man but I want you to think about what I am saying. We both love you very much."

I assure my Dad everything will be just fine. I tell him we are getting married in three months. My Dad bows his head . . . then slowly he stands up and says "I hope the best for you . . . always and forever . . . you are my beloved daughter Anuska."

I was determined my wedding would be more simple and not feel onerous as my sister's wedding had been to me. We have limited the attendees to fifty which was not easy to do. We are to be married at an Anglican church where Don's grandfather had been a canon.

Sandra suggested our engagement pictures be placed in the society page of the major newspaper in town. Since I came from a working class family I felt uncomfortable in doing so but agreed to Don's family wishes in the end. Our engagement notice prompted a series of invitations to teas, lunches and dinners from Don's aunts, uncles and old family acquaintances

I discovered many of them were curious to meet me. Was it because I was "the foreigner Don was marrying?" Unfortunately I overheard someone saying "her family are foreigners." I was born in this country. I admit I was momentarily irked by the remark. Though Don's family was extremely courteous and gracious, their interest in who my family was and what my father did often felt intrusive and uncomfortable. I began feeling insecure in the splendor of their homes. I could not help but notice the sense of entitlement they sometimes displayed, a characteristic I had occasionally witnessed before among the wealthy.

Sandra continued to be down to earth. She remarked more than once the relatives meant no harm and they always behaved this way. She said they were used to peppering people with questions, never aware that perhaps they shouldn't. Don shrugged his shoulders and said "I guess in their own way they're trying to be nice . . . don't let them bother you . . . I certainly don't."

Don's out-of-town sisters only contact with me were congratulatory letters when our engagement was announced.

During a conversation with Mr. James, my new boss, he asked me if I had a prenuptial agreement. I told him I didn't even know what it was. He explained in great detail the importance of having such an agreement emphasizing none of us knew what the future held. He strongly recommended I meet with an attorney friend of his that had handled his daughter's agreement. Since Mr. James treated me like a daughter, I recognized he had my best interests at heart. I also knew that my father was not educated as Mr. James was to advise me in this area.

I met with the attorney advising him the only assets I had at the present time was the money Aunt Sofie had left me some of which I had invested in some stocks. The attorney kindly explained the reasons for this agreement in more detail than Mr. James, patiently giving concrete examples of what would happen in a specific situation versus what did happen because the individual had a legal document. The counsel was effective and I acknowledged that I should have a prenuptial agreement. Don said he didn't see the point of it all since neither one of us had anything of real value . . . besides my diamond ring . . . and my stock investment. He said "sure, I'll sign it . . . it doesn't matter."

Prior to our wedding Don advised me he was getting a large contract for some part time advertising work. I was excited for him. He asked if I could help him cover the cost of material since he was a little short on money due to related wedding expenses. I felt uneasy but rationalized that it was right for Don to come to me, his future wife. I glossed over the fact that Don had assured both my father and me that he was looking for a full time position. I convinced myself that this new contract would provide the security my father wanted for me. It would enable Don to more easily transition to something more permanent without the burden of worrying about money.

As the wedding date approached, I was becoming more anxious. Surely I wasn't having second thoughts. Don was wonderful . . . we loved each other . . . we were meant for each other. Didn't everyone say most people got the jitters before the wedding? . . . but a little voice inside of me whispered "do you really know Don?" I shooed it away . . . Don was my prince charming.

On my wedding day, I remember taking my father's arm to walk down the aisle. His deep blue eyes were filled with love "you look beautiful Anuska" . . . then quietly laughing he said,

"Anuska get ready, this is the longest church aisle I've ever seen." I could hardly breathe . . . what on earth was I doing? Everything felt surreal. I couldn't go through with it. Should I tell my father before it was too late?

What was I thinking . . . I would shame my family . . . my mother would never forgive me or die of shock. All of a sudden I realized we had reached the altar. There was still time to stop the wedding. I kept my head bowed and couldn't look at Don afraid he would read my mind. This wasn't happening . . . it was a dream and I would shortly wake up. My reverie was interrupted with the minister's words. It was time to take the marriage vows . . . I tried to speak . . . it was time to repeat the minister's words. I couldn't. I started sobbing uncontrollably. The minister paused trying to reassure me. The wedding would continue in spite of my tears. There was no turning back. I valiantly tried saying my marriage vows. I heard Don's subdued giggle. Amid the sobs, the only words I recall ever saying were "I do."

Was my behavior a bad omen of things to come? The clap of thunder and lightning at Maria's wedding certainly was. But this was different. Though the day was slightly overcast, the sun did make its appearance every now and then.

Don was smiling . . . he looked relieved and happy. I prayed that the wedding reception would be a success and so would our marriage. Was it my imagination even the guests looked relieved that we finally walked down the aisle as man and wife. Most people attributed my sobbing to a bad case of nerves but I did hear several persons say they didn't think I was going to make it through the ceremony.

Ours was a Slovak wedding reception with an overabundance of food, drink and polkas to dance to. My earlier concerns were how would Don's relatives and guests respond to our traditions. I believe Don's family surprised themselves. The Slovak guests mingled with the English guests totally unabashed by their conservative demeanor, inviting them to dance the polka. Everyone had an exceptionally good time including Uncle John. The English said it was the best wedding they had been to. The Slovaks said the English weren't so bad once they loosened up.

For Uncle John to let go of his inhibitions was close to a miracle. Uncle John, Don's uncle was responsible for delaying my wedding by fifteen minutes. He said he was unable to escort my mother down the aisle without the proper dress attire . . . the poor man had forgotten his grey gloves and dashed home to get them. We were pleased he lived close by.

You can imagine how delighted we all were when at the reception he and Mrs. Novak twirled around the dance floor in complete abandonment and sheer joy. This didn't look like an easy feat since Mrs. Novak was a very large woman and Uncle John was tall and very slender. Uncle John who had been taught ballroom dancing as a young boy in England told Mrs. Novak she was so light on her feet, he felt he was dancing with an angel. Mrs. Novak told this story many, many times ending it by always asking my mother "how is Don's Uncle John . . . what a dancer."

After a brief honeymoon, Don and I commenced our married life. I found it ironic that I couldn't remember what vows I had taken but presumed it was "to love and cherish till death do you part."

I went back to work and resumed my marketing classes, paid for by my company. Don learnt his advertising contract had been canceled. I expected he would say something about the money he had borrowed from me prior to our marriage since now there were no materials or expenses to cover. Upon discussing our mutual financial situation Don finally advised me that the money was gone . . . he had many other expenses he had taken care of.

After several months of marriage, I found myself paying most of the bills. I decided not to take any evening classes for the coming new semester. I would now concentrate on my marketing classes since Mr. James advised me if I excelled, and he knew that I would, he would recommend me for the next opening as a marketing representative. He was confident I had a great future ahead of me.

Uncle Tom was a former professional hockey player that Don greatly admired. He was a widower and lived alone in a very large house. While he did not attend our wedding, he sent a generous check with a note suggesting Don bring his young wife over to meet him. Uncle Tom was the general manager of a prestigious manufacturing firm in women's clothing. I suggested to Don we visit Uncle Tom per his request. My ulterior motive was to get Don talking about his hopes for the future, which he usually did sooner or later, hoping that Uncle Tom might recognize Don could use some help. I was open with Don about my motives and he appeared pleased that I cared so much.

Uncle Tom helped Don get an administrative job at his company at an exceptionally good salary. We could both tell he was pleased and proud that he could assist Don. We were astounded at our good fortune and Don said "our financial worries are over."

With Don working at a full time job, the goals I had submerged resurfaced and I happily enrolled in night school again with Don's blessing. It felt wonderful to have achieved a measure of happiness and stability in our relationship. Don's long working hours were not a problem since it gave me time to study. Our love continued to be passionate, amorous and sexual in no way fading even when we were confronted by the exigencies of daily life.

Don got fired from his position . . . he had worked there for approximately two years. His uncle called me and said that he had warned Don several times to change his behavior. He was very sorry but headquarters had made the final decision. Uncle Tom was very upset and said he did accomplish one thing for Don . . . the company would give him references and say he had been laid off.

I approached Don immediately advising him of Uncle Tom's conversation with me. He responded by saying it was all a ridiculous misunderstanding. He had not approached certain ladies in the plant, rather they had approached him and upon being rejected had reported him to Personnel.

Don was taken aback when I stated "your uncle never mentioned your behavior was related to ladies . . . he just mentioned as I stated to you that you had been warned several times." I told Don I was having a hard time believing him. Then I asked myself since we were passionate lovers, why would he be seeking affection elsewhere? Don said "I'm really hurt that you would even think I would do such a thing."

Jeannine, my childhood friend, was still around . . . she had not yet been disillusioned by love to become a nun. She called to say that her cousin, Solange, worked at the same company as Don, and did I know what was going on? Everyone in the company was talking about it but not openly to spare Uncle Tom who was respected by all the employees. Jeannine struggled with this information and whether she should tell me. Then based on our long friendship and the fact that we were never reluctant in being honest with one another, she felt she had to tell me. I knew her loyalty to me was unquestionable.

Apparently Don had been soliciting sexual favors from the employees with the promise of advancement and salary increases if they obliged. He had been smitten by a happily, married woman who rejected his advances. He became very aggressive and told her she could lose her job unless she was more cooperative. She went directly to senior management bypassing Uncle Tom and revealed everything that had been going on in the plant. Then as Jeannine said "the rest is history."

Jeannine was concerned about me and concerned about my marriage for some time. She had always been a straight shooter but I could tell how difficult it had been for her to make this phone call. I knew that in her heart she was hoping everything would turn out all right.

Later in my life I would realize how fervently I needed to believe that Don was the man that possessed the characteristics I had imbued him with. The event of my sister, Maria, and her daughter, Jennie returning home exacerbated my need to be the most important person in someone's life. Feeling secondary to Maria once again, I was vulnerable and yearned to fall in love. I refused to be disenchanted with Don and my need to love him did not diminish for a long, long time.

Don was very fortunate and got a selling position in a major chemical company where for many years he actually achieved more than a modicum of success. I too had achieved one of my goals . . . I became a marketing representative in an up and coming technology firm. By leaving the past behind us, or so we thought, life was pleasant and we were happy lovers. Don informed me he wanted us to start a family.

I always knew that someday I wanted to have children but was not certain we were ready for the responsibilities of parenting a child at this time. As Don and I talked, the concept of a happy family was generously fulfilling and our mutual appreciation of each other seem richer as we discussed becoming parents. I was filled with joy. The birth of our child would be a profound symbol of our love for each other.

Nine months later our first son named Daniel was born. I fell in love with Daniel the minute I saw him. I now knew how my father felt when he said he loved me from the minute he laid his eyes upon me. Don was ecstatic, a loving father who spent hours talking about his wonderful son to anyone that would listen. I felt that we had rekindled our happiness to a level of passion fantasized only in romantic novels. We were radiantly happy. Why had I been afraid to start a family?

Don started traveling out of town frequently due to his changing job requirements. Our separation was hard to bear. I sublimated my feelings of loneliness by enhancing our home and toyed with the idea of taking classes again. I was filled with guilt that I was not content with my life. I loved my son, Daniel beyond description and knew I did not want to leave him for others to care for while I worked.

Unexpectedly, I received a long distance phone call from a lady asking for Don. I told her Don was out-of-town. She said she hadn't seen or heard from Don in over two weeks, really missed him, and would I please have him call her. Prior to her words, instinctively, I knew this was not a business call. She ended, saying she hoped she hadn't disturbed me, Don's mother. I told her I was his wife upon which, crying, she quickly hung up.

Had the universe intervened on my behalf? I felt betrayed. How could I continue our marriage under these circumstances? I was despondent and tearful and I found myself reminiscing about memories of my lost love. I was angry. I shouted "I will never trust you again" to the empty room. I was in pain. My body ached all over . . . my head hurt . . . my heart felt broken . . . I was certain it was because of the pain in my chest that refused to go away.

When I confronted Don, he immediately attempted to mollify me telling me she is only a friend and nothing is going on. "I love only you." I shouted back "you don't even lie well anymore . . . stop it . . . I don't believe you." Don pleaded with me to forgive him while proclaiming his innocence. I asked myself why does he need my forgiveness if he is innocent?

I knew I was in a vulnerable position. I had become financially dependent on Don since Daniel's birth. I was loathed to tell my parents about my situation as they were still dealing with Maria's divorce and their living arrangement. Marie and Jennie still lived with them. My father's conversation with me, prior to my marriage, regarding his fears about my future with Don were haunting me. I had listened to my father but had not heard his wise words. I was ashamed.

I had been totally devoted to Don. I knew I must now think more fully about the future and determine what is best for my son, Daniel. I knew any choices I made would impact all our lives.

I tried to suppress my anger and ignore my negative feelings. I decided I would sublimate much energy into extra studies that I believed would eventually open the door to my financial independence, thus solving many of my problems. Nothing would deter me from this goal.

Even so, I found it impossible to ignore that I was disenchanted with my marriage. Inwardly I knew the emotional attachments that Don and I had in the past that once felt so deep, had been seriously damaged. I also felt confused because our sexual bond had always felt strong even in the worse of times. Now I wondered because I had responded sexually to Don, had I just presumed I was in love or had I fallen in love in the first place to overcome a sense of aloneness and separateness from my own family?

Don went on a quest to recapture my love. He was exceptionally attentive to all my needs and was amorous which was a constant reminder of the passionate sexual relationship we had both enjoyed prior to this recent argument.

His affection created new feelings of warmth and attachment and, once again, he succeeded in seducing me. I acknowledged to myself that I was still committed to the marriage because

Daniel needed his father. Only later would I recognize I was choosing to overlook Don's faults, my own shortcomings as well, that were extremely detrimental to our relationship.

Much was yet to come in all our lives and at a certain point, I would well remember the following:

> *Imagination, that dost so abstract us*
> *That we are not aware, not even when*
> *A thousand trumpets sound about our ears!*
>
> Dante, Purgatorio

Chapter Six

Joy, illusions, betrayal and death

Oh yet we trust that somehow good
Will be the final goal of ill.
      Alfred Tennyson

Father Francois had been unfrocked by the Roman Catholic Church and now lived with his mother in our neighborhood. He continued to wear his black frock whose hem was ragged and appeared to be beyond repair. There were also numerous patches on his frock as well as many tears and holes. Father Francois wore a large wooden cross and always carried a bible that he read when sitting on a bench in the park. In the wintertime, he still wandered around in his sandals a sharp contrast to the large brown woolen scarf he tied around his neck. His hair was always unruly as if never combed, his eyes glistened and he had a beatific look on his face.

On occasion the children teased him when they were bored or followed him around as if he were the pied piper. They admitted liking him but didn't really know why. He seemed pleased when they followed him though he never talked to any of them. The children said they could hear him constantly praying under his breath. No one was afraid of him and everyone agreed he wasn't dangerous. There was constant speculation as to what Father Francois had done to get into this position yet no one dared question his mother who daily attended the local church. We were so used to seeing Father Francois around that we were surprised when somebody new visited the neighborhood asking "who is that poor soul?"

I admit I am at a loss to understand the many faces of love. Perhaps my friend Josie's sister's love story contributes to my confusion. Josie's sister, Celine fell in love in grade school with Denis. They grew up together and seemed to be totally oblivious of other people and the world around them. Celine and Denis had talked about marriage since they were children. Celine's mother accepted it was just a matter of time before "God joined them together." She was convinced it was a match made in heaven long before they came to earth. When you met Celine and Denis, you could feel their connection, their profound devotion and loyalty to one another . . . it resonated powerfully within you as well.

Who can explain their thwarted love? Denis was the eldest son of a French Roman Catholic family. The eldest son's destiny was often determined at birth by many families. Denis would become a priest "his true calling from God." So many stories circulated regarding Denis, embellished by every story teller, it was difficult to ascertain what the true facts really were. All Josie knew was that her sister, Celine, and Denis, the priest, were lovers. While they both suffered tremendously from guilt, their love prevailed. They momentarily dismissed their self doubting and self torment whenever they wished to be together. Both endured the pain in their overriding need for each other that was often followed by abject repentance.

There came a time when Celine felt that her love for Denis would destroy him if she did not find the strength to leave him. She accepted that the nature of their relationship was far too complex for her to understand. When they united in love, she knew their two souls were as one. How could their physical intimacy be a sin in the eyes of God? While she reflected upon the impact her determined decision to leave Denis would have on both of them, and she was filled with sorrow and pain, her love for Denis was so intense she quivered like a wounded animal who feels an impending death. She prayed to God to make her strong in the face of the torment and agony they would both experience by her decision to leave Denis. She prayed fervently that Denis be saved so he could continue his life serving God. Whenever she saw Father Francois, she worried even more that Denis must not suffer the same fate. No amount of pleading from Denis swayed her in changing her mind.

With the passage of time, with Josie's help, Celine made an effort to socialize something she had never done before. Since Celine was very attractive, before too long a young man by the name of Jacques Lambert started taking her out to various events. He was curious about Celine. He had heard rumors that she had never dated before having always been with her childhood sweetheart who was now a priest. He was not concerned about her friendship with a priest since he felt that her past relationship had been a spiritual bonding of a religious nature. He fell madly in love with Celine and proposed marriage. Jacques's passionate intensity created an interest in Celine but she remained certain she would never again experience the in-depth intimacy she had with Denis.

She was fond of Jacques. She convinced herself by marrying Jacques she might learn to love him and perhaps quell her yearning for Denis and quell his yearning for her. Celine agreed to marry Jacques. Denis was grief stricken . . . he said he would leave the church to marry Celine. Celine remained resolute . . . she married Jacques.

The marriage did not break the attachment between Celine and Denis. Within a short time they were lovers again. Several years went by before Jacques discovered Celine's infidelity with Denis. He loved Celine and their children. He was at a loss in knowing how to deal with a Roman Catholic priest from his parish. Celine assured him she loved her family and was sorrowful about the pain she was causing Jacques.

Celine and Denis's love always reminded me of the great love story of Tristan and Isolde.

As a child I would have written the following fantasy . . . Celine really fell in love with Jacques and they lived happily ever after, walking hand in hand towards the sunset . . . Denis acknowledged his love was greater for God than his love for Celine and rejoiced in serving God. The reality was that Celine and Jacques remained married and Denis stayed in Celine's life until his death. I, the incurable romantic, chose not to judge them.

As I reflect on the complexities of these three lives, I rationalize how fortunate I really am to have Don in my life and my wonderful son, Daniel.

Don is in an automobile accident and totals his company car. This is the second accident this year. Each time it is not his fault. I tell Don I am concerned that he is drinking a lot more than usual and I hope this had nothing to do with his accident. I am hopeful he understands that I don't want anything to happen to him or anyone else. He states the accidents are not related to drinking. He is belligerent and tells me everything is under control.

The three of us attend the company Christmas party. I like Don's boss, his wife and family and I am pleased to see them again. In the past, we were invited to their home and all enjoyed each others company. Today they are very cordial but I sense they are uncomfortable talking to me. I get a strange feeling in the pit of my stomach. I know without a doubt something is about to happen.

After the New Year, the company lets Don go. They have assured him that because he is a family man, they will provide good references. This time I have nothing to say to Don that I haven't already said before. I am beginning to feel like a nagging wife or shrew. I'm sure Don views me this way. Our arguments are now followed by unbearable days of silence.

Don is indeed fortunate that he always interviews well. He displays an affable personality and his handsome good looks are definitely a plus for selling positions. To date, he has managed to maintain good references. He lands a new job within a month and is extremely enthusiastic about the opportunities he believes this company can provide to him. My research of the company confirms they are a prestigious organization with an excellent reputation. This is by far the best position Don has ever had. Don says he feels his luck is changing. I very much want to believe in Don and hope we can save our marriage.

Don and I decide to have another child. We are highly pleased when I am pregnant and Daniel is really happy. He has asked many times "when am I going to have a brother or a sister like the other kids in school?"

"We always have puppies . . . everyone else has kids."

Daniel can't wait for the baby to come. He listens to the heart beat with his ear against my stomach. He asks questions all the time about how the new baby will come out of my stomach. He tells me his best friend says babies do nothing but eat, sleep and cry but Daniel still stays excited in spite of this latest information about babies.

I am overjoyed when my second son is born. We name him Matthew. Daniel is fascinated with his new brother. I hope they will always be close to each other. As I watch Daniel peering down at Matthew, I am filled with tremendous love for both my sons. I realize they are my greatest treasures. I know I will fiercely protect them from danger and I will try to build a life for all of us that is filled with hope, love and promise.

We purchase our first home with a down payment that is a loan from my father. We have settled into a life style that suggests security, success and happiness. Unfortunately, our life style will be shortly interrupted again by Don's problems in keeping a job.

This time he informs me up front he resigned from his job due to a major disagreement with his boss. He tells me he already has another job lined up with a competitor of his now previous company and expects to start working next week. He will need my car since there will be no company car.

Exactly, one month later, I accidentally find out Don has been leaving the house every morning pretending to go to work . . . but there is no work . . . he doesn't have a job. Things are going from bad to worse. Though I feel numb, I wonder what else is going to happen?

I am saddened that Don finds it necessary to hide the truth from me. I feel responsible for the serious breakdown in our communication but I am at a loss as to what else I can do. I know I must keep trying to make things better.

"Loneliness is never more cruel than when it is felt in close propinquity with someone who has ceased to communicate."

Don is recalcitrant in my attempt to find out why this charade? I blurt out "Did you think I wouldn't find out?" I ask myself if there is really any point in trying to talk about this matter. I quickly decide to drop the entire subject when I notice Daniel is now present, listening intently, looking very sad and unhappy.

Don responds by saying "I didn't want to upset you so soon after Matthew's birth."

I am grateful I have been frugal and saved enough money to pay next month's bills . . . but then what?

The telephone rings. I am advised that I have thirty days to pay my three months mortgage payments plus accumulated interest or I lose the house. I am flabbergasted. I have given

Don money for the payments on a regular basis. There must be some mistake. I take the bus to town, a one hour drive, to the mortgage company. I try to be calm but feel I am on the verge of hysteria. A kind gentleman listens to my story without interruption then sadly says, "there is no mistake . . . no payments have been made by your husband in three months."

I walk around down town for close to an hour. I am unaware of the sights and sounds around me. I reach a park and find an empty bench to sit on. Laughter and joyful voices eventually penetrate the capsule I have created to endure this fearful time in my life. I am humiliated but I have come to the conclusion that I have no recourse but to see my father and ask him for a loan.

In front of my father I break down and cry. Details about my life are spilling out rapidly between sobs. My father never interrupts even when there are occasional pregnant pauses in my tirade. He doesn't say a word. He listens attentively to what I am saying. He gives me his handkerchief to blow my nose and wipe my eyes. When I am spent, he writes out a check for a larger amount than I asked for and says "You don't need me to tell you this is not a good situation . . . you already know. There must be trust in a marriage. Right now you must save your home for the boys."

I am vociferous beyond belief and emphatically advise Don that from now on things will be different. I will pay every single bill and I don't wish to hear any excuses from Don why he didn't make the mortgage payments. Don starts to cry and says he is sorry. I find myself being unresponsive to his apology particularly when I smell liquor on his breath.

Inside a little voice is saying "thank goodness your father suggested you put the house in your name."

I sell my stocks and make a good profit. God bless Aunt Sofie . . . little did she know how much her gift to me would mean.

I contact Mr. James, my old boss and tell him I badly need a part time job but must work from home because of the children. I manage not to cry but my voice is shaky and I know Mr. James can tell something is very wrong. He promises to send me a marketing assignment that has just come up. He asks if he and Mrs. James can help me in any other way? I am grateful to have these good people in my life.

After I put Matthew down for his nap, I cry in complete abandonment for lost dreams, hopes and expectations. I still believe I can overcome my financial problems and provide some stability in my sons' lives. I think back to the girl I was in high school . . . she always believed in the impossible dream. There is still a kernel of hope within me. Somehow I must nurture it so it may grow.

I no longer question Don about his activities. It is less painful not to hear his lies that he so easily tells. I don't wish to argue with Don in front of our sons. I am convinced I am in a holding state and I now acknowledge to myself that our relationship and marriage may not survive.

I am relieved that Matthew is now five years old since I realize I must go back to work full time. I don't want to leave him with a sitter for lunchtime and after school but I barely have enough money to buy groceries every week. I have supplemented my part time salary by doing product market surveys at night when the children are asleep and I still can't pay all my bills. I get a job as a secretary close by so I can get home quickly.

I have an hour for lunch. Matthew doesn't like having lunch at the neighbor's house. I make his lunches but still pay her to babysit him. He isn't happy. I know Matthew is having a difficult time. For an entire year, by juggling my working hours, I manage to come home and have lunch with Matthew. It takes forty minutes to drive home and back to work so I may have extra time to be with my young son. On the verge of exhaustion, I obtain a better job close by with a better salary. I am thankful

I will be able to maintain more of a presence in my sons' lives during the working week since I can be home in ten minutes when necessary.

Daniel made his school football team and Matthew made the junior soccer team. Their father states he is very proud of them both. Consequently they get to see Don some of the time when Don goes to their games. Matthew is less outgoing and prefers spending more time with his friends catching tadpoles, minnows, frogs and garter snakes. So far both are deemed very intelligent by their teachers and better than average students.

I am very sad when I think of my parents. I feel I let them down. I also feel I let my sons down. My mother's lament has become "what did I do wrong as a mother?" At times, I sense I am a failure as a daughter, wife and mother. My love for Don feels shattered. I feel I cannot pretend much longer that Don and I have a life full of mutual promises.

Lately, I have turned to prayer in search of strength and guidance. Don has turned more and more to drink. I believe he is trying to drown his emotional pain that I'm sure he has. Don has forfeited most of his old friends. I am concerned about the men he now spends time with . . . they do not appear to have jobs and are becoming Don's steady drinking buddies.

Don appears to have buried the past as if it never happened. He believes our issues are typical of most families. We live our lives by not discussing any of our problems. My now occasional attempts to do so are not successful. I am getting more discouraged about our relationship and I am deeply concerned about our sons.

My social network has become limited. I realize I must expand my horizons in spite of my responsibilities. To begin with I must forgive myself for any of my misjudgments in the past. I must find the courage to trust myself that I will more than survive in living my life.

I come across a small advertisement that a group is being formed for young mothers who are interested in meeting on a regular basis to foster intellectual growth. Books will be identified and selected by the group for discussion. I go to the first meeting and meet many young women with children that are interested in being a part of this group. Among the women I meet, I particularly enjoy Jane Spencer's intelligence, exuberance and humor. I will discover she is a kindred spirit and we will become life long friends.

Our group pares down to eight ladies, meeting every two weeks with a designated book that is required for discussion over a two to three-hour period of time. I find out I am the only one without a university degree and wonder if I will be qualified sufficiently to deal with the serious subjects we plan to study. The range is broad . . . philosophy, religion, various cultures, the role of women in society. We are an ambitious group. After our first meeting, I recognize that I am probably the most voracious reader in the group. I have a large repertoire of information that I have never had the opportunity to share with anyone to this extent before.

The eight ladies in the group are Jane, Barbara, Joyce, Joan, Laura, Margaret, Marion and of course myself.

Jane is our pseudo leader, enthusiastic, outgoing with two children under the age of five. She is currently separated from her husband for the second time. Her major struggle appears to be how she will divorce her husband since she is a Roman Catholic and retain custody of her children. Her husband continues threatening that he will take away the children if she divorces him.

Barbara is married to a dentist and seems to spend most of her time playing tennis or bridge. She is very bright and surprises everybody by her vast knowledge of authors such as Jean Paul Sartre, Rousseau, Nietzsche to name a few. She knows people think of her as a flighty socialite but she admits she doesn't care. "My life with Gordon and my daughter is what really matters."

Joyce is shy, very quiet, the mother of three young daughters. She is married to a very successful stockbroker. They are wealthy and Joyce never discusses that they are considered the upper class. She stated the reason for joining the group was "I need the companionship of young women who are mothers. I wish to keep growing intellectually."

Joan has five children, all under the age of five and is pregnant again. Initially she states "I just have to be with adults." Joan is direct, totally unpretentious and will share generously her wealth of knowledge in sociology. She is the only one in the group who has a Ph.D.. She never talks about her husband. In our early introductions she said "he's a crazy Irishman, this father of my children."

Laura has two sons, under ten years of age. She had a nervous breakdown five years ago. She is an artist and hopes some day to dedicate more time to her painting. She believes the group will inspire her in reading the types of books only she is interested in since her husband doesn't care for "heavy reading."

Margaret is a librarian, the oldest in our group with two sons in high school. Her husband is an engineer, an enthusiastic reader as well. Margaret is delighted to be joining a reading group again . . . "I joined this group since I missed the lively discussions of past reading groups."

Marion is divorced, the mother of a five-year-old boy. "I have been surrounded by books all of my life and I enjoy reading. I also want to make new friends." Marion is a very private person and I have the feeling she has been a people pleaser all her life.

What would I say about myself? I am married, have two sons

that I love dearly. I am striving to get a greater sense of self by expanding my horizons to include new people in an environment that stimulates emotional development and intellectual growth.

At this point in my life, I had a limited knowledge of group therapy. As I looked around the room, I knew that the focus of our group was to discuss books, but I intuitively knew that our interpersonal relationships might significantly affect our lives. The group would act as a social microcosm. We did not have a group leader per se . . . every member took turns in leading a discussion that seemed to promote an early sense of equality among the ladies regardless of wealth, education or marriage status.

Today I think of Harry Stack Sullivan's contention "that the personality is almost entirely the product of interaction with other significant human beings." His words ring true in my ears when I think of our reading group. In time, we became closely related to each other. We interacted more deeply and honestly as individuals firstly through our books and consequently through our personal experiences.

The group was providing a consistent and supportive environment that I very much needed. I was gradually restoring some of my self esteem and self confidence and felt I was developing a higher tolerance to the distress I experienced in my marriage. I was certain I was not Pollyannaish in my attitude to my relationship with Don; I was encouraged because I felt less obsessive about our circumstances. There were definitely varying degrees to these feelings at various times. But I knew in my heart I was getting stronger and more accepting to this challenge of learning, no matter how painful it was. I strongly felt my hope and faith were being renewed. I also passionately believed that all human beings are meant to accomplish something in their lifetime and that my sons and I would prevail.

Colin, the young black man who once walked me home from a dance, was now working at The Lakeview Mental Institution as an orderly. Angela Bryson, the young lady who was in my class in high school, was a patient at the hospital. Her recent attempt at suicide was denied by her family. It was only an accident. She swallowed too many pills because she had been drinking.

Angela spent most of her time drifting in and out of her own personal daydreams paying as little attention as possible to her environment. She's been here before. If she behaved and gave the nurses and doctors no trouble, they would pronounce she was fit to go home.

Colin noticed Angela feeling certain he had seen her before outside the context of this hospital. He eventually remembered that he once met her at a high school dance after a basketball game. He had also danced with her. Then he never saw her again until now. He was truly touched that she had such a serious problem.

Colin was aware that Angela responded to no one's attempts to talk with her except for the doctors and nurses. It was evident to him that she was playing a game that she had played before. His compassionate curiosity about Angela prompted him to place a new magazine on her night table with the hope that she might respond to his efforts. Angela didn't look up, but later in the day Colin saw her browsing through the magazine. Colin walked by her room every day for about two weeks until one day he finally said "hello."

Angela startled him when she said "he speaks . . . the black knight in white."

Colin was very much aware of the stringent rules about commingling with patients but was drawn to Angela experiencing feelings that were foreign to him. She reminded him of frightened bird with a broken wing. She was wounded and fragile . . . so very vulnerable.

Colin became very creative in spending time with Angela in a manner that did not violate the hospital's rules. Angela learned to trust Colin and it felt strange since she hadn't trusted anyone in a long, long time. She gradually opened up and told him about the baby she gave up for adoption when she was in high school. Colin responded to her torment and agony that he saw in her eyes by listening, not judging and just being. His unquestioning support was a sharp contrast to the onslaught of questions people usually asked her.

When Angela was released from the hospital, Colin asked if they might continue being friends. Angela said yes "you're the only friend I have."

Colin was afraid to broach the subject about his being black, how her family might react but knew he must to avoid causing Angela any more pain. Angela's humor, that he loved so much, was still intact "you're a black knight . . . you can slay any dragons that are out there."

Angela's parents were prepared to meet Colin with an open mind. They were so relieved Angela had an interest in someone, an emotion and characteristic she has not displayed since she was a teenager. They prided themselves on being loving, caring people who always did the right thing.

Angela's mother was reminded of the movie "The Man Who Came to Dinner" with Katherine Hepburn and Spencer Tracey and was certain she could handle this situation as well as the movie parents did in the film. Her husband said "it's time we let Angela live her own life."Mr. and Mrs. Bryson received Colin at their home with grace and cordiality. Angela was amused by the whole situation but appeared to actually be enjoying it all. Angela's mother was delighted that Colin was so good looking . . . better looking than Sydney Poitier. Angela's father found Colin to be an interesting, intelligent conversationalist and was pleased when he heard Colin liked to play chess as he was a chess enthusiast.

Colin and Angela became the closest of friends. They mutually cared for each other and their deep intimacy provided a love that diminished much of the unresolved tension and conflict in Angela's soul. They openly discussed the challenges of an interracial marriage and both agreed together they would cope and overcome any problems that might come their way.

Colin's presence in the Bryson family was a positive catalyst that changed family perspectives and ultimately family behaviors. Everyone communicated more openly and honestly and they started experiencing a compatibility they never thought was possible. For the first time in her life Angela was able to communicate to her parents the depth of her sorrow, her feelings and thoughts about giving birth to her daughter . . . then giving her up for adoption . . . and for the first time, her parents heard her.

When Colin and Angela married, the Brysons rejoiced in their daughter's good fortune. They felt truly blessed when a couple of years later Angela had twins, a boy and a girl.

My entire family, including my parents attended Colin and Angela's wedding. You may recall, Colin's family went to the same united church as my parents. It seemed like I had known Colin forever though we were not close friends . . . and of course I had gone to high school with Angela. I was convinced the world was not that big in spite of the numbers of people in it. I was fascinated how peoples lives connected at unexpected times.

It had been a long time since Don and I attended a wedding. Perhaps I was being maudlin when I suggested to Don we try to spend more time together as a family. Inwardly, I knew I was deeply concerned about the long term impact of our relationship on the children. Several days later I suggested to

Don we seek couple's therapy. I told him I would be willing to find the therapist if he agreed to come. He reluctantly said he would. I made an appointment for the following week. Don was to meet me there after work. He never showed up.

After I had a few sessions with the therapist, ever hopeful Don would come around and participate, the therapist stated directly "you may need to consider that if someone doesn't want to help themselves, you can't do it for them." I knew the therapist was right and with a heavy heart I went home.

Daniel started having problems in high school. He also started experimenting with drugs. I was frantic. He had always been a good kid and suddenly he was disappearing before my eyes. When I expressed my concerns to Don, he dismissed me by saying "boys will be boys . . . it's just a phase."

Over a four-year period, Daniel left high school several times, got in trouble with the law and was a juvenile delinquent according to society's standards. But he was still my son and I loved him. I sent him for counseling to no avail. I was desperate. All that was left was prayer . . . so I prayed and I prayed. Matthew developed a nervous tic in grade three. I believed we, as a family, had let Matthew down. Daniel created so much havoc I wondered if Matthew often felt he lived in his shadow. Matthew had a gentle personality and was a delightful young boy. The doctor prescribed some medication and assured me there was nothing to worry about. He stated tics were common in young children. Matthew was probably stressed because of school and friends. It would pass. I told the doctor his Dad and I were having major problems and I was sure this wasn't helping Matthew. The doctor was sympathetic but concluded with "children are far more resilient than we think. He's going to be fine."

Several weeks later Don came home drunk. We had a terrible fight and he struck me in the face. I was in total shock and disbelief. He had never hit me before. When the boys came home, I told them I hit my eye on the stairwell bannister while painting too ashamed to admit what their father had done. I was certain they didn't believe me. Both of them were sullen. They went to their rooms not saying anything. The next morning Don looked at my battered eye and said "I can't believe I hit you. I've never done this before. I promise I'll never do it again. I guess I was drunk. Please forgive me."

Memories of my sister's abuse come hurtling into my mind. I knew I should leave Don at once. How would my parents react? I'm not ready to tell them yet. I can't let them see me like this. From now on I'll stay out of Don's way. The boys are having a difficult time. I'm sure this is an isolated incident. Don definitely looked like he didn't remember striking me.

In spite of my personal problems, I was doing well at work. I was promoted and received a substantial salary increase. In the past I shared my monies with Don but not since the mortgage incident. Shortly after Don's physical abuse, a series of events took place that propelled me to make a long overdue decision to separate from Don.

Don tells me he won a vacation for ten days in the Bahamas that ties in with his national sales conference. He knows I can't go with him because of the boys but since it's mostly work, it's understandable why he plans on going. While I am suspicious, in view of our recent circumstances, I decide to accept what he says. Coincidentally, a colleague tells me on the telephone of Don's good fortune. "Isn't Don lucky? So sorry you can't join him." The call feels like a setup but I ignore my intuition that is telling me something just isn't right.

Several months later, the universe conspires to help me again. I happen to be home from work because I have a bad cold when I receive a phone call from a travel agency that recently booked the reservations for Mr. and Mrs. Don Watkins. I am advised by the agency payments for our two tickets and hotel reservations have not been paid. The young lady on the phone asks if I am

Mrs. Watkins? "Yes, I am."

"We hope you both had a wonderful time. Please tell your husband his account is overdue."

It may seem mundane to say this was the straw that broke the camel's back. I am in a blind rage. I pay for the food Don is eating, the home he lives in, the clothes on my children's backs, dental bills . . . I pay for everything by scrimping and saving to make ends meet. I shout at the top of my lungs . . . no more, no more. I forget my commitment that I will not aggravate Don in any way. I feel completely out of control. My anger is so intense my entire body won't stop shaking. I rush around the house picking up anything personal belonging to Don. I gather all his clothes. Perhaps I have gone mad when I destroy one of his shirts. I am having trouble breathing. I drink some water to calm myself and I wait.

I tell Don to get out of my house or I will call the police. I contacted my friend, Jane who is standing by in case I need her. She is coming over as soon as she gets a baby sitter for her children. Don looks at me in shock as if I am stark raving mad. "What's wrong with you? Why are you so upset? I've never seen you like this."

"Just go" I scream louder than I knew I could "the travel agency called because you haven't paid your tickets and hotel for you and your wife . . . don't say anything . . . just get out. All your belongings are in one pile. Take them and go."

"Let's talk about this . . . we'll work it out, we always do."

"Get out . . . Get out." I know I continue screaming to get out over and over again.

I turn away. I don't watch as Don is packing the pile of clothes. Don says "I'll call you and the boys."

I don't respond and I don't watch him leave.

When Daniel and Matthew come home, I tell them their father is gone. I asked him to leave. Matthew runs upstairs to his room crying. Daniel goes to his room with a stoic face. My friend, Jane arrives and cooks dinner for us. We are rather silent throughout the meal that is mostly left uneaten. Jane leaves as quietly as she came promising we will talk some more when I want to perhaps when the boys aren't around. I hope I can be as strong as Jane is some day. I know how difficult her life is on a daily basis but she remains strong and hopeful, constantly finding tidbits of happiness every day. I am spent and just want to crawl into bed. I try to comfort myself by saying "I finally made the right decision."

Irvin D. Yalom, in his book entitled Existential Psychotherapy, talks about a client as follows:

"She had to accept the guilt (and the ensuing depression) for having thwarted her own growth. She had to accept the crushing responsibility for the future" . . . and then finally "One can atone for the past only by altering the future."

His words had a tremendous impact on me. At last I was struggling to alter my future and I would never turn back.

Within a few days I received the first of many phone calls regarding my "throwing Don out of his home." Ron was a childhood friend of Don's, an usher at our wedding and someone we both had not seen in a long time. He surprised me by stating Don was staying with them and he was calling on his behalf. "Don is in bad shape . . . he's distraught . . . he's sorry . . . he wants to go back home."

"I'm very sorry Ron but there is no way he is ever coming back. I don't want to talk about my personal problems with you. I know you are just being a good friend to Don."

The next call was from Don's sister, Sandra. "Anna, Don is beside himself. I'm sure you can work things out. He loves you and the boys."

"Sandra I don't wish to be rude but you know nothing about our lives. He is not coming back."

"Anna, who will take care of him? You know he can't manage without you?"

"Please Sandra . . . I have to think of Daniel and Matthew and the impact our relationship is having on them. I know you mean well but please stay out of this."

There is a local gas station where I buy my gasoline on a regular basis. I know Max, the owner quite well and appreciate how hard he is struggling with his wife's terminal illness. In the summertime, I occasionally brought flowers from my garden for his wife. Max was truly touched by my actions and we now enjoy a pleasant repartee whenever I need the station's services for my car.

"Anna I feel awkward talking about this but Don has been buying gasoline on credit for some time. I turned him down the other day since his bill has been outstanding for over sixty days and is quite sizeable. I don't expect you to pay for it. You always pay cash for your purchases and this has nothing to do with you. I wanted you to know why we won't sell to Don anymore. He is your husband and I'm really sorry."

I tell Max I asked Don to leave and he is gone. I am sorry for this situation and I hope Don will pay him back.

"If I or the boys at the station can do anything for you, besides fix your car, let us know."

Suddenly, there was a new group of phone calls from various creditors threatening to take my house and furniture away if

I don't pay Don's outstanding bills. I couldn't believe this was happening. I was desperate and called Jane who put me in touch with her family attorney, a personal friend, who is a divorce lawyer. When he asked me if I had a prenuptial agreement, I was truly grateful that I did have one. I thank God that I had good people in my life when I was so naive. The first thing the lawyer said he would do, and he did, was stop the threatening phone calls.

My parents appeared resigned that their second child was also getting a divorce. In my mother's eyes I knew she saw our family as truly disgraced. How often had I heard these words "what will people say?" While I am sad knowing I am a disappointment to them, I know it was the only course of action left for me to take.

Once Don's physical presence, his ways, his tenderness, however momentary were no longer enough to engender in me again all the old love and yearning in my heart, cold criticism told me he had altered for the worse. Don's lying and behavior, not trifling events, had completely destroyed my trust in him.

Eddy meets Maria downtown. She is quick to tell him I have filed for a divorce. Eddy is engaged to be married within the month. He phones saying he would like to see me and help in any way he can.

"Eddy, there's nothing you can do. This is a happy time for you . . . enjoy it . . . know that the boys and I will be just fine."

The wedding is out-of-town and I have never met the bride to be. Even though I am disconsolate, I am pleased Eddy is in love. If anyone deserves to be happy, he does.

It will be another ten years before I see Eddy in person again.

During the divorce proceedings, Don tries to get the house. He fails since it is in my name. I also am able to prove I made nearly all the mortgage payments during our marriage.

I promised Sandra my engagement ring will be given to my eldest son to honor their family tradition. I am pleased Don's family accepts my commitment in good faith.

The day of the divorce, Don and I accidentally meet on the steps of the courthouse, each with our own lawyer. He tells me in a voice no longer confident "it's not too late to change your mind . . . you're the only woman I have truly loved . . . think of our sons and." He left his sentence unfinished. Had he acted on impulse that was a part of his character? No matter.

"Don it's too late. I am thinking of our sons" then I briskly walk away.

The judge asks my lawyer why I am not asking for child support. My lawyer responds "my client has been supporting her family for many years. She just wants her divorce."

The judge insists Don pay some child support. Don agrees with the judge and says of course he will. The judge grants the divorce. My sense of relief was somehow tempered with a curious feeling of unreality.

I have deep emotional feelings but my thoughts are centered around Daniel and Matthew. I am determined to be strong for them and not be fearful of the future. I will not allow myself to succumb to a nightmare of possibilities that wish to crowd my mind thereby destroying my hopes for a better life for my sons and me.

I reflect on this choice statement that I read somewhere "When a marriage ends, who is left to understand it?"

I receive two child support checks after the divorce. No other monies are ever forthcoming from Don and I support myself, Daniel and Matthew until they are grown men.

The ladies in our book group are supportive in a caring, compassionate, non intrusive way. The bond between us is strong. We have all had our share of laughter and joy as well as pain and sorrow, some of us more of it than others. We have now been together for seven years.

I get a telephone call from Lily's father telling me Lily was killed in a head-on collision a block away from the hospital where she was a cardiologist. I don't know what to say to this gentle man for whom I have genuine affection. I am grief stricken. No matter what I say I feel the words will be inadequate.

I get the details from Lily's father to attend the funeral. How ironic life is. Lily became a heart specialist because her mother had a heart condition since Lily's early childhood. Now Lily is gone and her mother lives on.

Two months later I receive a small packet of cards and letters that Lily and I exchanged over the years. I am particularly fond of the letter she wrote just before she graduated from Harvard . . . "Anna, for the child of a Jewish shoemaker, this ain't bad." Not bad indeed. Her parents were so proud of her and so was I. Lily and I were kindred spirits. I'm glad she was in my life. I will miss her.

My fond memories of Lily include dancing the Horah at some of her family gatherings as well as sharing Sabbat with Lily and her family. Lily always laughingly said I had a Jewish heart and pronounced me to be an honorary Jew. Her family agreed. Though I had not seen Lily very often in past years, we maintained contact and when we did get together, we celebrated our special bond. Since childhood we knew we were kindred spirits. Shalom Lily.

God has given you a spirit with wings on which to soar into the spacious firmament of Love and

Freedom.
                    Kahlil Gibran

Lily's death is a jolt to my being. I feel strongly reminded that life is so fragile and precious. I find more time to reflect upon my own life. I realize that I am still filled with hope and faith for the future, acknowledging I have many blessings to be thankful for in the present.

Chapter Seven

Choosing life . . .
reflections on yesterday, today and tomorrow

He that loveth not knoweth not God;
for God is love.
1 John 4:8

The following incident would reaffirm that if you mustered the strength to seek help and deal with outstanding issues in your life, you could create a loving atmosphere in sharp contrast to an atmosphere filled with fear and hostility. I had often wondered how individuals managed if they constantly stifled their own feelings or desires kowtowing to others. Did they forsake their dreams by burying their potential?

I am in a bookstore when I bump into Gary, my first high school crush, for the first time in at least ten years. He looks wonderful. He tells me I am more beautiful than ever. We are delighted to see each other and we decide to have a coffee and catch up on our lives.

I can't help but remember Gary's authoritarian mother. I am not surprised to hear that Gary married Fannie but I am surprised he divorced her after three years. They had no children. He realized he did not want to become like his father "weak, dependent and submissive." It was a rude awakening when he came to admit he never loved Fannie and had married her to placate his mother. "I don't blame my mother. Her behavior was the result of her unresolved childhood problems."

I sense Gary has had professional help to deal with his issues and now appears to be in a good a place in his life.

Gary tells me he is madly in love with a wonderful Hungarian woman by the name of Leda Burne. Did Gary say Leda Burne? Is there more than one Leda Burne in this world?

Can it possibly be the same Leda Burne that taught me to dance the tango? I was sorry we lost touch with each after she got married and moved far away. We sporadically wrote to each other for awhile. Her letters were always rich and colorful reflecting so well parts of her that delighted my soul. I missed her fun loving personality in my life. The last time I heard from her was when Daniel was born.

"Gary does your Leda tango?"

"Yes, she does the tango better than anyone I know. She has been separated from an abusive husband for the last three years and is in the process of getting a divorce."

Gary takes a picture out of his wallet. I can't believe it. It is my long lost friend Leda.

Gary must be reading my thoughts. "I have learned a great deal about myself and my family through therapy. I no longer have a need to gain approval from others. Of course it's an ongoing journey, with many challenges, that I now look forward to with hope and faith. My life is exceptionally wonderful now that I have Leda to share my life with. We plan to marry as soon as her divorce is final."

Will Gary have the same problems as Joanne Barnes and Keith Segal? This is a negative thought and I chastise myself for thinking it yet my unspoken words seem to have reached Gary. "Believe it or not my mother was in therapy as well. My father passed away five years ago . . . it was a very difficult time for my mother . . . she had so many losses that she had never sufficiently grieved but she was smart enough to know she needed help. My mother and Leda get on very well . . . better than well . . . she loves and adores Leda."

Gary and I reach for each other's hands across the table at the same time. "It's wonderful to hear such happy tidings. I'm really pleased for you Gary."

"Leda is converting to Judaism. Her ancestors were Hungarian Jews and somehow over the years, they fell by the wayside in acknowledging who they really are."

We talk animatedly how incredible it is that Gary is in love with Leda who was only visiting Montreal when they met while she was living a thousand miles away. He recalled Leda mentioning she had lost touch with friends after her marriage started falling apart. "Little did I know you were one of those friends."

Gary and I hug. "I know the three of us will reunite as soon as possible. For sure, Leda will call you." I think of how extraordinary all this is. How wonderful it is that Leda and her family are embracing their true heritage at this happy time in Leda's life. It feels like they are relinquishing fears in their past that will free all of them to love more joyfully.

I wave goodbye to Gary and he blows me a kiss that I catch. This was an affectionate ritual between us during our brief romance in high school. Gary smiles at me "you remembered." "Yes I remember." I know I always will.

Seeing Gary reminded me of the young, innocent girl I was in high school. I recall some of the memorable turnings in my life that changed how I look upon the world. I have learned that you can't do all you may wish to do in order to be a responsible human being. There are inevitabilities of life that require compromises and yet my meeting Gary has reaffirmed that people can change and make their dreams come true. I am content and at peace. This was a serendipitous meeting.

I am further reminded of my early childhood friends . . . Aurora, Jeannine, Lily and Myrtle along with Billy. I recall my first marriage proposal from Whitey at age sixteen, teenage dating with Charlie, Russell and of course, dearest Eddy.

I recognize how fortunate I am to have the ladies in our book group in my life. Many seasons have come and gone. We have read and discussed books that have enriched our lives and in the sharing of ideas and different perspectives, we have grown both emotionally and intellectually. We are openly appreciative of the rich friendships we have with each other.

Jane went through a nasty divorce and fought valiantly to keep her children. She lost legal custody and suffered major trauma when her children went to live with her exhusband and his new wife. For too many years she was never free of her exhusband who appeared to be mean spirited. He seemed to use the children as pawns in his power game with her. When she refused to be used, the children suffered and so did she. In the fourth year of our group, Jane met and married a powerful businessman who somehow miraculously put a stop to her exhusband's shenanigans.

Over the years, Barbara's life appeared to be the most uneventful. She and her husband took many trips to exotic countries, attended dental conferences, entertained and enjoyed their family. Suddenly, in the sixth year of the group, Barbara's parents were both killed in an automobile accident. Barbara was distraught. As the only child, much was expected of her in handling this very public tragedy. Considered a socialite before her parents' death, her status changed to a "very wealthy socialite."

Barbara was non pleased about the money. The lawyers were doing something to set up a benevolent foundation in memory of her parents. We had several excellent discussions related to money, its power both positive and negative and we explored how it would feel to be wealthy like Barbara . . . and then we didn't talk about it anymore.

Joyce was becoming less shy as time went on. She contributed significantly to all our book discussions but never talked about her personal life. She was interested in our lives but was never intrusive. I still have a kind letter she wrote me after my divorce.

We were reading books of poetry when during the discussion Joyce admitted she sometimes wrote poetry. We asked her to bring her poetry to the next group meeting. At first she was reluctant but agreed to do so.

Her poetry was magnificent . . . it pulled the strings of your heart . . . you soared with angels . . . you heard the Angelus resonating through the skies. Joyce was our poet laureate.

Joyce obviously felt safe with our reading group when she told us she had been raped by a stranger when she was eighteen years old. She said "I do not feel like a victim . . . I am a survivor . . . but it has taken me a long time to get there."

Joan, our Ph.D., had her sixth child. She was now the proud mother of six boys. She admitted laughingly that perhaps they should adopt a little girl. She worked from morning till dawn, was very happy with her lot in life and always astounded us with her good humor. Joan was often invited as a guest speaker to organizations to discuss parenting issues. She was somewhat amused with her celebrity status but admitted she enjoyed being a speaker about subjects that were dear to her heart. Her husband was a regular guy who was delighted with his wife and family.

Laura redecorated her entire home using her artistic skills in a creative imaginative way . . . the end result being a warm and decorous home. She helped several of us wallpaper our foyers and helped us rearrange our indoor plants in such a way we were awed by the wonderful results.

At one point in our six years, Laura told us "I know when I am getting too close to the edge but now it's okay because I know what I have to do." Barbara invited Laura to exhibit her paintings in a gallery she knew very well. Laura was excited about the opportunity to exhibit and finally did so when we all convinced her she had nothing to lose. She agreed. Her paintings were well received and she was invited to exhibit again.

Margaret, our eldest member, discovered her eldest son, now in his first year of university, was using LSD. She was shocked, disappointed, but most of all very concerned. She and her husband found out that their son and four other young men in the neighborhood had been experimenting with LSD for an extended period of time. They insisted their son give them the names of the other young men. They wanted to talk to all the other parents believing they would be as concerned as they were about this situation.

Upon individually contacting the four sets of parents, they were speechless when they were told "maybe your son is using LSD . . . ours isn't." We asked our son "he has never used drugs in his life." "You have a nerve suggesting our boy would use LSD." The parents' hostility towards them was extremely severe but to be rebuffed by all the parents was more than they could handle. They went to see their parish priest. Unfortunately, they felt he didn't know what to do in this particular situation so they went to a psychiatrist.

Their son started therapy that eventually involved the entire family's participation at certain times. Margaret said the entire family grew closer as a result of this experience. Their son graduated with honors from his university. Margaret said she would always be grateful they had been vigilant when it came to their children's friends and whereabouts. She reiterated the importance of doing "what you believe is right"

Two of the other young men who had used LSD, along with Margaret's son, did not fare so well. They both dropped out of university. Margaret and her husband were ostracized by the other parents and they never reconciled their differences. Since we were much younger than Margaret and had younger children, we learned a great deal from Margaret. We felt privileged that she shared her experiences and knowledge with us.

Marion wrote a cookbook for her local church. It was extremely popular so much so she had copies printed to meet the demand. A reporter from the Sunday Times got one of the cook books as a present from his sister. He was so impressed, he contacted Marion asking her if she would be interested in submitting recipes on a weekly basis for publication in the Sunday Times. She accepted the offer and is still happily publishing recipes. Thanks to Marion we enjoyed many delicious desserts after our group discussions. We were always her willing guinea pigs.

These were all strong women who courageously faced life's many challenges. All of us wore a three-cornered hat . . . wife, mother, and person . . . sometimes it was person, wife and mother . . . and sometimes it was mother, person, wife. Our group became well known in the community and we assisted other ladies to start their own reading clubs. We provided them with lists of books and the programs we had developed over the years. We talked about the three-cornered hat . . . it was nobody's phrase and yet it was everybody's phrase.

When we disbanded our group, we knew we would cherish the many hours we had spent together. Our fond memories would sustain our friendships forever.

It behooves me to mention that during our many discussions in the group, we discussed the changing political climate in Quebec. As a result of Expo 67 in Montreal, a book entitled

"The Colour of Canada" with text by Hugh MacLennan was published.

Our group accepted there were many people who now acknowledged that there was talk about arising problems from some of the French population.

The following is a quote from the above-mentioned book:

> *"French" and "English" may still be two solitudes, but at least they are learning to respect one another. Their joint ownership of the land makes this necessary, just as, a century ago, it made it necessary for them to form a political union. They knew that if they could not hang together, they would hang separately."*

We all wanted to believe that our French/English problems would be resolved without any major upheavals in Quebec and the rest of Canada. We welcomed and embraced the words of wisdom such as quoted above that supported our beliefs and helped diminish our fears.

We believed Expo 67 had indeed been a visible symbol of what Canada could not yet believe she had become.

We knew Canada is "A land larger than any one person can hope to comprehend."

We now know we were misguided in our thinking. There have been numerous disruptions in the lives of many Canadians over these many years concerning the evolving political unrest in Canada. Canada has become a bilingual country but a majority of people in Quebec continue to actively pursue Quebec's separation from Canada . . . and our history continues to unfold.

Chapter Eight

Embracing the essence of life

Self-reverence, self-knowledge, self-control
These three alone lead life to sovereign power.
                    Alfred Tennyson

After the divorce I vacillate between hope and despair, faith and lack of promise for the future as I struggle with all my might to fight my disillusionment and disappointment for the many sorrowful events that have occurred in my life. I am determined to create a loving atmosphere for Daniel and Matthew now that I no longer have to tolerate an intolerable marriage. I reflect on how the linchpin of our family has been non existent for a long time . . . where was the respect, the kindness, the civility and the consideration?

I am totally aware that Daniel, Matthew and I needed to communicate our feelings of anger and frustration. I am very concerned about my sons. Children learn by imitation and emulation . . . what effects would their parents' behavior have on them?

"Any maladjustment or neurotic behavior in the parents contributes to the negative self-image of the developing child, who later takes that negative self-image to adulthood and thus to the marriage and the children."

My sons need to hear and believe, again and again, that I truly love them. My actions must demonstrate to them the words I speak are genuine. We need a family structure that assures each of us that we can find positive meaning in our lives.

I pray that I will have the courage and energy to do the right thing. Initially, my premise is that we start open discussions about whatever it is Daniel and Matthew have on their mind. My hope is that perhaps we may identify some goals and values, as well as determine our individual wishes. Our home environment has been chaotic and traumatic. I recognize I have been losing touch with my sons compounded by their experimentation with drugs.

We need consistency and some predictability in our lives to help reestablish the trust that has been eroded over the years. I want to help Matthew during his adolescence so he may become a responsible, caring man. I know Daniel has a compassionate heart and I hope he can learn more self-discipline.

I currently feel disconnected from my own parents but I do believe this is a temporary situation. Maria and Jennie are permanently living with my parents. As a result, I realize I am strongly motivated to be completely independent.

In moments of clarity, I know that I wish to restore hope and faith in our family so that we will do more than just survive in our lives.

Daniel is living on his own and recently dropped out of college. I am disappointed but more worried about the company he keeps. I remember Margaret's problems with her son and LSD and how difficult it was for the entire family . . . and she had a supportive, loving husband. In spite of Daniel's behavior we have an intimate conversation one day about his father and our divorce. His comment was "why did it take you so long?" I had tried so hard to protect my sons from what was going on only to discover they knew more than I thought.

Matthew is still in high school, getting good grades, but constantly in trouble. The school principal is finding it difficult to deal with Matthew since his behavior does not seem to affect his academic achievements. When the school gave all the students IQ tests, Matthew scored so high they thought he had stolen the exam prior to writing the test. Of course, the principal knew this was impossible since the exam was kept in a safe.

I reminded the principal that when Daniel had taken an IQ exam over five years ago, his scores were so high they made him take the exam over again.

While I am pleased my sons have high IQs, I am more concerned than ever that the potential they have is going down the drain.

My position at a large computer company is going well and I have been promoted, receiving a modest salary increase. I guess Matthew and I have something in common . . . in spite of the turmoil in our lives, we are super achievers in some of our efforts.

I will receive my B.A. at the end of this year. The group, as we are now called, knows how difficult it was at times to continue pursuing my academic goal. They plan a celebration party in my honor.

My life is very structured . . . I go to work . . . I come home . . . spend as much time with Matthew as I can . . . and Daniel less frequently. Maintaining the house is difficult but I am managing better all the time. Matthew helps me by cutting the grass in the summertime and shoveling the snow in the winter. He has always been a kind young man and I fervently pray that he will find peace in his life. I seldom go out socially but on rare occasions attend a concert or the theater with my good friend, Jane.

I still return to the place in my mind that questions "why did what seem unbearable have to be borne?" . . . yet there were happy times. We were happy when our sons were born. . . For many years, I experienced intense feelings of tenderness, elation, sexual desire, passion and ecstasy with Don that are deemed attributes of love . . . what happened to us? I want to understand but perhaps it will take more time.

I read recently that "people leave their original families with a level of basic self that is rarely altered by future experiences." I was troubled by this and relieved when the author further stated that "therapy is based on the observation that a directed long-term effort can produce some change in basic self." I am encouraged by these words of wisdom as I ponder the changes I wish to make in my life that will necessitate making changes in my basic self.

Occasionally I am maudlin and wonder if anyone will ever smile at me in a way that enlightens my life. I feel that sorrow has dropped a shadow on my life . . . but there is a stirring in my soul . . . I am certain I will dispel the darkness

I am invited to a Labor Day barbecue party. My first inclination is to decline but Jane insists that it will be fun and it's time I stop being a recluse. Daniel is living in another city and Matthew is going to his friend's house for the day. I search for reasons not to go . . . realize I can find many if I so choose . . . finally I decide I will go.

When I arrive at the party, I feel awkward, more so, when I realize there are several available single men . . . divorced men . . . without partners. I am reticent about getting involved in the lively conversations but feel I am adequately sociable.

Eventually I wonder down an incline towards the St. Lawrence River and notice a huge rock where I decide it's a great place to perch. The lapping of the waves against the rocks is soothing and I find myself feeling peaceful and in rhythm with the forces of nature around me. I listen to the birds wondering if they are swallows like those in our back yard. I'm sure the glass of wine I had with my meal has contributed somewhat to my relaxed feeling.

"Do you mind if I join you or do you wish to be alone?"

I turn my head around and see a pleasant looking man that I remember being introduced to as a colleague of Jane's at work ... but I don't remember his name.

"You're Anna ... Jane tells me you're good friends."

"Yes we are." For someone who likes people and conversation, I certainly am not behaving in a manner that validates this persona.

He sits down on an adjoining rock ... I stay perched ... there is silence but it feels comfortable. After a considerable length of time I say "I've forgotten your name."

"Stanley Kowalski."

We start talking. I ask Stanley what he would like to tell me about himself. I discover he has a wry sense of humor that I enjoy. He talks about his life ... he was abandoned by his parents when he was a baby and left at a local orphanage where he grew up. Because he was exceptionally bright, he won several scholarships. He obtained his doctorate degree in physics and engineering. He is considered an international expert in this field. I tell him that I would have a problem understanding all his technical jargon. He is amused and laughs. "You're not alone, most people don't understand ... but at least you're honest."

He has never been married "just never met the right lady ... I never had the time." He related the facts of his life with such beautiful simplicity and I was touched by his candor.

"Well now that you've heard my life story . . . what about you?"

"Stanley, let's talk about me another time. I just want to watch the sunset tonight, okay?"

"You're the mystery lady tonight . . . when the sun sets perhaps we can continue our conversation if our host doesn't think we're being too antisocial."

"Stanley, don't let me keep you from the party . . . there are a lot of single people here tonight and you are a very eligible bachelor."

"Really, Anna . . . has anyone ever told you you're a delightful, bright person and attractive as well?"

I laugh . . . "you just did."

We return to the party and over coffee talk about the books we like to read, the music we like to listen to and what we enjoy doing best. I recognize I am having fun for the first time in a long, long time.

"May I call you? We could have dinner, maybe take in a concert, or just talk some more. It will be my turn to listen to you about your life."

I feel anxious . . . this nice man that I just met is asking me out. Stanley Kowalski is asking me out.

"Well, are you still considering my invitation? You haven't said a word. I know this will sound phony since I just met you, but there's something special about you . . . and I want to get to know you."

"I'd like that" . . . and I give him my telephone number at work. I can't believe I actually did that.

"I'm pleased . . . for a moment I thought you hesitated and I was hoping I was wrong. I don't date very often because of my work and related travel . . . I'm not too good at this sort of thing."

I'm thinking you did just fine. Stanley will be my second real date since my divorce from Don. The blind date I went on was a disaster and surely not indicative of things to come with Stanley.

Jane is excited when I tell her what happened. "Anna, he's really a nice guy, considered one of the smartest men in our company. That's really impressive when you realize how huge our company is. He is definitely slated to go places. In fact he's already on the fast track. The guys say he's probably not married because he is too intelligent and the ladies probably feel intimidated by him. Also, it seems he has very high expectations."

"Jane, I wasn't intimidated by him. What are these high expectations?"

"Anna, I'm not sure. Never mind. You got to first base. Just enjoy the experience."

Stanley didn't call me for two weeks. I was ready to write him off and go back to my "not dating" status that felt safe, when I heard from him. He was very apologetic, explaining he had to fly to Switzerland the day after the party and just got back yesterday. I accepted Stanley's invitation to an intimate French restaurant. During the dinner he told me "I have been thinking about you for the last two weeks. Now who are you? Tell me everything about yourself."

I tell him I am divorced and I have two sons. I tell him about my career and my hopes for the future. I tell him about my parents and some of the things that I think are really important. Stanley is very attentive but I sense his demeanor has changed. It is a subtle change but I feel it is there. When he takes me home, he gives me a sweet, tender kiss. What is it that I sensed before our kiss while at the restaurant? Had I imagined the subtle change that I observed in Stanley? While fleeting, I'm sure it was there.

Stanley calls me a week later. We spend a wonderful evening together, sharing our hopes and dreams so openly I am convinced I misread his behavior the last time we had dinner. We kiss and hug fervently. I am very much aware that Stanley is attracted to me.

He validates my inner thoughts about his feelings for me when he ends the evening by saying "Anna, I know I could fall in love with you."

Was Myrtle right when she said I had inherited my mother's charm and was attractive to men? While I was married, I never thought about whether I was attractive to anyone else. Of course I knew how Eddy felt about me but I thought that was different.

Stanley and I continue seeing each other. He invites me to his apartment and cooks dinner for me. We spend the evening listening to his favorite records and browsing through his book collection. We are both relaxed and happy. It is obvious we are very compatible and enjoy each other's company.

Stanley playfully tousles my hair saying "This has been one of the happiest evenings of my life."

I respond "It's been delightful . . . you're a wonderful host . . . I enjoyed it too."

We go out together quite often during the coming month and I feel we are getting more emotionally involved every time we see each other. When Stanley returns from a business trip, we meet briefly after work for a quick coffee. My intuition tells me immediately something isn't right. Stanley looks miserable.

"Anna, I care about you a great deal but we can't see each other anymore. My career would be jeopardized if I married a divorced woman with two children. I've worked too hard all my life to get to where I am. Our company policy is stringent when it comes to these types of matters. I've seen other men throw away their prospects for a successful future by defying the system. If only things were different. You're so right for me. I'm really sorry."

What spoken words would adequately communicate to Stanley the impact of what he was saying to me? Should I start by admitting I am attracted to Stanley. I like him but I feel I haven't known him long enough for him to be talking about marriage, a future and why we can't marry. Stanley's words sound like something out of the dark ages but then perhaps I just forgot the stigma of being divorced.

I hear him further saying "You're a wonderful person and I don't want to hurt you. It's best we just break it off completely."

While I appreciated Stanley's honesty and actually recognized he was sincere in not wanting to hurt me, I confess I was disappointed and more than surprised by his words.

In the immediate future, I wondered what might have been had the relationship continued. I felt very sad that this brilliant man was full of fear. When I occasionally thought of him, it was always with much compassion and hope that he might eventually find the right person to love.

Stanley never married and became an outstanding, successful, international business executive. His picture, interviews regarding his major accomplishments frequently appeared in business publications and magazines. Over the years, Jane had minimal contact with Stanley who she said was now way beyond her business league. Jane felt like he sometimes made a point of seeking her out and she conveyed to me that whenever they met he would ask "How is your friend, Anna, doing?"

During their last encounter he mentioned "I noticed Anna was appointed to the Board of Directors of the Computer Science Management Association." Jane said he appeared genuinely interested in how my career was progressing but he never asked her about my personal life.

Though Stanley was a very private man, over a rare business luncheon with Jane, he confessed that the biggest regret in his life was letting me go.

Jane said "Anna, I felt so bad for him. He's so successful, a leader in his field but such a lonely man, I felt I might cry. It's crazy but I think you two could have had something special. You know what, I think he knows it too. I guess it's just too late. All water under the bridge as they say."

"Short as it was Jane, I believe it was special but just not meant to be."

"Well, isn't it sad how things worked out Anna. His personal sacrifice for his career was a dichotomy. Our company policies were changed regarding executives marrying someone who was divorced, or executives themselves getting a divorce. It was no longer a deterrent to promotions and success. It wouldn't have mattered that you were a divorced woman" Jane said shaking her head.

> *It's odd to think what might have been*
> *Sun, moon and stars unto each other*
> *Only, I turned down one street*
> *As you went up another.*

When I was promoted to Vice President, I received a congratulatory note from Stanley. He read about my promotion in a business publication that had given me much coverage. I was truly saddened by the one sentence in his note that reflected his regret for our lost friendship.

I was always thankful that I met Stanley. Our brief relationship came at a time in my life when I was ready to dream again. I started to feel there was a possibility I could be happy if I met a kindred spirit. I confess for a while I daydreamed Stanley might be my kindred spirit.

After Stanley and I said farewell, I began thinking maybe I wasn't meant to be in a long term relationship. Our family track record seemed to support my thinking. After all, Maria was divorced as well. I thought two out of two is somewhat troubling. What was confusing to me my role models, my parents, had been happily married. What on earth had happened to Maria and me?

Myrtle was still with the same man though she claimed he had never been the love of her life. She said they were comfortable and both had always been honest about their feelings for each other.

Being the incurable romantic that I was, I on the other hand knew I would never settle for being in a long term relationship that didn't fill me with intense feelings of tenderness, elation, sexual desire and ecstasy.

I was sure Stanley's physical attractiveness had not played as dominant a role in drawing us together as had been the case with Don. More than that, Stanley and I had a commonality of interest as well as the same religious beliefs. We definitely didn't have similar family histories but our in-depth discussions in this area suggested this would not have been a problem in the future.

As I reflected on my current lot in life, was I much wiser when it came to affairs of the heart? The only thing I knew for sure love could not exist without trust and genuine concern for another's welfare.

I also concluded Myrtle's words from long ago "Anna, you're a dreamer and a realist. It's a tough combination" still applied to me today and for some unknown reason, I found myself quoting:

> *Ah, fill the Cup: - what boots it to repeat*
> *How time is slipping underneath our Feet:*
> *Unborn To-morrow, and dead Yesterday,*
> *Why fret about them if To-day be sweet!*

> The Rubaiyat of Omar Khayyam

Once again, I knew my spirit had aspired to move forward with hope and courage that continues to grow from my awareness of the fragility and uncertainty of life.

Chapter Nine

New beginnings . . . destiny and a lover's call

By bringing the past into the present, we create a future just like the past. By letting the past go, we make room for miracles.
      Marianne Williamson

A year later I met Joel. The first time I saw him, when our eyes met, I knew we would marry though I knew nothing about him, not even his name. It was the most overpowering feeling that felt both safe and exciting at the same time.

I remember coming home and wondering what had happened to me? If this was my bolt of lightning, why was I so calm? I had read so many psychology books trying to better understand who I was and why I behaved the way I did. Recently I had come to the conclusion I would not repeat the mistakes I had made in the past while I was Don's wife. I would also not be in a relationship with anyone that would prevent me from being a better mother to my sons. Thus you can imagine my surprise when suddenly I had strong feelings for a complete stranger.

Joel was an American, working in Canada for an extended period of time. Our first date was a luncheon unlike any I had ever been on before. I knew I had found my soul mate and felt my unexpressed feelings were mutual. While I was content and peaceful, my being was also exhilarated.

Joel was divorced with two daughters whom he loved very much. He knew I was strongly attracted to him from the start but he did not pressure me in any way to be anything but his friend. He sensed I was determined to know more about him even though he had already expressed his desire to be in a committed relationship with me. I wanted to know Joel exactly as he was not as I might wish him to be.

Joel was intelligent, witty, kind, compassionate, tender, loving, fun to be with and when he laughed, you heard the greatest, deepest laugh in the world that embraced your being. He had broad shoulders, dark brown hair and blue eyes, same blue shade as my father, and a smile that warmed your heart. Because my initial feelings for him were so strong, I was extremely cautious before I fully acknowledged that I was deeply in love with Joel.

I was certain Daniel and Matthew would like Joel who had the ability to bring out the best in people. I liked that Joel was who he was with the boys, as he was with everyone, sincere and loving. Upon meeting Joel, my sons were not hostile rather I would say they were cautious.

After several get-togethers, my sons agreed he was "a nice guy" and were now relaxed when he was around. Joel spent a lot of time with Matthew and as I watched the two of them together, I was pleased that Matthew now had a positive role model in his life. I often thought being the youngest son, when I was married to Don, must have been more difficult for Matthew since he was around our home more often than Daniel who had distanced himself, to protect himself from the chaos.

Jane and I had talked many times about women's success in business. How when their careers surpassed the males' careers, it often put a strain on the relationship. I had witnessed this situation not only with Jane but another lady friend in my company who was consequently getting a divorce.

I had surpassed Don in my career motivated by the necessity to take care of my family but acknowledged I enjoyed the sense of accomplishment in being successful. In the past, I had spent much time cogitating about this issue but realized our marriage had failed due to many other reasons as well.

Joel felt my success was an important part of who I was, that he loved, and was not intimidated. He had several MA degrees in mathematics and business and was successful in his field. I knew he would be returning to the United States when his assignment in Canada was completed.

We had been going out for a year and a half, when Joel asked me to marry him and move to the states with my family. He said he knew he was asking me to give up my family roots, my friends and my career but was absolutely certain we belonged together.

"Anna, I have a small confession to make. The first time I saw you I knew you were the woman I would marry. It was such an overpowering feeling . . . something I've never experienced before . . . and I thought what is going on . . . this lady could be married . . . I don't even know her name."

You can imagine how surprised Joel was that I had experienced the same feelings at the same time.

I said I would marry Joel and move to the states with my sons. I was certain that I could resume my career since I had worked with many American companies over the years. If not I was willing to start from scratch . . . "my personal life is more important than my career." Joel promised me that I would never regret my decision as long as he lived.

Some of my friends were delighted at my good fortune. They liked Joel and said "he just adores you." Most of them said as if by osmosis they could feel our deep love. Others said "are you crazy, Anna? . . . you don't know anyone in the states . . . you have to sell your home . . . leave your job." It was all true but for the first time in my life I knew if I followed my heart, all would be well for all of us.

My mother who was now a widow amazed me when she said "Don't listen to anyone. Listen to your heart. He's a good man . . . I can tell. Start a new life in a new country and I know you will be very happy. I see his eyes are filled with love for you and yours for him. Don't let this happiness slip away" It sounded more eloquent spoken in her native Czechoslovakian language.

I thought it was ironic. My mother had started a new life in Canada with her husband and baby, my sister, Maria. I was now contemplating moving to the states, a new country for me, to marry the man I love.

The next surprise came when my mother went on to say "I didn't always understand you when you were growing up. Your world has been so different from mine. I am very proud you are my daughter. You did so many things . . . you got a good education, your BA, even though we couldn't help you. I know it's been difficult for you having to work and raise your sons. Your father was so proud of you; the first in our family to go to university. You have two wonderful sons. I love them and I love you Anuska."

I had waited a long time to hear her words of praise and love. The tears that trickled down my cheeks were tears of joy. Her warm, loving embrace would sustain my memories of my mother that I truly loved.

My sister Maria was not enthusiastic about my moving to the states to marry Joel. While she liked Joel, she thought it would be far too difficult for me to be happy away from the life and friends I now had. "You don't know a soul in America. You're giving up a very good job. We're a small family and all you've got."

Certainly everything Maria said was true but intuitively I knew the right thing was to marry Joel and be with him and my sons wherever that might be. I had worked so hard to forgive myself and Don for the mistakes in the past. I knew I would not forget some of the negative experiences that occurred in my life with Don. I was at peace with the progress I had made and happy that I could love this good man. I was more hopeful for my sons because Joel was such a wonderful role model and I could see they were becoming less guarded when they were with him.

I felt sorry for Maria as she had never moved away from my parents after her divorce. I was pleased she had finally gone to work again when Jennie was older and my hope was that she would develop more of a social life for herself.

I noticed that most of the people that were rooting for me were individuals who were positive in their attitude and less fearful of new opportunities. Interestingly, they were by no means people who had not had pain and sorrow in their own lives. On the contrary, some of them had major losses. I was trying to accept some of the events in my life as gifts of growth. At times, it was not easy but I felt if I maintained a positive attitude I would come to more fully appreciate that my experiences have created a strength in my character that will serve me well. I certainly had learned that my happiness has to come from within.

I was strong enough to know I and I alone would make the final choice about Joel. I never once doubted my love for him; it was the impact of moving to the states on my sons that I was most concerned about. I spoke to Daniel and Matthew about Joel's marriage proposal and all of us moving to San Francisco. Daniel said he was happy for me . . . he liked Joel . . . but didn't know if he wanted to leave his friends. He said I shouldn't worry about him since he needed to make his own decisions and live his own life. Matthew said he wanted to leave Canada and start all over like his grandparents. He said "I promise when I get to the states, I'll stop smoking marijuana." It was the first time Matthew admitted smoking it.

Joel and I started making arrangements for all of us to legally enter the states. It would take close to a year before we moved from Canada. Joel's courtship was filled with spontaneous and planned activities. He showered me with flowers, books and music that we both loved but the best gift of all was Joel and his love. We went on picnics, climbed Mount Royal, visited museums and art galleries. Some of the best times were just hanging around the house with the boys and barbecuing outside on a sunny day. How wonderful life could be.

Joel's positive energy surrounded us all and I was delighted with our good fortune. I wrote love poems to Joel . . . "the first I've ever had in my life" he said. He bought me posters with Gordon Lightfoot's beautiful songs that we both enjoyed and beautiful cards with words like "I never imagined how completely fulfilling sharing my life with you would be, and I know that I owe a great debt to you for teaching me the value of making dreams come true." He particularly loved the following poem, one of many I wrote for him:

> *I now journey a road sprinkled with angel dust; hear the rustle of gossamer wings*
> *Once again all things are possible; dreams of love and joy*
> *Dance with me, if you will, among the flowers in my path*
> *Share my laughter, share my joy*
> *Hear the birds singing gleefully; my song joins theirs*
> *I celebrate my butterfly wings, they are delicate but strong*
> *Life is now, God is now, I am reborn*
> *No longer am I filled with sorrow and fear*
> *I rejoice in loving you.*

I knew Joel was very happy and deeply in love with me. He told me many times he had never been this happy in his entire life. Joel's marriage had been loveless for a long time and his wife was only interested in the material comforts he could provide. He had stayed with her because of his two daughters.

One day he realized that he could no longer live this way; it was also a bad example of a marriage for his daughters. His wife agreed to the divorce because of his generous financial arrangements he provided for her that he maintained throughout his life.

I always thought how fortunate it was for me that his ex-wife had not reveled in this extraordinary man . . . it seemed she had been oblivious as to who he was. I was delighted at my good fortune. I loved Joel . . . I had found my soulmate at last.

Joel returned to the states, found a place for us to live, and was eagerly awaiting our arrival that would take place in one month's time. The proper papers had finally all been processed and "we are coming to America."

Chapter Ten

We are coming to America!

Surely as I have thought, so shall it come to pass; and as I have purposed, so shall it stand.
                                        Isaiah 14:24

The three of us arrive in San Francisco on a beautiful sunny day. After clearing through customs, I see Joel's happy, smiling face waiting to greet us. I am filled with a peaceful joy knowing that Joel and I relate so authentically and humanly to each other. I recall Martin Buber saying that when this is so "God is the electricity that surges between them" . . . them of course being Joel and I.

Though we are all tired from the long airplane flight, we are eager to see our new home and immediate surroundings. Select possessions arrived safely from Canada and Joel unpacked everything and set things up "as best I could." We all take a long walk around the neighborhood that is very different from our Canadian suburbs where we lived. It is not too long before Daniel and Matthew relax with Joel once again and I sense all will be well.

After a couple of months, Daniel says he wants to go further north where there is less civilization. I recognize that he is restless and not totally at peace with himself. Joel and I discuss his plans with him, reassuring him that if he ever changes his mind, he may come home to us at any time. Daniel promises to stay in touch and inwardly I cry a little when he leaves.

Matthew's academic learning is beyond the level of his classmates and he is transferred two classes higher. I am concerned that emotionally he will not be on the same level as his classmates which unfortunately proves true. Matthew appears to be making a few friends and never complains about his new life situation. I recall Matthew's unsolicited commitment that he would change his life when he got to the states.

His father has telephoned him several times and tells Matthew he is planning to visit him shortly. We have now been living in the states for about three years. I have no contact with Matthew's father whatsoever, having made it clear to Don prior to our divorce, the boys are old enough to determine when they wish to see their father.

Don phones Matthew saying he is in San Francisco and makes arrangements to see Matthew. Don picks Matthew up for his visit . . . I ensure that Matthew knows he can spend as much time as he wants with his Dad. Matthew returns after one hour and goes to his room. I am concerned and ask "is everything okay?" Matthew says he doesn't want to talk about it. Many weeks later, Matthew says "we had lunch . . . he was with his girlfriend . . . I thought he had come alone . . . he never said anything to me about bringing someone else . . . we had nothing to talk about so I told him I wanted to go home." In keeping with my promise, I had nothing to say about Don's actions either.

A couple of years later, I received a telegram from Sandra, followed up by a phone call, telling me Don died from a heart attack while making a phone call in a phone booth. Unfortunately, he had forgotten his angina pills that Sandra said might have saved his life. It was late at night . . . he was out-of-town with a colleague who said there was nothing he could do. Sandra called me because she couldn't get in touch with Daniel and felt I would want to give the news to Matthew.

After I told Matthew about his father's death, he rushed upstairs and I heard heart rendering sobs emanating from his room that I could tell he was trying to muffle in his pillow. I too started to cry. Don had fathered both my sons . . . I remembered the early happy memories . . . I cried for his life and what he might have been and now could never be. I was filled with a quiet compassion for Matthew. When Joel heard about Don's death and I told him about Matthew and my own reaction he said "I would expect you would have feelings . . . he was a part of your life, Anna . . . you are not looking back in sorrow for your life, but his . . . I also see you counting your blessings." My wonderful, loving man, Joel.

I told Matthew he could go to Canada for his father's funeral that Sandra was taking care of. Matthew said without hesitation "I don't want to go."

When I finally located Daniel, I made the same offer to Daniel. He said no. "I prefer to remember him when he was alive. I did see him once with his girlfriend and at that time I wondered about his health . . . he always seemed to be out of breath."

Daniel asked me to contact Aunt Sandra. I told her Daniel and Matthew did not wish to go to their father's funeral, but Daniel said he would call her at a later date.

As I was pondering over this current event, certainly a trauma in my sons' lives, I remembered my mother telling me how surprised she was when Don once showed up unannounced at her door. She invited him in . . . made tea . . . he asked whether my life was going well with Joel . . . did she hear from the boys? This was the only contact he had with my mother after we were divorced and her feeling was that he was a lonely, unhappy man.

I am doing very well career-wise. I am now in marketing/middle management. The job is competitive but I have confidence in my abilities and always remember my father's advice "if a job is worth doing, it's worth doing well." Joel is also thriving and we are more than pleased with our status quo.

Matthew is excelling at school but I am becoming concerned about his lack of enthusiasm. He always tells me everything is fine whenever we talk. I ask myself if he is still grieving for his father?

I get an urgent telephone call from Joel to "please come home . . . it's important." I rush home immediately. Matthew had called me at work. I was unavailable as I was out on the road. Matthew then called Joel. He told Joel he was very scared because he had swallowed a whole bunch of aspirins. Joel rushed home and took Matthew to the local hospital.

After treatment, the hospital agreed to discharge Matthew in Joel's care provided he and I agreed Matthew would receive counseling. I am shocked but mostly devastated. I keep asking myself why, why, why, why, why . . . . I ask Matthew if he is all right before I ask him why? He says he doesn't know why. He really didn't mean to do it. The hospital stated "it's a cry for help."

I am besieged with feelings of guilt . . . I am a failure as a mother . . . my loving Matthew is not enough. Joel is very supportive and assures me we will both do everything we can to help Matthew.

Matthew starts therapy . . . we are invited to attend some family sessions. The therapist says Matthew is depressed and is keeping things bottled up inside. He is also angry.

The therapist asks me "what would happen if you said no to your son?" I ask him why he is asking me that question. Does he believe I am spoiling Matthew? I try to respond to his question and realize I really don't know how. The only thing I know is I want Matthew to be happy. I will make whatever changes I must to provide an environment where this is possible. "Surely, Matthew knows I love him?" The therapist believes I am fearful of saying no to Matthew's wishes. I do not perceive Matthew as a demanding young man. I struggle with this input for a long time. I am pleased that Joel's relationship with Matthew since this incident has grown much stronger. I believe Matthew recognizes Joel is really there for him.

When therapy ends, Matthew is applying to various universities. He has decided to become an architect. Joel and I can see his renewed interest in life. We are all talking more openly and we have all agreed to continue doing so.

Joel's daughters, Lindy and Pamela have visited us on occasional weekends . . . initially it was very difficult because of his oldest daughter, Lindy. She was trying very hard to create problems between her young sister and myself when she realized her young sister enjoyed my company and even said "you're nice . . . I like you." Pamela said Lindy often makes trouble. Joel dealt with the problem and peace reigned supreme for a while. Eventually, Joel and I agreed it would be best, if at times, he just visited with his daughters by himself. It became evident that their mother was influencing them in a negative way.

I remain convinced that children whose parents are divorced are less damaged than if they stay in a hostile, unloving environment. Joel's daughters got to see their father in a new light as did my sons see me. All the children saw and experienced what it is like to be with two people who love each other.

Throughout our marriage, Joel and I had many challenges to face regarding our children. Together we prevailed and never doubted that in the long run, our children would benefit from our mutual love for them. I will always remember when Lindy, Joel's eldest daughter said to me "I never saw my father hold my mother's hand like he holds yours . . . I never saw them kiss. My Dad sure is happy, isn't he?"

When I told Joel what Lindy had said, he was pleased that Lindy was able to recognize his happiness. Things improved between us all and life was more stable and pleasant for everyone. There were some inevitabilities that occurred that each life experiences, but I had reached a place, in my own life, where I viewed them as an opportunity to expand my vision and connection to the world.

Daniel keeps in touch with us and we are delighted to hear he is working at a regular job in a community center helping families on welfare. He is able to commute to his job from his cabin in the woods, as he describes it, and also mentions that he has met a nice young lady. He tells me he is turning his life around. He says "I hope Matthew is doing okay and you and Joel are happy." I assure him we are doing well. When I get off the phone, I give thanks to the all mighty for watching over Daniel

I continue reading psychology books as I have in the past and Joel laughingly says "I'm sure you could pass the necessary exams to set up a practice."I find it is easier to read knowledge than to put it into action especially with those I love . . . but I know I will keep on trying.

Chapter Eleven

Spiritual soulmates, courage and the power of love

Rejoice always.
1 Thessalonians 5:16

Joel and I decide that we will get married by a judge at city hall. Joel is a Roman Catholic who no longer attends church. I am comfortable with our plans. I have not become associated with any church in the states and don't wish a traditional wedding. Joel and I know our souls are already united and we are deeply committed to each other. This ceremony will just legalize our status in the world.

We pick a convenient date and the two of us go to city hall to be married. To avoid difficulties regarding our children's availability, or lack thereof, to attend our marriage ceremony, we decide to marry without them being present. Prior to our marriage, when we talked to our children advising them of our decision, they were very accepting and didn't seem concerned.

I have a beautiful cream-colored dress that I purchased for this special day. On the way to city hall, Joel asks me to stay in the car while he goes into a florist shop. He comes back smiling with a lovely bouquet of fresh flowers saying "every bride needs a bouquet . . . I hope you like them, my love."

The judge who marries us is a lady. Our witnesses are a young couple, we just met, who will be married after we are. I am delighted the ceremony is brief . . . I hear every word the judge says and repeat my vows to Joel in a strong, clear voice. I am full of joy and so happy I feel I am beaming like a light. Joel's kiss and embrace envelop me with emotions I cannot describe. We are now each wearing a wedding band.

After the signing of papers, we go back home to celebrate. Matthew comes home from school and is the first to congratulate us. To celebrate our marriage, Joel has made reservations for the three of us at an elegant restaurant. Matthew doesn't say much but looks pleased. The three of us have a lovely evening and we are all content. Joel and I have decided it would be better to have a honeymoon later on. We will go to Europe when it is more convenient.

I was certain our wedding ceremony would go well . . . all I wanted was a simple service; just Joel and me. Several people were surprised that I didn't have a church wedding since they knew I am an incurable romantic. What people didn't know was every day with Joel was filled with love and romance. I will mention here our honeymoon was one of the happiest hallmarks in my life.

We enjoy every day more and more and are filled with wonder and delight that our love keeps growing. I can't imagine loving Joel any more than I do. We both sense that our love is an exceptional gift and we feel truly blessed. Joel and I also celebrate the visible progress our children seem to be making in their lives.

My career is doing well, a lot better than I expected. I have had no major problems adjusting to the American working environment. Apart from the fact that I find Americans are more aggressive in their efforts to achieve their goals, things are pretty much the same as they were in Canada. I am now a regional manager, responsible for a large staff in southern and northern California. I am in the process of obtaining an MBA at night to help further my prospects in the future.

It is said the only thing you can be certain about is the unexpected. This was surely the case when my boss made some sexually embarrassing comments about me in front of some employees. I was extremely upset. When I discussed it with Joel, he asked me what I wanted to do about it?

Contrary to my experience in Canada, where a boss chased me around the office and I resigned the next day, I was not willing to give up a good position that I had worked so hard to achieve. I told my boss I planned to report this incident to Personnel unless he took some corrective action on my behalf. He had seriously undermined me as a person and a manager. I told him I wished to resolve this matter amicably without intervention from Personnel.

The behavior and decisions made by senior management that ensued were governed by dishonesty, cowardice and greed. Truth did not reign supreme until much later.

My region was the most successful in the entire company. We had recently acquired two major national accounts that would produce excellent revenue for the next five years. This outstanding achievement was realized primarily due to the excellent relationship I had established with these customers and the support I provided to my people working on these accounts. Letters were available from the clients confirming these facts, wherein they stated that it was not the product alone that had influenced their decision to buy from the company. I was due to get a high five-figure bonus in the next two months.

I was surprised when my boss took credit for some of my account activities at a recent conference. I tried to convince myself he was talking in general about all the regions that included mine. Why did I lie to myself?

Later I discussed the matter with Joel. He wondered if, perhaps, my boss was insecure about my success. I had been wondering the same thing myself but it didn't make sense. The more money I made for the company, the more money he made.

I was also aware that my boss was having an affair with his administrator. I felt as long as it did not affect my position and the people who reported to me, I did not have to deal with the issue. Since I was in a subordinate position, it was best that I stay focused on my work and leave things as they were. Unfortunately, I now realized my boss's behavior towards women was spilling out on me.

A week later my boss fired me without explanation. I was shocked. This was America with laws to protect its people. I decided to fight back. First, I made sure that the company knew I was entitled to my bonus. Had the company fired me to save the bonus for themselves? Then I asked that the company provide me with just cause for my termination since I had excellent personnel evaluations, the last one performed three months ago.

The company immediately set up a mediation meeting that would become the turning point in my business career. My attorney was well prepared and said we had a good case. I was flabbergasted at the lies that my boss told at the meeting. He lied, and lied and lied. I was furious but felt sure I stayed outwardly calm.

During a break I asked my attorney, how can he answer your questions with such blatant lies? My attorney said "Did you expect him to tell the truth? He planned on getting your bonus. The problem they're having is you hit the nail on the head. Your boss's only recourse is to diminish your success . . . he hasn't had any of his own lately."

The company paid my bonus, reversed the firing, and gave me an excellent written reference. They also provided a written letter confirming they would provide verbal references upon request.

A year later, my boss was fired for improper behavior, so grave, senior management couldn't cover it up. His wife filed for a divorce. I couldn't help but remember my parting comment at the mediation . . . "some day you will all know the truth and perhaps regret that you took part in this debacle."

I was temporarily disillusioned but encouraged that "the truth will out." I learned that I would not be unjustly intimated by authority . . . I had the courage to stand up for my rights and the courage to speak the truth

I had several job offers within a few weeks. I felt much wiser, stronger and more secure than ever before about my ability to perform successfully in the business world. I definitely was no longer the innocent, young lady who once got chased by her boss around the office in Canada.

I valued my excellent personal and business reputation. I chose to view this unsavory incident as a lesson that would help me in the future. It would serve me well to remember I had tapped into strengths I did not know I had and had prevailed in spite of the overwhelming barrage of lies thrust my way.

Life is multifaceted. I was dealing with issues related to my career yet concerned about my mother who had been ill for a while. During our telephone conversations, lately I noticed she seemed disoriented. My sister assured me my mother was getting proper medical care and kept me posted on a regular basis as to what was going on. Maria was often harsh with me that I knew was because I was not there to shoulder the burden with her. I appreciated her feelings but I was at a loss as to how I could help since I lived so far away. One day the telephone rang and I was told "Mother just died."

I got on the first flight to Montreal to attend my mother's

funeral. Joel and I had agreed I would go alone. Matthew was writing exams and I didn't want to leave him by himself. I was relieved that Joel would be staying at home with Matthew.

My sister had taken care of all the arrangements and together we planned to host what I call a "farewell reception" at her home, my mother's home. Perhaps it is similar to an Irish wake.

I know my mother would have been pleased with her funeral service, all the flowers and good turnout of friends and neighbors . . . she always thought such things mattered. She always remarked on them whenever she came back from somebody's funeral. It was very important to her.

Understandably, Maria and I were both stressed out. I was sensitive to Maria's feelings and tried to accommodate her as best I could. I knew Maria had been wholly responsible for my mother these many years but she seemed to ignore that my mother generously provided her home to her and her daughter, Jennie, since Maria divorced Frank. I had much compassion for Maria but I was also aware that had Maria made other choices earlier in her life . . . finding a home for herself and Jennie . . . she might not have been in this position.

During the years, we had talked about this several times. Maria always felt she had no choice . . . who else would have looked after our mother if she hadn't stayed with her? We would argue because I suggested that maybe mother would have become more independent if Maria and Jennifer lived elsewhere. Our sibling rivalry got us no where.

As time went on, even though Maria knew my mother had encouraged me to marry Joel and move to the states, Maria made it clear that I had abandoned my mother and left her in her care. I wanted to remind Maria when I left Canada my mother was well and thriving.

I had accepted long ago that you cannot change someone's

perception . . . it is theirs . . . and often far different than yours. I knew Maria had strong feelings as I did that were now being exacerbated by our mother's death. I tried to remember "feelings are neither right nor wrong . . . they simply are."

The best I was hoping for was to go back to California without further arguments. That was not to be.

My sister had my mother's old will and I had her most recent will that my mother had given me for safe keeping when she was having problems with Maria. I was surprised to hear they were having problems since Maria had always been the favorite daughter.

My mother's instructions were that I bring the new will, from the states, to be read after her death. She made me promise I would honor her wishes and never say a word to Maria. She explained that she had always felt guilty that her first will left everything to Maria except for a very small sum of money that she would have left to me.

My mother said she had a lot of time to think and sort things out. She said when she made her first will after my father's death, she was very distraught and knew she had been influenced by Maria as to its contents. The more she thought about it, the more she felt the will was unfair. She only had two daughters . . . it was only right that she leave everything equally to each daughter including her home that was her biggest asset.

"Yes, Maria has done a lot for me over the years but she has forgotten that I have provided a home for her and Jennie since her divorce. I am grateful to her but I need to change my will and make things right."

I told my mother she should do whatever she wanted to do. I did not want to influence her in any way. In my heart, I knew if my mother changed her will, which she did, my sister would blame me, and she did.

To minimize a laborious segment of my life, it behooves me to say my sister bought my interest in our family home . . . we settled the details of the will per my mother's wishes . . . after which my sister did not speak to me for over five years.

I often thought about our father's lessons regarding money and wondered whether we had both failed in appreciating how divisive money could be. Had my promise to my mother been devious? I had entirely forgotten about my mother's new will until her death. I knew intuitively my sister and I would have problems as a result of my mother's decision. I also struggled with the fact that the very things Maria was accusing me of doing . . . influencing my mother to change her will . . . she had done when my mother made her first will. The only thing I knew for sure was that I was saddened by all these events.

Jennie and my sons maintained contact, agreed this was a situation involving two sisters, their respective parents, and each of us had a different story to tell. They decided not to get involved in any of this . . . I believe it was a wise choice.

I wrote Maria several letters over the years and I eventually contacted her by telephone, asking if we could put the past behind us. It took some time before she agreed to a reconciliation. Our relationship is tenuous as Maria is unable to let go of the past. I have accepted that we have many unresolved issues. I am still vulnerable to hurt and pain when it comes to my relationship with Maria but remain hopeful that someday we can be less fearful and more loving to each other.

My dear friend Eddy telephones to say he is sorry about my mother's death. He is living in Montreal again and was wondering if we could meet for a coffee or lunch before I go back home. I haven't seen him in ten years and would like very much to see his friendly face especially since the recent turmoil with my sister.

Eddy hasn't aged except for the grey sideburns. He looks rather handsome. He walks towards me quickly with outstretched arms that embrace me in a warm hug. "You look more beautiful than ever Anna."

"Eddy, my eyes are withered from crying so much . . . but thank you."

We get settled in a restaurant booth and I say "okay Eddy, tell me what you have been doing in the last ten years? Do you have children? When did you move back to Montreal?"

"Anna, I was married for five years. She was a good person but I made a serious mistake in marrying her. We are now divorced. We never had children and maybe that's a good thing. I'm a stockbroker and doing very well. It's a lot easier living in the city I love where I still have some of my old school friends . . .now what about you?"

I tell him about Joel, Daniel and Matthew though I know Maria may have told him about my life. I ask him to visit us in San Francisco and I tell him I have talked about "my friend Eddy" to Joel. He looks pleased and sad at the same time. I well remember that look.

"I thought by getting married, and I really did care for her, I might fall deeply in love with her."

"Anna, the heart doesn't work that way. I can't change how I feel about you and I don't expect you can do anything about it. That's just how it is. I've learned to accept it. I still love you. I always will."

I feel tears rolling down my cheeks. I know I am very vulnerable because of my mother's death but it is more than that. I remember Celine and the priest, Denis, and the pain and sorrow they felt for loving each other . . . and the overwhelming joy when they did.

"Eddy, I do love you as a person but please know I passionately love Joel as a man and my soulmate. I will always treasure the gift of your love."

"Thank you, Anna, for loving me in any way you can. It matters a great deal to me."

I fly back to California into Joel's passionate embrace at the airport. I am filled with joy to see him.

> *"Love gives naught but itself and takes naught but from itself. Love possesses not nor would it be possessed;*
> *For love is sufficient unto love."*

These words go through my head as Joel is driving us home. I read them to him when I gave him The Prophet by Kahlil Gibran.

Over the years, life with Joel is an ongoing delight. I never imagined I could love someone so deeply, with all my heart and soul. Some days when I wake up in the morning, and see Joel's face and tousled hair on the pillow next to me, I ask myself what did I do in my life to deserve the love he gives me? Joel cherishes who I am and I feel cherished and loved. He celebrates my achievements and those of our children and is compassionate when I need his support and understanding.

When Joel and I first met and we discovered our mutual interest in gardening and flowers, I happen to mention I thought it was better people give flowers to the living rather than to the dead. That way the person who gave them had the joy of seeing the happiness in the person who received the flowers. Joel must have taken my casual comment to heart and during our marriage, he spontaneously brought me flowers every month of the year as well as on birthdays and special occasions. I always knew he had a bouquet of fresh flowers hidden behind his back when he lovingly grinned at me in a certain way that I fondly recognized.

On one of his birthdays I bought him flowers and enclosed a love poem I had written to him. He looked like the happiest man alive and in fact, told me he was.

Joel marveled at his good fortune. "When I wake up in the morning and the first thing I see is your face on the pillow beside me, I ask myself why the gods are so good to me. You are my beloved . . . when was the last time I told you I love and adore you?"

Matthew appeared to be faring well in his studies to become an architect. Like me whatever was going on in my life, I still managed to perform my work and studies. Matthew seemed to be able to do the same and I recalled that he had always been an excellent student even during his difficult times.

He graduated with flying colors. We now were the proud parents of an architect, the first in our family. We were both excited when Matthew stated he would be working for a large firm, here in the city, as we both hoped to see him more often. While Matthew was living on campus, he continued to see us during all the holidays and often came home for dinner on weekends. We loved Matthew and enjoyed his company. I felt my relationship with Matthew had become more relaxed and I felt that we were getting to know each other as adults.

I got my MBA and was pleased I had achieved another major goal in my life. It seemed an awfully long time ago when I was sixteen, and realized I would be going to work, instead of going to university. At that time, I remember I promised myself I would achieve this goal but it was just going to take a little longer. Joel was so proud of me. He took me out to celebrate. We also had a dinner party for a few close friends.

Daniel got married to a young lady, Jackie, who has a five-year-old son, Adam. We had a small church wedding for them in San Francisco attended by Joel, Matthew, myself and young Adam. Jackie has no family and is alone except for her son. Something about her reminds me of Stanley in Canada who was brought up in an orphanage. Adam seems to really like Daniel and Daniel appears to be comfortable with his new role as stepdad. They plan on living in Daniel's log cabin.

My heart is filled with a peaceful joy as we wave goodbye. Something good is stirring inside of me and I feel Daniel, Jackie and Adam will have a life filled with much happiness and joy. I am truly thankful Daniel has fought his demons and won.

Joel and I spend a lot of time outdoors exploring northern and southern California. I learn about all the different flowers that flourish in this climate and environment along with the birds that inhabit the various trees. We take many trips along the magnificent coastline and also inland to visit the splendid vineyards to taste and purchase their delicious wines. Joel is a voracious reader, as I am, but also an exceptional teacher that helps me to appreciate the beauty of nature more fully than ever before.

We take several extended trips to Europe that complement our local traveling and knowledge of the world. I always recognize these trips are especially wonderful because Joel is there to share everything with me.

Our children visit sporadically and we are always delighted that they are all making progress either at work or university, whatever the case may be at that time. Matthew sometimes joins us in our nature walks and I am always so pleased at how close he and Joel have become.

With the passage of time, I notice Matthew seems to be less open and appears more distant in his behavior towards me. I can't help but wonder what it is I may have done that is causing the changes . . . they are subtle but evident to me. Joel suggests that perhaps Matthew is just being more independent since he has not experienced any change in Matthew's attitude towards him. I try talking to Matthew, asking how everything is, and he brushes me off by saying everything is okay.

Matthew advises us that he and his girlfriend, whom we have never met, are moving in together. He had once mentioned that he was going out with a young lady once in awhile and that was it. I am surprised but try to be pleased that he has a girlfriend and his personal life must be happier. I try hard not to be intrusive by asking too many questions but do ask "when are you planning to introduce us to her?"

"Soon" he says . . . "she wants to meet the two of you as well."

I am encouraged.

Several months later we meet a very nice lady called Katherine. She is an occupational therapist and an only child. Katherine is well spoken, appears to be shy and somewhat nervous in our presence. I notice she pays a lot of attention to Matthew during all our conversations as if to gauge how he is reacting to what is being said.

Many months go by and then I get a call from Katherine suggesting we have lunch. I am pleased as I want very much to know the lady my son is living with. Katherine is more at ease than the first time I met her and we have a delicious lunch and pleasant time together.

Every couple of weeks Katherine calls me and we either talk on the phone or get together for lunch. She tells me "your son is busy becoming a successful architect and has little time to call you." I suggest her career as an occupational therapist must also be demanding . . . she replies "I monitor my schedule very well so I have free time quite often."

The next time Katherine and I meet she tells me Matthew and she had a terrible fight. I am very uncomfortable listening to the details and tell her so. I also state, I think it best she not discuss their personal matters with me. I feel she is disappointed with what I have said and I do not hear from her for a long time.

They say . . . whoever they are . . . which reminds me of my mother's favorite saying "what will people say" . . . that events, bad things, good things come in bunches. They seem to be right.

Joel is offered a promotion that would involve relocation and extensive traveling away from home. He discusses the offer with me even though he has decided he is not going to take the job. He feels it is only fair we talk about it since his decision affects me as well. Joel tells me he has no interest in being away from me about seventy percent of the time, which would be the case if he accepted the position. He also feels the new job is not as challenging as the one he currently has. He also feels it would not be good for our children, his as well as mine. I tell Joel I am happy with his decision and more than pleased he is going to be around.

I get a big promotion; I am now a senior vice president in a major American corporation. With time, I will realize that I have reached the glass ceiling that everyone talks about. At this moment, I am pleased with my past performance and that my accomplishments are being acknowledged. I look forward to the new challenges that lie ahead.

When I show Joel the formal announcement of my promotion that is being circulated within the company and that will be submitted to the press, he kisses me with much passion, then gayly twirls me around the room, saying "you did it; I knew you would . . . haven't I been telling you all along you're the best." Indeed he has always encouraged me when I hit major bumps along the road.

Joel tells me he will enjoy being married to an executive. We both laugh when I remind him when they have spouses' activities for the conferences that I attend, he will be the only male with all those lovely ladies. This does come to pass, and Joel is a hit with all the executives' wives. He has a lot of fun being the only male in the group. I can tell he enjoys the surprised look on people's faces when we are introduced at company functions and people find out he is the "spouse of" our senior executive, Anna Adams.

Joel was always proud of my accomplishments and never felt threatened by my success. While he was extremely successful in the world of technology, he maintained a clear sense of priorities in his personal relationships. He had this wonderful quality of unconditionally accepting people's thoughts and feelings. Joel had learned early on in his life what was really important to him . . . family, friends and colleagues . . . honesty and integrity, and being responsible for one's behavior . . . as well as not abandoning your principles under any circumstances. I loved who Joel was with all my heart and soul. When we weren't together, I was just happy knowing he was in this world.

A welcome surprise was a phone call from Myrtle in Canada. She was coming to Los Angeles for a week to visit a friend, and wondered if we were available for a weekend visit from her in San Francisco. After all these years, I was delighted that I would see her dear face again.

Myrtle had been involved for a considerable period of time in activities pertaining to human rights and racial issues. She felt that Canadian blacks had not experienced problems to the extent that American blacks had and became interested in identifying what the significant differences were in the two countries. She contacted various groups in America who were involved in these matters.

As a result, Myrtle and her brother drove to the states and participated in the Martin Luther King marches that took place in Arkansas. During the march, she met a man named Samuel. "We had so much in common . . . he pulled the strings of my heart . . . it was the first time I ever felt attracted to a man this way." Unfortunately, Myrtle found out Samuel was married.

Myrtle was going to Los Angeles to meet Samuel who had contacted her a year after his wife died of cancer. They had maintained no contact whatsoever over the years but she told me she never forgot the feeling she had when she was with him. Since her childhood boyfriend and she had parted company years ago, after what Myrtle described as "a steady, long relationship that served both of us very well," she had no qualms about flying to Los Angeles.

"Anna, you know what a realist I am. It's not like me to do something like this but my heart is telling me to go to L.A. This may be a major disappointment but I'm willing to take the risk. Needless to say, I was on pins and needles waiting for Myrtle to arrive after her visit with Samuel. Joel and I met her at the airport and as she was walking quickly towards us, I whispered to Joel "I think it went well . . . look at her face." Joel whispered back "you haven't seen her in years and years . . . how can you tell . . . let's hope you're right."

Joel was right, I hadn't seen Myrtle in years, but I had known her since elementary school and could tell there was a positive nuance in her face that was there before she spotted Joel and me in the airport.

I wanted to jump with glee when Myrtle finally recounted what had happened when she met Samuel. He had aged, as she expected . . . we all have . . . and now had grey sprinkled throughout his hair. They knew each other immediately . . . and "yes, Anna, he pulled at the strings of my heart once again."

She said "we talked about everything . . . his wife's long illness, his children . . . my life, my job, that I had no children . . . politics, religion, Canada, the states . . . food, movies, theater . . . you name it . . . we talked about it."

Eventually, we started talking about what was really on our minds . . . and Samuel told me why he had asked me to come to the states. He had never forgotten the enthusiastic, young lady from Canada, with the firm belief that everyone could make a difference in the world . . . that's why she traveled from Canada to the United States to march for black rights. He admitted he had been attracted to her but was a married man. He knew she deserved to have someone in her life that was totally available and not committed to someone else. He also remembered her saying she had a boyfriend back home.

"There has been so much pain and sorrow in the past. I was hoping you were free and were pleased when you told me you were. I wanted you to come here so that we might find out if we are meant to be together for the balance of our lives. It has been a long time and I know we need time to get reacquainted. But in my heart, Myrtle, I confess I believe I do know you."

Myrtle said she decided to be totally honest and tell him, as well, why she had come. "I was not being flirtatious or acting seductive, but I sensed, at this time, my honesty was far more powerful than any feminine wiles that I possessed."

The end result was very good. Samuel will be visiting Myrtle in Montreal for a month . . . staying in her apartment . . . and Myrtle happily said "we'll see where we go from there after his visit."

The three of us wandered around beautiful San Francisco. Joel and I showed Myrtle all the San Francisco sights that she was seeing for the first time. It was wonderful; we were relaxed, laughed a lot and just enjoyed the simple pleasures of the day . . . we had a happy, memorable time.

Myrtle and I reminisced about some of the crazy things we did growing up causing Joel to chuckle several times. Joel and Myrtle talked a blue streak about music and I played my Billie Holiday records for Myrtle.

"Remember, Myrtle, the first time I heard Billie Holiday was at your house?"

"Yes, so it was. I remember. Do you remember we both predicted Oscar Peterson would be famous some day?"

"We were right, weren't we" I replied.

Before leaving Myrtle said "Anna, Joel is so madly in love with you I can feel it just being with the two of you. He is a wonderful man . . . he's kind and caring. I can see how happy you are and how much you adore him as well. I'm really happy for both of you"

"Well Myrtle maybe it's your turn now . . . it sounds like you may have found real love at last. Just make sure you keep me up-to-date."

Matthew called to say he and Katherine were engaged and planned to be married. I invited them over to celebrate. Matthew said they were busy and would call when they had some time. The wedding would be medium sized. Katherine would be wearing a long, white wedding gown and was going to have three bridesmaids. Matthew asked Daniel to be his best man. The reception was to be held at Katherine's father's private club that is very prestigious in San Francisco.

Katherine's parents went all out for her wedding that was lavish but in very good taste. No expense was spared in order that their only child had an exceptionally beautiful wedding, one she and everyone would always remember. I thought it was such a contrast to the wedding Daniel and Jackie had but then Daniel was a primitive man who didn't much care for the sophisticated life style. Nevertheless, he was doing an incredibly sophisticated job at being Matthew's best man. It was obvious Daniel and Jackie were both having a good time at the wedding and were very happy together in their life. Adam was also enjoying himself with the other children at the reception.

As our lives continued, Joel and I were seeing less and less of Matthew and Katherine but hearing more often from Daniel and Jackie. I still sensed something was different between Matthew and me whenever I saw him but couldn't identify what it was I was feeling. I would cope by putting my thoughts and feelings aside and tell myself "as long as he's well and happy; that's all that counts."

A year later Matthew and Katherine had twin boys that they named Joseph and Michael. Katherine's parents were ecstatic and generous to a fault when it came to the twins. I enjoyed the twins tremendously but wished I could see them more often.

Two years later, Matthew and Katherine had a daughter they named Pamela after Katherine's grandmother. Katherine's parents doted on this little girl as they had on their own daughter. Katherine's father set up trust funds for all the children's education suggesting the kids would not be as strapped financially if he took care of this.

The same year Pamela was born, Daniel and Jackie had a son they named John. We were proud grandparents and I was beginning to realize being a grandparent was maybe a lot more fun than being a parent.

Joel's daughters weren't married yet but dating different young men. It was difficult to keep track of whom they were dating. We occasionally got to meet their most recent boyfriend but not very often. Both of them said they weren't in a hurry to marry.

Joel's parents came to California to visit their grand daughters and Joel as well. I met them once before but only for a short time. Joel was very much like his father who I found to be kind and considerate. His mother was very courteous to me but I felt she lacked the warmth her husband had. Perhaps I had been influenced by Joel's input about his parents but I didn't think so. I knew he loved both his parents. It always showed in his loving behavior towards them. His father said with pride "Joel was always a good son who never gave us need to worry." Joel once said his mother had been a strict disciplinarian that you didn't want to cross when she was displeased with someone or something around the house.

During our conversations, I realized that Joel's mother had still not become reconciled to the fact that Joel had divorced his first wife, the daughter of Joel's mother's best friend. This sounded too familiar and I instantly remembered why. Gary in Canada had married his mother's best friend's daughter . . . then got divorced. He later met my friend Leda, got married and lived happily ever after. Maybe when parents got involved in affairs of the heart, regarding their children, things just didn't work out too well.

I recognized it didn't matter whom Joel married after his divorce, his mother was still pining for the past and her first daughter-in-law. Joel's father accepted me from the beginning and told me he was pleased his son had finally found happiness in his life. He was a bright man who knew how his wife felt about Joel's divorce and marriage to me.

I felt compassion for Joel's mother and under the circumstances, I was pleased that I maintained a cordial relationship with her all the years of her life. I believe that was the best we could both manage.

Chapter Twelve

Madness, chaos . . . survival

*The One who is full of grace
Will find the ladder to the sky.*
                          Rumi

Joel and I have enjoyed many wonderful years together. We have remained aware how precious our love is and together celebrate the coming of each day with deep appreciation. It's hard to believe how quickly time flies when you are with your beloved.

Joel has been fortunate in his work that he thoroughly enjoys, and I am pleased he made the right career decision years ago. He is well respected in the field of communications technology and his business colleagues speak highly of him.

Over the years, as an executive I gained much satisfaction from my work but recently I found myself getting disillusioned with what I saw happening in the corporate environment. It is the era of acquisitions and mergers and common practice for powerful executives to make cutthroat decisions that too often result in competent, good people losing their jobs.

Short term profitability is the name of the game. The competition to win is fierce and brutal as executives vie to keep their jobs. Unfortunately, I observe and encounter individuals who, when they feel vulnerable, are willing to sacrifice their principles to forge ahead. They have forgotten, or perhaps never knew, that "the highest reward for a person's toil is not what they get for it, but what they become by it."

I witnessed several major takeovers wherein I was responsible for implementing all aspects of corporate marketing in these newly acquired companies. Consequently, I had close contact with many employees whose positions eventually became obsolete. In some instances, thousands of people lost their jobs and were traumatized as a result. It was obvious to me that final decisions, made in the ivory tower, were based on financial data and highly impersonal when it came to the effects of a particular decision. I am not suggesting that rhetoric did not exist as to what would happen to employees that became "displaced" . . . what I am suggesting is it did not reverse decisions that had been made for financial gain.

Thomas Hobbes wrote these words more than three centuries ago: that the life of man is "poor, nasty, brutish and short." I certainly believed that we had made progress since then but couldn't help mulling over why sometimes "man behaved in a nasty way." Being the eternal optimistic I didn't want to believe Hobbes's words. I far more preferred these words by Confucius: "the more man meditates upon good thoughts, the better will be his world and the world at large."

I maintained a positive attitude in spite of the growing pessimism I was encountering in many divisions of our corporation. My position was highly personal . . . I was dealing with vice presidents and managers who often felt they saw the writing on the wall when I and my staff arrived from corporate headquarters.

Many knew it was a matter of time before their jobs became obsolete due to corporate restructuring that often created a need for different capabilities they did not possess.

There were discussion and serious activity pertaining to our organization being sold in the near future. I likened what was happening in the corporate world as follows: the little fish got gobbled up by a bigger fish; then the bigger fish got gobbled up by a large fish; the large fish got gobbled up by a giant fish . . . and on and on.

In view of possible pending changes, and the massive reorganizations that would take place, I cogitated for a long time whether this might not be a good time to take an early retirement. Joel said "you're at a point in your life you can do whatever you want to do."

Based on a gut feeling, I finally decided to resign; it was the right time to do so. I felt I had reached all my goals, beyond my wildest expectations. I had worked full time since Matthew was five years old plus I had worked part time in the evenings when the boys were babies . . . a little voice inside me said it's time to move on.

I was unemployed for the first time in a very long, long time. I found it interesting to be Anna, a person, wife and mother and not a senior vice president as well. I took long walks enjoying the ocean and beautiful sights around me . . . I wrote poetry and letters to old friends in Canada . . . I visited my grandchildren and played with them for hours on end . . . and best of all, I surprised my beloved Joel with many more little acts of love now that I had more time.

When word got around in the business world that I had resigned and was taking an extended vacation, I received several good job offers. As a result of these offers, I came to the conclusion I did not want to go back to corporate America. After several months, I started to ponder what it is I would do for the rest of my life? What was my purpose to be? When I declined the positions, I recognized I was heading in a new direction but not quite certain where it would take me.

Joel and I were having our picnic supper, I had prepared,

sitting near the ocean so we could watch the brilliant sunset. We talked of many things . . . were silent . . . reflective . . . and joyously happy in the moment.

Joel eventually asked me if I had gotten any closer to figuring out what I wanted to do. I surprised myself when I said "if I had my druthers, I'd like to go back to university and get a degree in psychology. As you know, I've been reading psychology books all my life and I would be interested in pursuing this professionally. All my past experiences in dealing with people in the business world are bound to be helpful as well."

Joel said "that's wonderful Anna . . . there's no reason why you can't have your druthers . . . think about it . . . what's stopping you?"

"Maybe I'm too old . . . everyone will be so much younger."

"All the more reason to start soon. I think you will discover your age will be an advantage along with all your life's experiences. Say you're about fifty years old; would you want to visit a therapist that is as young as your daughter?"

The more Joel and I talked, the more excited I got. I enrolled and was accepted in a Master's Program in Clinical Psychology at the local university. My life was heading in a different direction and once again I was filled with faith, hope and anticipation in what I might accomplish. I genuinely looked forward to developing the necessary professional skills that would enable me to help people.

Going back to university was an incredible experience. Usually, I was the oldest person in the class but within a short period of time, I was just one of the many students. I discovered the field of psychology attracts many people who are searching for answers about their own life and quickly realized that this was probably true for me as well. I would learn that the "helping profession" is a demanding one that is very gratifying.

While I read psychology books most of my life, the depth of my learning would be expansive and greatly increase my compassion and caring for all mankind. Suffice it to say, becoming a therapist deeply tapped into my basic human qualities.

Dr. Ernest S. Wolf aptly describes the motivation for seeking treatment that, in his description, also explains why I was motivated to gain the necessary knowledge to work in this field:

> *"There is the hope of leading a less painful way of life, the hope to achieve some potential for creative endeavor, and the hope to finally be what one always really could and wanted to be--one's own self expressing itself. But mostly, there is the need for an ambience of being understood, for a self-sustaining self-object experience that remains always out of reach as long as the archaic defensive patterns get in the way."*

My purpose here is not to discuss the heart of psychotherapy; rather briefly mention to you, the reader, a few highlights that may help in understanding how significantly my life's journey was changing and why. The process of therapy is an intimate relationship between two people. The therapist recognizes that the person has reached out for help and the therapist wishes to give the help with respect and genuine care.

Everyone in our program, planning to be a future psychotherapist, generously shared with their classmates their past experiences . . . families . . . traumas and so on. The courage and honesty in describing their lives were truly inspiring and a monumental contribution in our learning.

I remember Jonathan, a black man, who was the eldest son of a distinguished judge in the city. He was a recovering drug addict and alcoholic who had lived in skid row for five years.

Greta had been gang-raped when she was fourteen years old . . . became pregnant as a result . . . and had an abortion.

Nancy and her two brothers had lived in a car with their mother for one year. Prior to that, Nancy said they had moved around constantly as the police were looking for her mother. As a result, none of them went to school. Nancy ran away from her mother when she was twelve years old . . . she had decided she didn't want to live this way anymore.

Madeleine was a disillusioned attorney seeking a new career. Her brother had committed suicide when he was sixteen years old.

Fred was a retired police officer that wanted to help people. He said "saying my family was dysfunctional is an understatement."

Janice had just graduated with her BA and wanted to work with young abused children. Her mother was bipolar and "life was hard for my sister and me."

I heard so many poignant stories that in comparison, I started to think perhaps my life hadn't been so bad after all. I had Joel, two wonderful sons and many grandchildren who loved me . . . these were wonderful blessings.

Final exam time rolled around and given my excellent results in past semesters, I was confident I would be graduating shortly. I did exceptionally well and was eager to spend more time working at my new profession now that I had graduated. I continued my internship at a free clinic until such time as I was licensed to practice on my own.

During my internship, I became a close friend of a medical doctor, Nathan, who did pro bono work at the clinic once a week. He told me he was a homosexual who was in a sexual relationship that included commitment, trust, tenderness and respect during the last seven years. This really was the first opportunity I had to be friends with a gay person. I accepted Nathan for whom he was; an intelligent, caring, compassionate human being with a wonderful sense of humor. His partner, Geoffrey, was also a doctor, and together, along with Auntie Sarah, they were raising two young daughters of mixed racial origin from Vietnam where they had both served in the military.

My friendship with these men enhanced both my personal life and psychological profession. I had read extensively the different psychosocial and biological theories that attempted to explain the development of homosexuality, but Nathan and Geoffrey simplified everything for me . . . "we had no choice." Parenting patterns, life experiences, or psychological attributes of the gay patients I worked with did not support their sexual preference. They also felt it was not a matter of choice.

I continue to believe that further exploration in the theories of biological causation that looks to genetic causation, or prenatal or adult hormone differences, may lead us to seriously revisit our thinking about homosexuals and lesbians. In the meantime, I hope we can accept them as God's children. These two doctors were not alone in making a positive difference in our world. I was grateful that I too was now in a position to help people who were seeking help.

Two days before Christmas, little did I know I would suffer unbearable anguish and pain followed by guilt, remorse and grief. I believe it was the closest I ever came to having a nervous breakdown.

Katherine called to say the children were sick with colds and they would not be able to see us this Christmas. She was bringing over the Christmas gifts for Joel and me. I invited her for a Christmas lunch at a local restaurant. Joel was home on vacation but decided not to join us. He was going to wrap presents and put up the tree.

During our lunch, I finally got the courage to ask Katherine if she knew why Matthew seemed so distant towards me.

She said "you know why" then looked away. I sensed she was uncomfortable . . . but why?

"I wouldn't be asking you if I knew why? Please help me understand what's going on. I want to know."

"I can't tell you . . . it wouldn't be right" said Katherine.

"Katherine, what's not right is you tell me I know . . . then you leave me hanging in the wind."

We bantered back and forth until Katherine reluctantly said "Matthew was molested by his father when he was a child. He recently started having flashbacks. He believes you knew it was going on."

I am dumbstruck. I feel like somebody just punched me in the stomach. I can't believe what I just heard. I gradually find a voice and ask Katherine "Did I hear you correctly? Did you say Matthew's father molested him when he was a child?"

Katherine says "Yes and Matthew believes there's no way you couldn't have known about it."

"Katherine, do you know what you're saying? I can't believe this. Matthew would have told me. We have always been close."

"His father threatened to kill you if he told anyone. He had a knife that he held to his throat when he molested him. He told him that was the knife he would use to kill you."

There is a ringing in my ears. I have trouble breathing. I feel nauseous. My heart is pounding so hard it feels like it might explode. This is a bad dream. None of this is happening. I start sobbing uncontrollably. When I finally stop, I utter to Katherine "I can't believe this. My poor Matthew. How is this possible? How can Matthew possibly think I knew anything about this?" I am overcome with anguish as I clearly see in my mind my beloved Matthew, the adult, as a sweet innocent child. "You mustn't say anything to Matthew about our conversation. I promised him I would never tell anyone. He will be very angry that I told you. You shouldn't have made me tell you."

Though I hear the words, I know they are not registering. Dear Lord, my precious, little child, Matthew was protecting me when I should have been protecting him.

When Katherine and I get home, Joel's greeting smile disappears when he sees the distraught look on my face. He is both baffled and concerned but before he can say anything, I blurt out "Katherine just told me Matthew was molested by his father when he was a child and I knew it was going on." I start sobbing leaving Joel with Katherine as I run to the bathroom overcome once more with intense sorrow for my young son, Matthew.

When Katherine leaves, I tell Joel everything I remember Katherine said. I ask him "do you believe me? I didn't know anything about it, if I had, I would have stopped it?"

"Of course I believe you Anna. I know you never would have allowed this to go on. I know how loyal you are to your sons and how much you love both of them."

I remain very agitated. "I knew something was wrong lately. Matthew has been acting differently towards me. Poor, poor Matthew. Why didn't he tell me this was going on?"

Katherine didn't say how long Matthew had been having these

flashbacks. I am certain they started when I noticed he was acting differently. Had Matthew remembered anything when his father died? I have so many questions and thoughts I feel my head is spinning out of control. What kind of a mother was I that I didn't see what was going on? Children are supposed to be safe in their own homes. What kind of a monster was Don?

I go on berating myself but feel no relief. I did not protect my child. How horrible this must be for Matthew. I am obsessed in reviewing the past. Don was a womanizer. We had sex on a regular basis in spite of our many arguments. He didn't fit the profile of a child molester. I keep looking for something but don't really know what it is while knowing full well it won't change the past.

When I look in the mirror, I don't know who I am. It had taken me such a long time to become the person I liked after I divorced Don, the person Joel fell in love with. Where is she? I believed I was intelligent, fairly self confident, liked by most people who said I was kind, caring and compassionate. I guess I'm none of these things. I don't know who I am anymore. The only thing I know is that my son believes I knew this dreadful thing was happening to him. I am a complete failure as a mother.

Joel is very concerned about me. He is also worried about Matthew and Katherine. We both agree Katherine must be telling the truth as there would be no reason for her to make up such a story. I tell Joel I have to speak to Matthew about the molestation. We must talk.

I never promised Katherine that I wouldn't call Matthew. Since I appreciate her position in this matter, before I talk to Matthew, I decide I will call Katherine and ask her to tell Matthew she has spoken to me about the molestation. She begs me not to talk to Matthew. I tell her I must. We can't continue our lives having these types of secrets from one another.

As my conversation is at an impasse, Joel intervenes on my behalf. He calmly tries to explain to Katherine that we can't hide this. We need to discuss it, particularly for Matthew's sake. Joel tells Katherine I will wait a week before I talk to Matthew, giving her enough time to approach the subject with Matthew. I then tell Katherine I will speak to Matthew after a week whether she has spoken to Matthew or not. I passionately pray for all us and ask God for guidance in finding the right words when I speak to Matthew.

I sleep very little, hardly eat and worry that my state of mind will affect my patients. In the past, what is interesting, in spite of my life's circumstances, I have always been able to perform my work satisfactorily, possibly because I am able to sublimate what little energy I have left entirely to the task at hand . . . perhaps a throwback to the Christian work ethic instilled in me by my parents. I talk to my supervisor/mentor regarding my concern for my patients. We review my caseload and what is happening with each client and I am reassured that I am doing excellent work.

I phone Daniel to tell him what has happened. He is shocked and tries to assure me that he definitely knows I didn't know what was going on. "My God, I can't believe this. I am Matthew's older brother . . . how come I didn't see anything? . . . why didn't Matthew say something to me?" I can hear Daniel starting to feel guilty that he let his little brother down.

I ask Daniel "Did your father molest you as well?"

"No Mom. He never did. Remember I was the tough kid no one could push around." I get off the phone in disbelief that I just had this type of conversation with my eldest son."

I wait for Katherine to call me to no avail. The week is over and with Joel at my side, I call Matthew. My body is shaking inside and out. My throat is dry but nothing will deter me from speaking to Matthew. I know it is very important for his welfare that he believes I knew nothing about the molestation. I know it also matters to my well being. Matthew is very angry and cuts me off during the conversation. He lashes out at me "how could you not know?" More words are spoken better left unsaid in this writing and I hang up crying hysterically.

I decide to write Matthew a letter telling him how sorry I am that I failed him but reaffirming that I did not know about the situation. I tell him I accept responsibility for my ignorance and want him to know that I love him with all my heart.

The response letter I get from Matthew is vitriolic and states emphatically he does not believe a word I am saying. As far as he is concerned "my mother is dead."

I am devastated and start worrying again about my ability to function. I write Matthew more letters and receive more replies that in no way suggest Matthew and I will ever have a relationship again. I even try to explain to Matthew that I was not the person I am today when he was growing up. I was somewhat naive. Matthew vehemently dismisses everything I say. I keep apologizing for my ignorance. I am guilty because I did not know.

I go back over the years trying to remember everything that I possibly can when my sons were growing up. It is excruciating but necessary that I review the past . . . it's as if by doing so, I might change it.

My obsessive efforts resulted in my remembering when Matthew had developed a nervous tic. I persuaded Don to spend some time talking about our children. I recalled how calm I was when I asked him to put our differences aside, and to please answer me. I was desperate . . . what did he think we're doing wrong as parents? . . . and in particular what I was doing wrong. I remembered distinctly saying "something is terribly wrong . . . Daniel is having serious problems . . . and now Matthew has a nervous tic."

Previously, I had only remembered that he agreed with Matthew's pediatrician, that it was probably due to school and was a common thing in kids and he would outgrow it. But now I remembered that Don never looked me in the eyes during the entire conversation. I also remembered when I said "I know something is terribly wrong, I just don't know what it is" Don left the house, without saying a word, and drove off in his car.

Matthew refused to stay at the summer Y camp. Was it because he was afraid his father would kill me while he was gone?

The other thing that had never made sense before, Matthew and some boys in high school were in trouble and one of the boy's mothers asked to meet me at the school to talk about the problem our kids were having, something related to her son's misplaced bicycle.

I met this lady for the first time who went into an immediate tirade about how evil our home was. When I asked her why our home was evil, she ranted and raved and was never specific about anything. At the time, I thought she was mentally ill. That evening I told Don about her and he shrugged his shoulders saying you can't help what sick people will say. Was the evil she was talking about the incest in our home and she was trying to warn me?

Joel was concerned. He said he was worried I would drive myself crazy with this type of thinking. I knew he was right and trying to recreate the past in this manner was not solving my problems. He was kind and compassionate in reminding me that no matter what I remembered, it would not change the past. He believed me beyond the shadow of a doubt that I knew nothing. I needed help and went into therapy.

I did not see Matthew, Katherine and my grandchildren for two whole years. Joel maintained contact with Matthew through phone calls and occasional business lunches. He always told me how Matthew and his family were doing and once or twice brought home the most recent pictures of our grandchildren. Joel was very careful not to pressure Matthew in any way always telling me he believed Matthew and I would reconcile some day.

After much time, I accepted, what I had always known, that I cannot undo the past. I love Matthew, always have, and I am saddened that I did not see what was happening to him. My love did not protect my child. I fervently prayed to God asking him to help Matthew and to give all of us guidance in healing our family.
The only way I can try to describe how I felt during those two years is to say a part of my heart hurt all the time. It was a physical hurt that, on really bad days, affected my entire body.

During the therapy process, I knew and witnessed people who suffered major traumas in their lives, successfully reinvented themselves and went on to live fulfilling, happier lives. I was at a complete loss as to whether I could ever change my present perception of myself as a person. I felt that whoever I had been before I found out about the molestation was scattered in pieces, like a puzzle that needs to be put together again . . . but for me it also felt like I had lost most of the pieces . . . and the puzzle no longer made sense.

Had it not been for Joel's loving support, Daniel's belief in me, my two closest friends' belief in me and the fact that I was still a competent, compassionate therapist (this confirmed by my supervisor) I probably would not have functioned as well as I did. My anguish and pain far surpassed anything I had ever endured in the past. I acknowledged that it was a good thing Don was dead . . . at one point, I honestly believed I would have been capable of killing him.

I spent as much time as possible with Daniel, Jackie, Adam and John. Daniel was struggling with his guilt that he too had not protected Matthew, his little brother. I listened to Daniel hoping that it might alleviate some of his pain. We talked at great length, both concluding and acknowledging we wanted to help Matthew. We loved him. At present, Matthew refused to discuss this matter with Daniel as well.

I was still joyous when I saw my grandchildren. They were always pleased and happy to see Grandpa Joel and Baba. They learned that my mother had been called Baba by their dad instead of grandma when I told them stories about their great-grandmother. They thought it was different and they liked it. Over time, I was called Baba by all the grandchildren. It pleased me as it reminded me of a happy time in my mother's life.

Chapter Thirteen

Mirrors of our souls . . . clients in treatment

*We shall not cease from exploration
And in the end of all our exploring
Will be to arrive where we started
And know the place for the first time.*
                                            T. S. Eliot

As a psychotherapist I felt privileged that clients placed their trust in me, sharing their deepest feelings in the hope that they might begin to interact with life more realistically and with greater satisfaction. Initially, most of them just knew they were "hurting."

We worked together so the client could differentiate between the self and behavior and become aware that inner self and feelings are more closely tied to their own actions and beliefs than to that of others.

The following is a brief overview of some of the clients I was privileged to work with. I believe it will more than adequately demonstrate what happens to people when there is an absence of authentic love in their lives. There is no in-depth description of the treatment that took place, only a brief summary of the outcome.

By sharing this information with you, I hope you will see more fully the mammoth changes that were taking place in my life both personally and professionally. I was filled with compassion for these courageous people who wished to make a resolution with their past.

In the process of helping my clients, I better learned to accept the most recent events in my life as gifts of growth that I knew ultimately create strength of character and strength of faith. It was an arduous journey. I kept hearing John Donne's words:

> *No man is an island, entire of itself . . .*
> *Any man's death diminishes me,*
> *because I am involved in mankind;*
> *And therefore never send to know*
> *for whom the bell tolls;*
> *It tolls for thee.*

These wise words were written in 1624 and are applicable today . . . and evermore.

Kelly

Kelly had been diagnosed with Bulimia Nervosa when she was in her late teens. Neither of her parents were obese but she recounted, ever since she could remember, that her mother was always on a diet. Kelly said her mother was always starving but made it quite clear it was important to keep your figure. She had also stated, many times, you can never be too thin.

Kelly's father had gained weight recently but was certainly not obese. Kelly stated her father claimed he was only a social drinker but she had noticed that he was drinking more frequently than he had in the past.

The first time Kelly came to see me she was twenty-four years old. She was not overweight, attractive with a large bone body structure that no amount of dieting would change. She had been in therapy, many times over the years, to deal with her problem but had never been hospitalized though she had at times required medical care.

Kelly had a persistent over-concern for her body shape and weight. She admitted early on that she was really afraid because she felt she was on the verge of binge eating again and had already started taking laxatives to control her weight.

Her parents had divorced during her teen years and she thought it was about that time that she first started her self-induced vomiting but only, Kelly said, "if I have eaten too much food."

She described her mother as an intellectual and a perfectionist. The house was always perfect and so was she. "My mother never showed her emotions even when my dad divorced her." Kelly said "I'm not like my sister who looks just like my mother and is very slim."

Kelly said she loved her father but was tired of his steady stream of young bimbos, who were often her age, that she had to put up with during her visits with him. Her father's life style embarrassed her but she never said anything about it to him. Kelly also came to realize, and felt certain, that her father loved the image of himself as a father more than he loved her as a person. He seemed weaker and more insecure to her the older she got.

Kelly said she knew she had an eating disorder . . . she had been to enough therapists to at least agree to that. She didn't think she was trying to live up to her mother's expectations but thought that maybe her perception of herself was not lovable.

What had prompted her to seek help from me at this time was her overwhelming fear that she was about to backslide into a destructive pattern of behavior . . . binging and vomiting . . . that she had now controlled for over a year. For the first time in her life, she had met a young man who loved her just as she was . . . unconditionally. "I don't know how to deal with this kind of relationship." Kelly had always been popular and had dated many men. The difference here she said is "he values who I am . . . and I'm scared."

Though Kelly had worked on enmeshment and conflict-avoidance of the whole family system in previous therapy, it was necessary for Kelly to again revisit the pathological system in which she and her family continued to function. It was important, as well, to revisit the behavior patterns in this family. Kelly's family felt this was her problem and continued to believe they were not contributing to her disorder in any way.

Kelly still did not feel lovable and was convinced she could never meet her parents' expectations. In therapy, she became aware and acknowledged that her parents made unrealistic demands upon her. This knowledge was a beginning in changing her concept of herself and her place in the world.

The power of true love frightened Kelly so much many of her fears from the past returned. She had enough insight to get help with her struggle by returning to therapy. I believe the unconditional love, she was experiencing for the first time in her life, shone so brightly it beckoned her to a place where she could heal her soul and rejoice in a truth that had long escaped her . . . "as a child of God, she was lovable and had always been lovable."

When I was working with Kelly, I remembered reading somewhere the following words:

> *"Your parents weren't simply the people who had given you life. Somewhere in the process of growing up, they became the measurement of the life you built for yourself."*

Steven

First and foremost, Steven was a sculptor and an artist as well. He came from a blue collar family where his father meted out discipline "with a fist in the face or a swift kick wherever it landed." His mother was completely downtrodden and was a shadow who performed her tasks with nary a word to anyone. Steven had two brothers . . . he was the middle son.

He had always been artistic and made sculptures from old pipes, tin and wood that he found around his house or in the neighborhood. His father said he was growing up to be a faggot. When Steven was sixteen years old, he sold one of his sculptures to a local gallery in town. Steven shared his good news with his family. His father insisted he give him the money he had received. Steven refused . . . he felt the money was his . . . he had earned it. His father beat him up and took the money away from him. Steven was angry and frustrated that he hadn't been able to protect himself against his father to save his earnings.

After this incident, Steven said he finally acknowledged that he hated his father. Steven hated him for the way he beat him and his brothers and treated his mother like she was a slave. How he constantly verbally abused them all. He was a tyrant. Someday soon his sons would be much stronger and things would be different. His oldest brother was already fighting back and Steven noticed his father wasn't pushing him around as much.

Steven was spending more time visiting the gallery whenever he could. The owner of the gallery became an interested friend, asking him what his plans were for the future. Steven replied he would probably land up working at the foundry like everyone else in his family.

The owner suggested Steven apply for a four-year scholarship since he felt Steven had tremendous potential to be successful. He stated prestigious universities often provided opportunities to people like Steven "so what have you got to lose by applying?" Steven was dumbfounded when he got the scholarship.

Steven was happy to leave home but was sad for his mother and concerned at her lot in life. His brothers would manage somehow . . . they were learning to stay out of their father's way as much as possible until they too could leave home. Prior to leaving, Steven's mother sneaked him some money, wrapped in a handkerchief, and managed to say "take care of yourself, Steven." He noticed the tears in her eyes. They did not hug. She quickly disappeared for fear Steven's father might show up.

Steven did well at university, and shortly after graduation, to his surprise he became fairly successful in the art world. His work was described as outstanding, original and full of passion. Consequently, he was reaping the financial rewards that come with success.

Steven came to see me because "maybe I'm using cocaine a little too often." He would inhale it through his nostrils but had also smoked it as well. He didn't think he was an addict. Steven said "I know addicts and how they behave and that's not me." He smoked marijuana regularly and did not consider it a drug.

Since early childhood, he had never dealt with his feelings of frustration, anger and helplessness at the hands of his father. He loved his mother and felt that she loved him but had never had the opportunity to express herself in any way because of his father. He clung to the brief episode in his life when his mother had given him the money before he left for university as an affirmation of her love.

First, Steven had to deal with cocaine and marijuana dependence before he could start dealing with the issues in his past. He admitted he liked using cocaine . . . he experienced intense feelings of self-confidence, power, energy and euphoria. He had exceptional stamina for his projects and worked grueling hours accomplishing "major sculptures" with little or no fatigue.

Steven admitted it was great to feel no pain, thus finally admitting he was in pain. Recently, he wondered if his body was starting to react differently to the cocaine but said, if it's true, it's probably worth the risk because of the feelings you experience which "are the best I've ever had."

Steven's resistance was primarily due to "fear of being traumatically injured again." His wavering motivation to stay in therapy and remain abstinent were major challenges that he faced prior to learning new coping styles to deal with rage, guilt, anxiety, low self esteem and depression. He had difficulty with intimate relationships; was often promiscuous attributing his behavior to "it's just a man thing."

Steven learned and recognized that he avoided celebrating his accomplishments and success because in some ways it reminded him of bad things in his past. He had to first consider, then resolve his destructive patterns in spite of the pain and sorrow associated with this revelation.

With much work on his part, Steven got to the place where he no longer wanted his father's brutish behavior to deprive and hinder him from living his life successfully now and in the future. He was learning why it is important to let go of the past.

Steven actually started healing his soul and making tremendous progress in therapy when he also joined a religious support group for people who were addicted to cocaine. Initially, he was skeptical about being there but stayed when he remembered at the age of five years old his mother had told him the Holy Spirit is always with you. Now he was hearing these same words spoken at the group meeting.

The transformation that took place in Steven was really miraculous as he separated truth from illusion and came to believe that God is truth. I saw before me a man who now believed "All power is of God. What is not of Him has no power to do anything."

Steven turned his life around. He continues to be one of America's outstanding sculptors. To the best of my knowledge he has been totally drug free for the past seven years. He has set up a foundation to help children from impoverished families who wish to go to university and study art.

Christine

Christine was an exceptionally attractive tall, blue-eyed blond about thirty-five years old who demonstrated a pervasive pattern of excessive emotionality and was prone to much exaggeration. She came to see me because she was extremely upset with her lover of several years who had just broken off their relationship.

"Our relationship was absolutely fantastic. I can't believe he did this after all I did for him."

She started sobbing and finally, when she stopped, she lifted up her T-shirt . . . was not wearing a bra . . . and said "look at me . . . I had breast implants just for him and now I'm scarred for life . . . there was really nothing wrong with my breasts before . . . I wanted to make him happy . . . .and then what does he do . . . he dumps me."

She started sobbing again and when she stopped immediately said "everyone assured me there would be no scarring . . . yes, he paid for the implants . . . but can you believe it? . . . he already has a new girlfriend . . . she's about twenty years old. I've called him a couple of times and he says 'it's over; it was great ride while it lasted . . . don't call me anymore.'"

Christine was the only daughter of an upper class family. She managed to get a university degree but had never really worked at any job for a substantial period of time. "I get bored plus it interferes with my traveling." She was impulsive, manipulative and frequently got angry. Christine was pessimistic that no man would want her with these terrible scars. "He made me do it."

Christine's father had a very bad temper and physically abused Christine every time he was in a fit of rage. This went on until she was sixteen years old when her parents got divorced. Her mother was a self-centered woman who had emotionally abandoned Christine early on in her life and had never attempted to protect her from the physical abuse she experienced. Christine felt it was because she was afraid of her husband and he might turn on her if she said anything.

Christine did not believe in God. "Where was he when my father used me as a punching bag? My father believes he's a God-fearing man and actually goes to church once in awhile . . . he's all the more reason for me to not believe in a God."

By the time she went to university, Christine knew how to manipulate men through sex and sought love, praise and attention in this manner. She accepted generous gifts from her boyfriends and had developed a strong sense of entitlement for everything they gave her. She admitted she trusted no one . . . "everyone has their own hidden agenda."

Christine lived with different wealthy men for certain periods of time at which time she traveled extensively with them, spent their money in wild abandon and professed to love them while she was in the relationship. The longest relationship she ever had was five years and she believed this had been her "one real love." Unfortunately Christine said "he broke my heart when he married someone else. He said he didn't see me as the mother of his children. I had been a part of his wild days that were now over."

During this recent relationship, she had started worrying about her age and looks. "Men still say I'm beautiful so I guess

I shouldn't be worrying yet. After all, there is plastic surgery."

Christine was denied the ability in childhood of idealizing her parental figures so that she could identify with a positive image. Her inability to experience pleasure in accomplishments and activities, along with the absence of or devaluation of an admired parental image, lead her to alternate between an overvaluation or idealization of significant people in her life as well as a sense of disappointment and devaluation of them.

Christine stayed in therapy long enough to deal with her panic but had no further interest in dealing with the more arduous task of examining and modifying long-standing attitudes and behavior. "My life may be filled with crazy emotions and strife but at least it's not boring. I am who I am . . . take it or leave it."

When Christine left therapy I thought of what I had learned from Winnicott's writings:

> *The calamity of childhood trauma that rejects the child's experience as 'bad' results in the substitution of a 'false self' for the child's own 'true self.'*

My hope for Christine was that someday she would go back to therapy to deal with the anguish and pain within her soul. Her "false self" prevents her from realizing there is no pain or sorrow that cannot be healed. Perhaps, like Steven, Christine may eventually experience the gift of love from the Holy Spirit and find peace, happiness and moments of grace.

> *"For thou hast delivered my soul from death, mine eyes from tears, and my feet from falling."*
> Psalm 116 :8

Lisa

Lisa came to see me because of Vaginismus, the inability to have sexual intercourse due to muscle spasms in the outer part of the vagina. Prior to this condition, on occasion when she had succeeded in having intercourse, she had experienced pain before and after.

Lisa was twenty-five years old, a European model from Germany now living in the United States. She was five foot ten inches tall and had an angular body. She spoke in a soft, modulated voice and was extremely nervous at our first meeting.

Lisa's parents divorced when she was one year old. She was the only child of a prominent German businessman and a socialite mother who had remarried and spent most of her days partying. Lisa became a burden to her mother's life style therefore allowing Lisa's father generous visiting time with his daughter. Lisa remembers at the age of four spending the entire summer at her father's home in the country.

Her father first fondled her genitals during that summer. When she cried because it hurt, he laughed and said she'd get used to it. Lisa did not understand because she was so young. The fondling continued and at age seven, her father decided it was time for her to learn all about sex . . . what little boys and men wanted. He made her watch while he had intercourse with his girlfriend and that became a regular event in her life. He told Lisa it was all a part of her education and she would thank him someday.

When she was ten years old, he stimulated her genitals in preparation for intercourse. There was no one around to hear her crying at the pain she felt. Several days later when his girlfriend came back, he said Lisa would participate in making love to both of them. After it was over, she remembered throwing up in the bathroom until her stomach and throat hurt.

Lisa was now living with her father per the arrangement that her mother had agreed to. Her parents would let Lisa live with one of them alternating every couple of years. This would enable Lisa to really get to know both of them equally well. No thought was given to how disruptive this would be to her schooling or her life.

Lisa was terrified every time she heard her father's footsteps. When the intercourse was regular, she begged him to leave her alone. This would make him very angry and he would punish her by making her perform oral sex in front of his girlfriend. She remembered fainting several times and when she came to, she couldn't figure out what had happened to her.

When she was fourteen years old, she told her mother about the molestation. Her mother was furious and asked her to stop making up ridiculous stories about her father. Lisa could not believe her mother didn't believe her and she thought she was making up stories.

Lisa then asked her mother if she could go live with her elderly grandmother who lived in another city in Germany, far away from her father. While her grandmother was ill, she needed someone to live with her. Because it solved her mother's problems, her mother arranged for Lisa to move to her new living quarters. Lisa believed her father agreed because he thought it was only temporary.

Lisa refused to visit her father again. Her grandmother was very fond of Lisa and the living arrangement continued until Lisa came to the United States a couple of years ago.

Lisa told me that repetitious thoughts and memories of her molestation were overwhelming and she felt guilty, ashamed, disgusted and saddened.

When she meets young men, she is fearful and anxious. When she thinks about the incest, she feels she lost something because of the incest and she is filled with grief. She tries not to think about it but always does especially when she wonders what it will be like for her to have sex with someone she loves.

I'm pleased to say that Lisa's therapy was successful for many reasons. She was able to eventually think and feel about the incest without being overwhelmed. She was able to reprocess and reconceptualize the incest in a way that enabled her to experience increased self-esteem and increased trust and confidence within herself. There was an alleviation of her strong emotions associated with the incest.

Lisa was a gentle, loving person. She fully understood evil had been done to her. She had no wish for revenge; rather she wanted to heal her soul and free herself of the burden of her anguish, pain and sorrow that were within her.

This process of working with Lisa was done both in individual and group therapy. She also found a good medical doctor that she trusted. Belonging to a group provided Lisa a place where people who had also been victimized understood how she felt because they felt the same way.

Lisa fell in love with a nice young man whose loving support was an added motivator in her courageous efforts to deal with her past. Several years after we ended our therapeutic relationship, I received a birth announcement from Lisa and her husband, Mark. They had a beautiful daughter named Marilyn Ann . . . the Ann named in my honor.

The clients I have described all had to deal with losses in their childhood. They learned to survive by building powerful defenses that acted as controls against their anger and frustration, guilt and shame . . . that they could never express. Theirs were not the ordinary challenges that we all face in everyday living.

"When one does not see oneself clearly, one cannot see others clearly, and one remains caught in a world of illusion where genuine presence and authentic contact with others is impossible."

In my own life, I realized some of my healing would come in giving up "the fantasy that there is a way of rectifying the evil" that had been done to Matthew.

Hannah Arendt, who fled from Nazi Germany, is a social philosopher who wrote "the wish for revenge can never be truly fulfilled." Someone else wrote "those who understand this, if they are to make resolution with their past, turn to the task of giving to others."

I gave thanks to the Lord that I was now in a profession where I could assist people in their healing process.

I also wish to share the following story that beautifully demonstrates as well what can happen to people when their circumstances change and they are treated with respect and dignity.

I remember a story a psychology student at Berkeley told me in the late 1950s, when psychotropic drugs were first being tested. At the mental hospital where she worked, a long-term, chronic psychotic named George was picked to ingest an experimental dose of thorazine every day. No one had paid George any attention for years. Now doctors, attendants, and nurses all talked to him, and watched eagerly to see what effect the drug would have. His condition improved rapidly.

After only two weeks of the drug treatment, he was moved to a ward for less disturbed patients, where he took part in a number of activities. Soon he was doing so well that he was promoted again. By this time he had lively relationships with the other patients and many members of the hospital staff. He began to spend several hours a day with paints and clay, using them to express the rich fantasy life that had previously interested no one. His doctors marveled. Attendants praised his skill.

George was released from the hospital 38 days after his first dose of thorazine. While he was signing out, he remembered that he had left something behind, went back to his room, and returned with an old sock. When a puzzled attendant asked to see it, he found 38 thorazine pills carefully stashed inside the sock.

Chapter Fourteen

Struggling with devastating sorrow and tragedy

Eye hath not seen, nor ear heard, neither have entered into the heart of man, the things which God hath prepared for them that love Him.
                                             1 Corinthians 2:9

Joel was working on a major project and under a lot of pressure to meet specific deadlines. I noticed he was looking very tired and asked him when he thought he might get a break to take some time off. He was always able to leave his work at the office so I was getting concerned that he didn't look well. He was due for his annual company medical within two weeks and told me to stop worrying . . . "Anna, everything will be just fine."

After his exam, Joel came home early and told me he had to have further tests. "At the moment, there's nothing to worry about." I went to the hospital with Joel for his tests. My intuition told me that something serious was happening to Joel but I prayed fervently that all would be well. Joel's diagnosis was cancer of the pancreas and the prognosis was not good.

My person had been shattered when I heard about Matthew and I constantly gave thanks that I was still functioning effectively in my work. I was finally in a place where in spite of the permanent pain in my heart, I enjoyed the sunrise and sunset with Joel, the flowers, the birds . . . our life.

Once again, I was completely shattered. Surely, the doctors had made a mistake. Joel was young and healthy. They would come back and tell us they had read the wrong report. All the denial in the world did not change the reality.

The doctor suggested Joel spend as much time with his family as possible and recommended he leave his job immediately. I tried to remain calm for Joel's sake who was serene during the entire discussion. It was very difficult . . . I was holding Joel's hand and he kept squeezing it to reassure me. The doctor needed me to leave the room for a while so he could attend to Joel. I ran into the ladies' room down the hall. The pain in my chest was real and severe. I was positive my heart was broken and cried until I actually ran out of tears. I had previously learned that I had an unfathomable amount of tears that would well up again and again and again.

Joel's daughters were in complete disbelief about their father's condition. Daniel who is a warm hearted man was extremely upset and got off the phone with a shaky voice . . . I knew he was crying.

Joel asked that I call Matthew; he would call him later on. I was scared to call him but would never have refused Joel's request. It was the first time I spoke to Matthew in two years. I remember starting the conversation by saying this is your mother and sobbing profusely throughout the dialogue. I felt myself repeating over and over that Joel was terminally ill and the doctors said he might not have much time left.

I heard a primal cry followed by the most anguished sobbing I have ever heard in my life. I was overly concerned for Matthew's well being . . . Joel had been his father since his earliest teenage years . . . I knew Matthew deeply loved, admired and respected him as he had no one before.

Matthew saw Joel every day for the next five months until Joel's death. During this time they talked together alone quite often. Joel said he told Matthew more than once how much I loved him and he knew we would reconcile. Had it not been for Matthew's tremendous support, I am certain I would have had a nervous breakdown.

Daniel and Jackie, their children Adam and John visited Joel several times staying the weekend before returning to their log cabin. Matthew's wife, Katherine and the twins, Joseph and Michael, and their daughter Pamela also came for short visits that meant a lot to Joel. There was a constant flow of people . . . friends and colleagues who were all devastated by news of Joel's terminal illness. I remember Joel's boss saying to him during a visit "how can you be so brave?" Joel replied "I'm not brave . . . what choice do I have . . . we're all going to die someday . . . I just know my time is coming sooner . . . but life has been good . . . and maybe this new journey will be too."

During Joel's illness during the five months, Matthew and I probably spent more time together than we had in previous years. We were obviously both stressed out. In all fairness to my clients, I gave up my practice. Whatever time Joel had left to live, I wanted to spend my time with him. Some of my clients wanted to put their therapy on hold until I came back . . . I recommended they continue their progress with the excellent therapist who took over my practice.

A month prior to Joel's death, Matthew and I got into a ridiculous argument about something unimportant that today I cannot remember. While we never discussed any events that had occurred prior to Joel's illness, I felt certain when Matthew was ready we would openly discuss our differences. I was feeling optimistic that we would reconcile.

As we argued back and forth, Matthew shouted at me "I wish you were dying instead of Joel." There are no words in the English language that I can use to describe how I felt. Joel was dying . . . I was overwhelmed and extremely vulnerable emotionally and physically. All I can say, it actually felt like someone had just stabbed me in the heart . . . I felt physical pain in the heart area. I know it sounds melodramatic, but I also felt once again that I must be going mad. I didn't sleep all night which was not unusual anyway since Joel had to take medication every four hours. In the morning, the pain in my heart had abated somewhat but not entirely. I wanted to believe that I had imagined last night's nightmare but knew this was impossible.

Matthew phoned to apologize for what he had said. I listened but found nothing to say. I was still in shock and total disbelief. My wound was so deep that I now felt I had to protect myself from any other attacks from Matthew. My number one priority was taking care of my beloved Joel. I tried not to feel resentful towards Matthew perhaps because I remained fully aware that resentment would sap the energy I needed for other areas of my life. But I could not forget. I wondered if trust would be reestablished over time but I believed that now was definitely not the time. I found it ironic . . . Matthew didn't trust me because he believed I knew about the molestation . . . and now I didn't trust him because I believed he really meant what he had said, that he wished I was dying instead of Joel.

Joel and I were together every day until his death. I read love poems to him, played his favorite records and sometimes I would just lie with my head against his shoulder, his arms around me and we would be still in the moment, both aware we were embraced in love as one.

I bought Joel fresh flowers, plants and herbs that he enjoyed smelling. When Joel was very uncomfortable due to his illness I did imagery work with him or we meditated together for long periods of time.

The first week we all arrived in San Francisco, Joel gave me a huge poster with abstract trees on it with these words that I loved:

*"When we touch
each other with love,
The world, too, becomes
a more loving place."*

The author was not identified and I was pleased because I felt these were Joel's words that he had spoken to me many times.

Joel told me he was not afraid to die. He said "remember all those talks we've had over the years about life, the spirit, the soul. Anna, our spirits have soared together in this lifetime. That can never be destroyed."

I told Joel I loved him and that he would be in my heart forever. I expressed the tremendous joy and happiness I had enjoyed in loving him. He had always believed in me and brought out the best of whom I was. I thanked him for loving me and delighting in the essence of my being.

Joel endured the pain and discomfort of his illness never complaining to anyone. He died as he had lived . . . courageously, with dignity, and to the very end, with appreciation for all the joys that life had brought him. Just before he died, Joel thanked me for loving him and said "you gave me the happiest days of my life . . . our spirits were intertwined from the very beginning . . . you brought me so much joy, delight and passion . . . you were my hummer . . . my sweet, sweet Anna."

I told Joel I truly believed that our souls were united for life. His love had reshaped who I was and his being would influence me all the days of my life. My love for Joel was endless. Joel had reminded me during his illness that I had much love to give. I must go on with my life once he was gone. I understood what he meant but at that time, as I stroked his cheek, I did not want to face the reality of my life without Joel.

It is not surprising that a wonderful man like Joel had touched so many people's lives in a positive way. They traveled long distances to pay their respects. They shared inspiring stories about their experiences with Joel and how he had influenced their lives. They had enjoyed his wit and laughter, appreciated his kindness and intelligence as well as the gentle strength that he possessed.

Young men said he was a role model . . . some of them made major life decisions after they talked to Joel. They said he was a wise man who never gave them directions, rather helped them gain insights in their business and personal life. They all agreed Joel always knew what was most important in his life . . . Anna, his family and his friends.

Senior executive staff also liked and respected Joel for the strength of his convictions. All acknowledged he was an affable, trustworthy man of integrity that they admired.

I was in despair and I didn't think there would be much point to living without my Joel? Yes, I loved my sons, their wives and my grandchildren, but they had their own lives to live. I was convinced they would all get along just fine without me. I had also done enough family therapy to know first hand the damage lonely widows can do to their children without intention. I was determined not to fall into that category . . . I felt that was the least I could now do for my family.

Initially, I got through my days by remembering the many wonderful memories of Joel but they were so poignant I would become overwhelmed with my grief. I longed for Joel with such intensity as if by doing so he might return.

Prior to my becoming a psychotherapist, a graduating student sang a song at my graduation with the words "you're the wind beneath my wings." At the time, I thought the song more than aptly described some of my feelings for Joel. I can remember him proudly sitting in the audience, with that wonderful smile on his face, as I went up to get my diploma. I was so fortunate;

he was my lover, my best friend . . . always supportive . . . my soulmate on earth . . . . . . "the wind beneath my wings."

Today I recognize it was a blessing that I had much to do after Joel's death. I did all the administrative tasks that needed my attention by rote. Matthew and Katherine assisted me in many ways and I was thankful to both of them but every time I saw Matthew, I remembered his dreadful words. Would they plague me for the rest of my life? As a therapist, I certainly knew how destructive this could be unless there was a resolution. What would happen to Matthew and me now that Joel was gone?

Daniel and Jackie phoned every week and invited me to their log cabin, suggesting I could stay as long as I wanted. The grandchildren wanted Baba to come too. I longed to accept their invitation but knew I wasn't ready to do so. I did appreciate their kindness in inviting me.

After the reading of the will, Joel's daughters contact with me was minimal. Lindy stated she was surprised that all the children in our blended family received the same inheritance. She had expected that she and Pamela would be treated differently because they were Joel's biological children. Joel's ex-wife had always had a negative influence on her daughters, especially Lindy, the eldest, but I felt Joel's loving influence had diminished the damage significantly.

I was saddened by their behavior as we had shared so many great times together and I knew that Pamela, Joel's youngest daughter, had learned to love me over the years while Lindy came close to really liking me. I was aware they were grieving over the loss of a loving father. I could only hope perhaps with the passing of time, we would resume our relationship.

Myrtle and Samuel phoned me immediately upon hearing that Joel had passed away. It was good to hear from both of them, particularly Myrtle that knew me so well. Myrtle wanted to know what she could do "Joel was a good man and I will always remember my fun weekend with the two of you in San Francisco."

You may recall Samuel was planning to visit Myrtle in Montreal after their reunion in Los Angeles. Samuel fell in love with Montreal and after two years of going back and forth from their respective cities, Samuel permanently moved to Montreal. His grown children lived in Virginia and South Carolina so he didn't feel he was deserting his family by leaving L.A.. Myrtle and Samuel were married in Montreal, and honeymooned in Quebec City. Myrtle's parents loved Samuel and welcomed him with open arms into their family. Samuel would often sit with Myrtle's aging father and listen to stories about the railroads across Canada that he knew so much about.

Over the years, many English-speaking residents had moved from Montreal to the Provinces of Ontario and British Columbia because of the ongoing French situation. It was an extremely difficult situation for many people who had been born in Quebec and had lived there all of their life. They sold their homes, their businesses or gave up their jobs. Some people were more fortunate because they got transferred out of Quebec by their companies. Canada had become a bilingual country but problems still persisted in the Province of Quebec. Samuel's decision to move to Montreal surprised many people but endeared him to the French-speaking population when he learned to fluently speak French.

Myrtle and Samuel were not concerned about the French situation in Montreal that was becoming increasingly more volatile. They were both interested in politics and history and spent much time exploring the current situation in Montreal and its evolution to its present state. They did not feel nonplused about living in the Province of Quebec . . . "We're a black couple, definitely in the minority who understand discrimination and know what it means and feels like when you do not have equal rights. We are interested in understanding the French situation in Canada." Since Samuel was retired, he had time to go to political meetings where be found himself becoming an active participant in the local discussions.

Samuel felt the large Hispanic population in California was causing California, though not legally as yet, to become a bilingual state. Would the Hispanic population in California start demanding similar rights to the French in Canada since they were, or fast becoming, the majority population? The education system was currently dealing with many serious issues that involved the rights of Hispanics. Now that Samuel was retired, he planned to do much research in Canada and the United States regarding human rights, supported by Myrtle who like me, going back to when we were children, always believed you could make a difference in the world.

Early on in life, I had been fascinated with people's lives and how, because of the choices they made, whether well thought out or compulsive, affected their life's journey. I am sure my fascination started when I listened, entranced, to the many stories my mother and father told me about their lives and the decisions they made. Definitely my two Russian uncles, Uncle Mike and dear Aunt Sophie also contributed stories that piqued my curiosity why they did what they did.

Here was Samuel, an American, married to a Canadian, now applying for Canadian citizenship, permanently living in Montreal. I, a Canadian, now a proud American, was now living in San Francisco. Both my sons were now Americans and their children as well.

In these two instances only, it was interesting that our environments had drastically changed but more importantly, the love in our lives had motivated our choices then ricocheted affecting the lives of our families and friends.

My dear friend Eddy heard about Joel's death from my sister's daughter, Jennie. He called to say how sorry he was for my loss and that he planned to visit San Francisco next year and hoped we could get together at that time. In the meantime, if he could help me in any way, financially or otherwise, I was to call him at any time.

After Joel's death, things settled down. I knew this was considered par for the course. There were no more sympathy cards in the mail to respond to, the telephone calls became fewer and people who had been around for me resumed their own lives. I became more fully aware that I am alone. I even had a new title . . . I am a widow.

I recognized people are far more sympathetic when you are a widow rather than a divorced woman. I did not like being labeled a widow...I preferred people saw me as an independent person. My reality was that I was gradually experiencing the world I functioned in as a widow in a couple's society . . . not a surprise to me . . . that I was now coping with it still was. I had to face the truth that my presence created an imbalance in their couple's world. I got invitations to many lunches from my lady friends but very few invitations to dinners. Many couples while pleased to see me, were uncomfortable when they saw me since I reminded them of their own mortality. I believe it was particularly difficult for them since Joel was one of the youngest husbands in a group of friends that we had.

I knew my grief and pain had transformed me but the only visible signs of my sorrow were in my eyes that only people who had experienced much pain and anguish often saw.

The perceptions of my much younger friends were more in keeping with Anna is my friend who has lost her love . . . we feel for her . . . yet they had far less problems in accepting me into their world. An extra dinner plate at the dining room table was okay . . . you didn't have to have even numbers to have a social get-together.

It pains me deeply to suggest that men who have lost their spouses are treated with far more consideration than the female population but it has been my observation that this is so. It is not my intent to create ire as I appreciate the pain and anguish men suffer at the loss of a loving spouse. Much of our society contributes to this attitude and perhaps we can all individually reflect where we stand in regards to how we embrace those who have suffered traumatic losses, be they male or female.

I often had such vivid dreams of Joel I would wake up thinking he was back. Occasionally, when I walked down the street and I saw a broad-shouldered man, with dark brown wavy hair, I thought it was Joel. Several times I am certain his spirit caressed my face when I was in silent prayer. I also remember waking up wondering if it was a dream or a reality when Joel had made love to me . . . I again heard his precious words of endearment.

I decided to attend a grief group for professionals who had lost a loved one. I needed to talk to someone about my anguish and pain. As a professional, I knew that groups can be very helpful but unfortunately this was not the case in this instant. The group leader was an academic, and while a compassionate man, lacked the required skills to deal effectively with the people in our group. After several months, I had to admit this was not working for me and I contacted a colleague to discuss my feelings.

Grief has many characteristics. . . anger, despair, hopelessness, sadness, helplessness just to name a few. When you are in acute pain, it doesn't always help knowing others are in pain as well . . . you're too focused on your own pain. For example, I could easily acknowledge that I wasn't the first woman who had lost a loved one. I could acknowledge that some men died even younger than Joel. I could acknowledge how fortunate we had been to have loved each other so deeply . . . none of it helped . . . I hurt badly . . . I had a broken heart . . . and though I knew it was impossible I wanted Joel to come back.

I felt there was nothing left to fear having survived Joel's death. The journey ahead of me seemed so barren and yet lately, I was aware that I was not devoid of joy when I saw my sons and their wives and my grandchildren.

Also, the last time I sat by the ocean by myself, watching the glorious sunset, I thought of Joel's comment about a sunset year ago . . . we had been talking about a business acquaintance of his who was very ill. Joel said "what price can anyone put on what it means to experience the beauty of one more sunset?" We both had agreed it was impossible.

At that moment, there was a deep stirring within my soul . . . I was alive and my life had purpose. I knew, beyond the shadow of a doubt, I was meant to see God's magnificent panorama before me. I wept in complete surrender to God's will.

> *In his heart a man plans his course, but the Lord determines his steps.*
>
> Proverbs 16:9

Joel had a business friend by the name of Glen that he had known for at least twenty-five years. I only got to know him during Joel's illness. He was a loving, compassionate man who spent much time reading to Joel and helping me in any way possible.

After Joel's death, Glen who was retired, would often take me out for long walks whether I felt like going or not. We ambled down towards the ocean, then sat and looked at the waves whose steady rhythm I found comforting.

Glen talked about his wife and children, his interest in the arts and gradually, as I became more attentive, I realized this was an incredibly lonely man. I was grateful to Glen because our walks, our cups of tea, forced me to take stock of my own life. Here was a man in a completely different position than I, who was sharing the losses in his life that he had yet to resolve and still he was trying to help me.

It was a rude awakening. It was really quite simple . . . the words were anyway. I must learn to live without Joel . . . he was not coming back. I must move on. I was thankful for Glen's quiet, peaceful presence in my life at a time when I needed serenity and calmness.

A couple of years had gone by at which time, I decided to return to the field of psychology. I started working with many teenage survivors of incest and became well known in this area. While my peers felt I had a special gift, all I knew was I wanted to help people in their healing process. Since I could not help my own son, Matthew, I would help others.

Working again, I was acutely aware I was letting my spirit be free to soar as high as it had when Joel was alive. Remembering Joel was no longer pain and agony . . . my memories of him and our time together were once again joyful and happy. I recognized that the dark clouds that had loomed above me were fading away. I felt much of my healing had actually started that day at the ocean watching God's beauty and accepting his will. I now understood the stirring in my soul was the holy spirit working within me.

I have always enjoyed reading Joseph Campbell's work. He once said "the privilege of a lifetime is being who you are." He has also written about the need to find one's meaning and to live in joy, and that the truest form of remembrance is rejoicing. I am heartened by his words as I do feel joy when I think of my beloved Joel.

I was calmly continuing my search for truth and in the process was becoming more accepting of myself and others. I respected and completely understood that "there is an unchanging silent life within every man that none knows but himself."

Joel's spirit was with me as I found myself reflecting more

often on the blessings in my life rather than the losses. That is not to say that I did not ponder over other truths in order to be a better person and a better therapist. I wondered to what extent can fear be dissolved by love? . . . is there no negativity that forgiveness does not transform? . . . and other.

I kept thinking about what makes a family particularly when my caseload of families was such at times that you couldn't help but wonder why they were all still functioning as a family unit. In these families, the members were not compatible, they did not have similar interests but they did share a past no matter how painful it may have been. It was obvious there is a connection that links each member of a family and each member of that family usually remembers his experiences differently. I thought of my sister Maria and our family. I thought of my sons' families and the numerous families I had known throughout my life; how different they were and yet so similar in many ways.

Matthew occasionally called me but I sensed he felt uncomfortable and never had much to say. Katherine was busy with their three children and was now only working part time as an occupational therapist. Katherine's parents had moved to Ireland where her dad was building a manufacturing plant. I knew Katherine missed her parents very much.

I invited them over several times but after my attempts failed, I decided that I would stop and let them decide if and when they wanted to see me. I missed the grandchildren but regularly talked to them on the phone. I could not dismiss the fact that the only reason Matthew and I were talking was because Joel's illness and death had precipitated our contact. Since then, Matthew and I discussed nothing. I had asked Matthew on several occasions if we could discuss the problems we had before Joel's death. He said no . . . he didn't want to talk about it.

As the years went by, Matthew and Katherine maintained

contact with me during special holidays and on my birthday. I longed to see my grandchildren but accepted the circumstances of this situation. I felt that Matthew was doing what a dutiful son does when it comes to having a mother as far as holidays were concerned, but he did not recognize that getting in touch with me once every month or so by telephone was not the type of relationship I hoped to have with him. It felt dutiful not loving.

Since I knew Matthew was an exceptionally bright person, a kind and loving man, I made up my mind to get rid of my expectations for our relationship. There is no doubt, my behavior was influenced by knowing Matthew had a perception of me that I found intolerable. While I respected Matthew and understood why he perceived me as he did, in order for me to continue loving myself, I needed to remind myself his view of me was not the absolute truth.

As a psychotherapist, I knew the psychoanalytic process explores the client's experiences. I also knew, in fairness to Matthew, I would not presume to analyze his feelings or his experiences. First and foremost, I was his mother. I would not be intrusive in his life and continue to hope that, someday, the abyss that I feel exists between us will be destroyed.

Occasionally I heard from Glen but we had discontinued our walks now that I was working again. The last time I talked to him, he was getting ready for a community art exhibit and said he had done a lot of painting. Glen was very talented and Joel had told me he thought Glen could have been an artist if he hadn't become an engineer. Many months went by and I wondered how Glen had done in his art show. He also traveled a lot, visiting his grandchildren, so I figured when he had the time, he would call me. He usually called every three months or so just to say hello and bring me up-to-date.

A friend called saying he had bad news for me. I steeled myself to hear what it was. Glen had committed suicide in the morning after his wife went to work.

I was surprised and saddened at the same time. What lead Glen to end his life remains a mystery to this day. There was no suicide note. I appreciate "the processes which lead a man to take his own life are at least as complex and difficult as those by which he continues to live." I prayed for Glen's soul. I prayed for his family who was desperately searching for answers to this most difficult thing that had happened.

I will always fondly remember Glen for his many kindnesses to me during Joel's illness and after his death. Glen believed in God and the heavens above. Peace unto you or as the Jewish people say "Shalom Aleichem."

Chapter Fifteen

More trauma . . . family changes

There are places in the heart which do not yet exist, pain must be in order that they be.
                                        Leon Bly

Matthew calls me to say he and Katherine are getting a divorce . . . they have agreed it is in the best interest of their children. I am reluctant to ask the questions that are springing up in my mind. Matthew appears to read my mind; "we haven't been getting along for a long time and this constant quarreling in front of the children has got to stop. I don't want my children to suffer any more than they have to; after all, I know what it feels like to be a kid when your parents are getting divorced." Matthew ends the conversation by saying "I will call you as soon as I am settled elsewhere to give you my new address and telephone number."

Katherine calls me the next day, telling me Matthew and she are getting a divorce. I tell her Matthew has already called me with the news. Katherine starts weeping but manages to say "it's the only thing to do for the sake of the children." I love Katherine . . . she is a good, loving mother. Katherine has always been kind to me and I respected the boundaries she clearly established early on in our relationship.

Katherine feels she has been nagging Matthew for quite some time, but does not say why. She says he no longer hears anything she says. Matthew has told her he feels she needs help ... Katherine feels he needs help. I ask whether they might consider couple's counseling? Katherine states "it's too late for that" and that is the extent of the information I receive on their pending divorce.

My heart goes out to the twins, Joseph and Michael, and their young daughter, Pamela. Matthew is a very good father and he and his children are very close. I am hopeful they can get through the divorce with as little animosity as possible since it is a mutual decision. Matthew is a generous person and since Katherine is financially comfortable because of her parents, there should be no major financial complications to hold up the proceedings. Matthew and Katherine have agreed to joint custody and plan on being cooperative regarding other access to their children on special occasions.

I cannot help but reflect on the fact that Matthew has unfinished business in his life and wonder to what extent this may have contributed to his pending divorce. I am contemplative and sorrowful about the entire situation.

Daniel calls me to say Matthew called him about the divorce and he did not blame Katherine. Rather, Matthew stated he was finally facing the truth and taking responsibility for his life and that of his children. He was grateful that he had his kids. He told Daniel they were a constant source of joy and happiness to him.

Daniel said "Mom, he sounded really good . . . he even said they were both responsible for the breakup of the marriage . . . and he knew it was necessary to give up his false expectations of the marriage and move on."

My conversation with Daniel gave me renewed hope for Matthew's future peace of mind. If he could face life openly, accept himself and accept others as they are as well, he could create a dream for a better life and commit to it.

With all my heart, I hoped that I, as well as Matthew would learn to relate to each other in a non-guarded way instead of a guarded way that is the posture of fearful expectancy.

After Matthew's divorce, he and the children started visiting Daniel and Jackie up north on a regular basis. Matthew's children loved the log cabin and particularly enjoyed sleeping in sleeping bags on the floor. They were happy there were no guest rooms . . . this was more fun.

Daniel and Matthew took all the kids fishing on a regular basis. There were ongoing discussions as to who caught the biggest fish and who would get to clean the next fish that was caught.

They roasted marshmallows over the fire, just as my sons had done when they were young in Canada. Matthew's children were learning important lessons, mostly by example, from their Uncle Daniel and Aunt Jackie. You didn't have to live in a big house and have lots of stuff that you never really used . . . you could have more fun in a log cabin singing songs and telling stories with people that loved you.

Their cousins, Adam and John knew many neat things. They knew the names of a lot of different birds and where they made their nests. Grandpa Joel had been a good teacher.

They knew where the skunks lived and where the grey owl usually sat when he hooted in the evening. They even showed their cousins a real porcupine that lived beyond their log cabin that they considered was a pet.

Adam taught the twins how to build a tepee out of branches explaining to them that the Indians had built tepees made of skins. Jackie helped Pamela find bird feathers. They made colorful head bands of old pieces of cloth placing the feathers in the bands that they wore with great pride. I remembered long ago what fun Jeannine and I had when we created so many wondrous things out of bits and pieces of odds and ends. I was pleased my grandchildren were using their creative imaginations and building treasures that they shared with each other.

Daniel and Matthew never talked about the past. When they were together, they lived totally in the present. One day when I was telling my grandchildren that I never had any grandparents . . . and why . . . I showed them their great grandparents' pictures on their father's side. Later on in the day, I saw Matthew looking at the pictures. He stated "my father, the monster looked a lot like his dad" as he walked away. It was the only time I ever heard Matthew mention his father since his father's death. Prior, he had made it quite clear, Joel was his father who had saved his life and loved him.

As a therapist, I knew that a person will only deal with previously concealed truths when he wishes to change his life. Some people go through life never dealing with their issues. I knew many clients that yearned to change, and did, only because there was too much pain in their past and they were filled with much anger . . . they no longer wished to tolerate their pain in the present as sadness and disappointment.

Matthew seemed a lot happier since his divorce . . . he looked more relaxed and was playful in a spontaneous way with his children. There was an expression that I remembered verbatim as I read it at a crucial time in my life with Don.

"If you sacrifice a part of yourself to keep a relationship alive, you will eventually leave the relationship to regain the part you gave up." I believed whoever said that, probably experienced what he had written. I am content with the beauty of life around me, fully aware that I am letting go of the past.

It is evening and I feel an eternal calm after a productive day. I plan to do some writing and reading before I retire. There have been fewer crises this past year in our family and everyone seems to be adjusting to their life's circumstances in a positive way. The telephone interrupts my revere and I am momentarily startled. Matthew has called to say he has bad news "Katherine has leukemia. Her parents are flying in from Ireland. I thought you should know. The kids are okay . . . Katherine's childhood nanny has moved in and is taking care of them."

All I can say is "I'm so sorry. What can I do to help?" I want to ask Matthew how long his ex wife has been ill . . . what is her prognosis . . . so many questions . . . but I know Matthew; I must wait for him to tell me when he is ready.

Katherine's parents will be in town for a couple of weeks and then they must return to Ireland. They are beside themselves full of fear and anxiety about Katherine. Katherine's father has contacted leading medical specialists in this field and we are certain Katherine will be getting the best of care.

Matthew moves back into his old home so he can be there for his children on a daily basis. The children are told, by Matthew, their mother is ill and he's back because it's easier if he's around to help them and nanny in the evenings. The children are overjoyed that daddy is home and Pamela, his young daughter says "I'm glad you're here even if you and mom don't get married again."

I love Katherine and I am truly sad that she is ill. I am also concerned about Matthew's well being as well even though he appears to be handling all his responsibilities without any undue incidents. He is very patient and loving with the children and very solicitous towards Katherine. From all appearances, I think Katherine is still in love with Matthew.

Katherine is despondent when her parents leave but lightens up when they state they will be coming back before too long at which time they know she will be well. On the heels of their departure, Daniel and his family come to visit Katherine providing a much needed temporary diversion.

Daniel and his family are staying with me for the weekend

while visiting Katherine. My quiet home is filled with noise, laughter and much activity that only emphasizes how tranquil my life style has become. Though the children are sad that Auntie Katherine is sick, it is obvious their worlds are filled with constant high hopes and expectations . . . as it should be.

When Matthew's children arrive to play with their cousins, their reunion is heart warming. It hopefully is providing a respite in their young lives that they sorely need. Recently, the twins asked Matthew if mommy is going to die. I believe they shared with me Matthew's answer to this question that was both honest and kind, trying to ascertain if I, their Baba, agreed with their daddy.

I reflect on the complexities of life and recognize that no matter how carefully I try to examine what is before me, it may turn out to be even more complex than I thought. Katherine is very ill and far too young to die . . . she has young children to raise . . . Then I humbly realize all I can do is pray and try to help wherever I can. I know for certain "God, thy will be done."

Katherine died nine months later due to major complications. Prior to her death, she had many loving conversations with her children and Matthew as she courageously faced death. The funeral service for Katherine was very dignified and loving perhaps considered lavish by some people's standards due to the overabundance of flowers, limousines, and dignitaries present. The same minister that married Katherine and Matthew performed the service.

I couldn't help but recall what an extravagant, beautiful wedding Katherine's parents gave their only child. I knew Katherine's parents would have willingly given away all their wealth to save Katherine's life. The pain and sorrow in their eyes were acute and they would mourn their daughter's death for a long time.

I thought of the following verse from Revelation:

God shall wipe away all tears from their eyes; and there shall be no more death, neither sorrow, or crying, neither shall there be any more pain; for the former things are passed away.

In 292 B.C. Menander said:
"Whom the gods love dies young."

In 159 B.C. Terence in his prologue in Eunuches said:
"In fact, nothing is said that has not been said before."

Matthew gave up his apartment. He decided it was best for the children they all live in their home, along with nanny who agreed to help him as long as he needed her. Matthew also made arrangements with his employer to travel less frequently in the coming year.

The children joined a young group dedicated to dealing with grief due to the loss of a parent. I well knew mourning takes time and everyone does it in their own way, in their own time. I could only reflect upon how the loss of their mother would affect Joseph, Michael and Pamela. I wept for my grandchildren that I loved so much.

Matthew and the children started spending weekends at Daniel's log cabin on a regular basis that I believe provided them with an environment that was conducive to healing. I felt I was too familiar with these words:

> *As the seasons past . . . Grief melts away,*
> *Like snow in May,*
> *As if there were no such cold thing.*

We gradually resumed our lives that had been severely changed. Katherine would never be forgotten. The children's loss of a loving mother would have a long term, major impact on their lives and would be an influential factor in shaping the people they would become. Matthew's life as a full time father would alter his life in ways he could not even imagine.

I always found comfort in these words:

> *They that love beyond the world cannot be separated by it. Death is but crossing the world, as friends do the seas; they live in one another still.*
> William Penn

I went to sit by the ocean to watch the sunset. In spite of the sadness within me, I was swept away by the magnificent panorama before me. A surge of waves flooded my being and I wept copious tears for my family followed by tears of joy that I was alive to see this beautiful sunset.

I thought of my mother and father . . . my friend Lily . . . and of course my beloved Joel. In many ways, they had greatly influenced my life and memories of them were with me. I accepted that I needed to believe in God when I was contemplating the spiritual side of humanity's existence. I felt by not believing in God, our inherent need for wholeness would be denied.

My beliefs had been reaffirmed when I studied Carl G. Jung's Analytical Psychology at which time I became more fully aware that he believed without God to aspire to, people are forever condemned to the incompleteness of their own existence. For Jung's theory the question of God's existence was nearly irrelevant because he believed it could never be answered with certainty.

The sadness I felt in my heart for Matthew and his family was somewhat quelled and I felt renewed hope for the future. I wondered if perhaps I was developing more tolerance for ambiguity. I laughed when I recalled, a long-ago conversation I had with Joel about "what price can you put on a sunset." I finally knew the answer.

Chapter Sixteen

The lonely heart

There is a destiny
That makes us brothers
None goes his way alone
All that we send into the lives of others
Comes back into our own.
                    Edwin Markham

In this chapter, I will briefly describe some of my feelings in being a single woman after many years of happy marriage. Four years have gone by since Joel's death and I have been attending the theater, concerts, museums and art exhibitions with female friends for several years. I am fairly satisfied with the amount of activities I partake in.

My private practice, some volunteer work and family require that I maintain a balanced life and so far, I believe I am doing just that. I have made some new friends, widowed as well, who are currently dating. A few of them feel it is time I also start dating.

Available data confirms that men die an average of eight years earlier than women and older males without partners often seek younger female companions, whereas women are still less likely to be involved with younger men. That being a given, as an older woman I recognize men may not be as available as they were in my young adulthood. Yet I know some of the most touching, successful romances have occurred in later life. For example, I am reminded by the well intentioned that I was not a young girl when Joel and I fell in love.

I readily admit missing the passionate love I had in my life . . . the touching, caressing, hugging . . . the sexual intimacy . . . and verbally expressing and receiving affection.

I acknowledge there are many types of relationships, including relationships without sex that sometimes progress into a sexual relationship or casual sex. I know persons may seek "companionate love" that is characterized by deep affection and attachment or "passionate love" that is characterized by intense, vibrant feelings. I am also aware that women consistently link love with sexual behavior more than men do.

While this knowledge is interesting, I believe it has no bearing on my current circumstances. To date I have not been in any relationship since Joel's death where I needed to make a decision to engage in a sexual relationship or not.

I confess I have not been enthusiastic about dating but I finally decided to be more open to the experience. My friends kept assuring me there were good available men of character, intelligence and warmth out there but sadly, all agreed, they didn't know any of them to introduce me to.

Nevertheless, several times last year I went out with an acquaintance of Joel's thinking it might be an enjoyable experience. I ended our brief relationship because I felt lonelier being with this man than when I was by myself. I also didn't think it was fair to continue dating him since he said he was looking for an intimate, committed relationship.

During another date, I felt I was being interrogated to see if I measured up to this man's expectations. I got extremely uncomfortable on our first date when he asked me some very personal questions about my financial situation and sexual preferences. Upon asking him a few questions, I concluded he was looking for a rich widow to support him. I guess I could admire his honesty but needless to say, I never went out with him again.

Since I am now a mature woman who has a broad array of past experiences as well as meaningful inputs in her life, and I have known true love, I believe I have a totally different perspective of how I wish to live the balance of my life.

First of all, it is possible that God gave me more than my fair share of romantic love when he sent Joel into my life. If I am to meet another kindred spirit, it will happen because it is God's will and it will happen in God's time.

Secondly, I don't think the balance of my life's purpose is to be searching for a companion. Rather, I believe that happiness is within my soul right now, with or without a man.

Thirdly, I remain open to new experiences and enjoy meeting men and women from all walks of life, different cultures and religions.

I celebrate that my life is already filled with love. All my grandchildren love their Baba. Daniel and Jackie love me. Matthew recently told me that he loves me. I want to believe him. Then there are a few friends, young and old, that love me as well. I know I am blessed with these gifts of love. I reciprocate love to them whenever I can.

Recently during a telephone conversation with Myrtle she said "Anna, whatever it is your mother had when she was a little old lady, you've got it too. I think it's called charisma. I've told you this before but I don't think you believe me."

It's not that I don't believe her but I just don't think about it. So what if it's true? When I look in the mirror, I am somewhat surprised that my face doesn't match the young spirit within me. Joel always told me I was beautiful . . . I matched my beautiful soul . . . but he loved and adored me. I know I am aging well . . . if that can be said . . . but I am less concerned about my looks as time goes by. Cultivating the spiritual beauty in my soul is very important to me.

I do know, in spite of my maturity, I am still the incurable romantic. I believe when true love exists, spirits are united and soar together. Lovers delight in each other's essence and illuminate each other's hearts. If I become attracted to someone in my golden years, will he know I need flowers, poetry, music . . . or courtly love? Joel knew.

I do not compare other men that I meet to Joel. I appreciate we are all unique and precious in our own way. Since I am still a realist and a dreamer, perhaps I recognize the difficulty, at this time in my life, of finding romantic love again.

Several months ago, I attended a conference where, for the first time since Joel's death, I was physically attracted to a man. He turned out to be intelligent, charming, and happily married. I was disappointed he was married but was pleased we met because I came to realize that I was still very much alive. It was good to know that so far I just haven't met a man who sparks my soul.

After marrying, several former widows came to therapy due to serious problems with adult stepchildren and step grandchildren. The common denominator in many of these cases was the fear that the children had that they would lose their inheritance to their stepfathers that was manifesting itself in unsatisfactory behavior. Initially, it was difficult for the adult children to admit that their money concerns were the driving force in their negative behavior. Financial matters and potential issues had not been discussed with the parent before the marriage due to the early blush of romance that was now quickly disappearing.

In many instances, I also saw the reverse of this situation when prenuptial agreements were signed prior to a marriage. Though the couple might be experiencing some problems related to blending the two families, there was less focus on the financial aspects in the relationship.

> *Will you gather daydreams,*
> *or will you gather wealth?*
> *How can you find your fortune*
> *If you cannot find yourself?*
> 　　　　　Gordon Lightfoot

Too many parents often found themselves being manipulated by their children and chaos prevailed before the sense of human love was restored but not in all instances.

On the positive side, I like to tell the story about Mac and Debbie who found each other in their late sixties. They had gone to high school together . . . went steady for years, attended different universities, got married to different people, had families and grandchildren . . . and then . . . Mac's wife passed away, Debbie's husband passed away.

They went to their high school reunion, each hoping the other would be there. They had not seen each other in over forty years. As Mac walked up the high school stairs, he was positive the lady in front of him was Debbie. It was. Nine months later they were married with both families attending their wedding.

Mac's wife had been ill for many years, as had Debbie's husband. Mac's children were compassionate and generous hearted. They had witnessed the tender loving care their father had given their mother during her illness.

Debbie's children exhibited similar characteristics and very much appreciated their mother's steadfast loyalty and love they witnessed when their father was dying.

Fortunately, all these adult children were good people who had experienced enough anguish and pain that they were delighted that Mac found Debbie or Debbie found Mac.

To avoid future problems, Mac and Debbie legally provided for all the children prior to the marriage. The children from both families were comfortable with the financial provisions that were made. They were genuinely pleased that Mac and Debbie were no longer lonely and in love. Mac and Debbie believe it was destiny they meet again in their sixties. Both admitted they each had loved their deceased spouses. They have been married for five years and are still madly in love.

While there are many wonderful stories, there are many sad ones that are sometimes never told. I have worked with mature people who married individuals they really didn't know because they couldn't stand the loneliness. It was overwhelming for them when they felt lonelier living with a partner that was a stranger to them. Many people married in haste and repented at leisure.

I believe in love but I am convinced that not all of us will have the opportunity to love more than one kindred spirit in this lifetime; yet I am inspired by these words:

> *Let those love now who never loved before;*
> *Let those who always loved, now love the more.*
> Thomas Parnell

. . . and will end the chapter with Sir Walter Scott's poem:

> *True love's the gift which God has given*
> *To man alone beneath the heaven;*
> *It is not fantasy's hot fire,*
> *Whose wishes, soon as granted, fly;*
> *It liveth not in fierce desire,*
> *With dead desire it doth not die;*
> *It is the secret sympathy,*
> *The silver link, the silken tie,*
> *Which heart to heart and mind to mind*
> *In body and in soul can bind.*

Chapter Seventeen

New song of love and happiness . . . and tears

How fading are the joys we dote upon!
Like apparitions seen and gone.
But those which soonest take their flight
Are the most exquisite and strong
Like angels' visits, short and bright
Mortality's too weak to bear them long.
     John Norris . . . The Parting (1678)

I haven't seen Eddy for a couple of years though he has always been forthright that he will come to San Francisco at a moment's notice when I am ready to see him. I feel the time is now right for me to spend some time with Eddy. I am quite excited that I will see him shortly. I can't imagine how I would have managed after Joel's death without his loyal support through ongoing letters, cards, flowers and regular phone calls.

Eddy has enjoyed a successful business career as a stock broker. Though he took an early retirement, he is financially comfortable. He claims his ulterior motive in coming to San Francisco is not just to enjoy my company but to watch "those fabulous sunsets you've been telling me I have to see." I can hear the lilt in his voice, his easy laughter and my heart is glad that he is happy just talking to me.

"Anna, I can't believe I'm finally going to see you tomorrow. I'm counting the hours."

"I'm really happy you're coming Eddy."

I immediately spot Eddy at the airport even though his hair is now practically all grey. The change appears to have enhanced his looks. One might say he is aging well. I think he looks very handsome in his jeans and blazer. His face breaks out in a broad smile when he sees me. He drops his carry-on luggage to hug me, picking me off the floor as he does so. When I get back on my feet, we are still holding on to each other. I feel really comfortable in his arms but I tremble a little as I am overwhelmed with happiness at seeing my dear Eddy from Canada. Why on earth did I wait so long to invite him?

"Anna, you look beautiful . . . you still have those sparkling diamonds in your eyes. Do you know how happy I am to see you" he says looking right into my eyes, his arms still embracing my shoulders.

"I hope as happy as I am to see you, Eddy. I've missed seeing you. I know, I know you would have come sooner. Anyway we wrote some great letters didn't we? . . . and your phone calls were often my life savers. You' re here now and that's all that matters."

Our first night, Eddy and I have a pleasant candlelight dinner at home. I bought a superb French wine for this special occasion that I know Eddy likes.

"Anna, you went to so much trouble. You even remembered the wine I like. This has been a wonderful evening. I don't expect you to wait on me hand and foot. I plan on taking you to a lot of the famous restaurants in this great city."

"Eddy, let me spoil you a little. It's time I did. You've always been so good to me."

Eddy's eyes appear to be dancing when he says "It's easy to be good to you."

With little effort, Eddy and I start enjoying a harmonious daily routine that includes pseudo planning what we will do for the day at breakfast time. More times than naught, we are spontaneous in our decision making. Sometimes we go to the ocean, walk around the wharf or ride the trolley enjoying the sights and the people. Other times we visit the city's highlights . . . art galleries, museums. We attend concerts, theaters and visit the botanical gardens . . . whatever strikes our fancy. Occasionally we get really dressed up and dine at a very elegant restaurant. Doing nothing more strenuous than watching the ocean waves rise and fall delights us both as well.

We are relaxed and comfortable with one another. I realize with the passing of each day how much I am enjoying Eddy's company. It feels good to have my home filled with Eddy's dear presence. Why did I wait so long to see him again?

One day after changing the bed sheets in the guest room and just tidying up, I see a bottle of pills. They are for angina pectoris. Eddy has a heart problem. Coincidentally, I start having palpitations. I take a few deep breaths, then I run as quickly as I can out to the porch where Eddy is reading a magazine. He looks up at my anguished face, starts getting up reaching towards me. I reach towards Eddy.

I must remain calm. "Eddy, I was cleaning your room. I saw your pills . . . Eddy are you all right . . . you know I care about you . . . why didn't you tell me?" I try not to cry, but the tears roll down my cheeks.

"Anna, Anna, please don't cry. I was planning to tell you. We've been having such a wonderful time, I didn't want to worry you. It's not that serious . . . it's a very mild condition. Anna honestly, as long as I take care of myself and take my pills the doctors say I'll be okay. You wait and see, I plan to live to a ripe old age."

I was afraid. I couldn't bear the thought of losing Eddy. As a family, we were still dealing with Katherine's death. Recently, a close friend of mine had also suddenly passed away. I missed her. Another friend was battling cancer. It felt like déjàvu. I distinctly recalled my mother in her old age saying, "every time the phone rings, someone I care about has passed away." I did not feel I was yet in my old age . . . then why did I now relate to what she had said?

Eddy lifted my chin upward so I was looking right into his eyes "Anna, I am touched I mean so much to you." He bent down and kissed me lightly on the lips. I clung to him and kissed him back passionately. Eddy responded at once to my passion with the depth of his love. It was a long kiss full of deep feelings that expressed a mutual desire to love even more. I was breathless when we drew apart. Eddy looked unbelievably happy.

"Anna, I love you . . . you don't have to say anything . . . you've known for a very long time how I feel about you. During the years, no matter what was happening in our lives, I never stopped loving you."

"Oh, Eddy, I don't know what to say."

Eddy kissed me on the forehead. "After that kiss, I am hopeful we can be more than friends. No more tears. We'll sit in the garden so you can gather your thoughts."

"Eddy, I enjoyed kissing you. I can't bear the thought of losing you. I just wanted you to know how much I care. My feelings for you are different right now. Eddy, the only thing I'm sure of is I'm so glad you're here."

"Anna, I've waited a long time for you. Right now when I look into your eyes, I just want to shout thanks to the heavens that we are together. We have all the time in the world . . . I'm not going anywhere Anna . . . don't be afraid to love me."

I fondly notice Eddy's shadow of a dimple in his left cheek

when he smiles and how his blue eyes seem to twinkle every time he looks at me.

Eddy put his strong arm around my shoulder as we walked towards the backyard. Sitting on the glider swing, Eddy encircled my body with both his arms as I leaned against his shoulder. The swing moved gently back and forth and the gentle San Francisco breeze quietly caressed our faces as if to soothe and not disturb the blending of two bodies united as one. I felt in the tranquil stillness of the moment, the only sound was the beating of our hearts.

The next day, at breakfast time, when I first saw Eddy I felt a warmth rush over me. I intuitively knew that Eddy could sense I was behaving differently. What had happened yesterday, was wondrous indeed. We both knew we had entered another phase in our long relationship. I could tell Eddy felt at long last my feelings for him had changed. He was right but I still couldn't believe I was falling in love with Eddy whom I had known since I was eighteen. Initially, I felt awkward and shy, like a young school girl and somewhat ridiculous . . . this was dear Eddy. He knew me better than anyone else in the world . . . in spite of all my trials and tribulations, he never stopped loving me.

Suddenly I appreciated and found attractive the many physical attributes that Eddy had that I had never really paid attention to before. He always had broad shoulders and a wonderful physique but only now was this strongly appealing to me. His blue eyes always twinkled when he smiled at me . . . now he sure was making my heart go pitter patter . . . and now in my eyes, his full head of wavy, grey hair just enhanced his strong profile. Though I thought I was being discreet in observing him as I made our breakfast coffee that was not the case.

After breakfast, Eddy held my hand and said "Anna, I plan to court you or in more modern lingo, sweep you off your feet for the rest of our lives. Beloved, we both know since yesterday things will never be the same again. You keep giving these darting looks, then hastily looking away. Darling, just look into my eyes and let me kiss you. I'm still your dear Eddy who has always loved you."

"Oh Eddy I feel wonderful. You're right things have changed dramatically between us . . . I feel like a young girl and not a mature woman. I always loved you as a friend but now it's as if I am really seeing you for the first time and Eddy, I have fallen in love with you."

Eddy gave me a big bear hug and the happiest smile I had ever seen before he passionately kissed me . . . "miracles do happen Anna . . . No matter what was going on in our lives, deep within my heart, I always believed we were meant to love each other."

Eddy gave me love poems written by Keats and Browning that he knew I enjoyed along with a glorious bunch of red roses. After an intimate dinner that evening, he read me poems that he selected that he said came from his heart for his beloved Anna.

We watched the sunset sitting on a lounge in the backyard and welcomed the moon that embraced us. Eddy stroked my hair, kissed my face . . . my eyelids . . . my lips . . . first gently, then passionately as he held me in his arms. He ignited a flame within me and I was completely enamored with Eddy.

He bought balloons that he festively hung over the swing, in the garden and in the house. He would sing "The more I kiss you, the more I want to kiss you. The more I hug you the more I want to hug you. If I keep this up, I may have a hit tune on my hands. What do you think Anna?"

We laughed for no reason just because we were happy.

"Anna, now there is nothing holding me back. It's as if the love I have for you was stored up and I can freely express it . . . yet it's an endless supply . . . my love just keeps growing and growing . . . and the wonder is you're loving me back"

I hug him and we dance around the kitchen. "Eddy, I love you, love you, love you. I was sure I would never love again. Thank you for never giving up on me."

During an evening when Eddy and I were enjoying tender loving kisses, he looked deep into my eyes and we both knew the time had come for our passion to be fulfilled.

Just like in the romantic novels I read as a young girl, Eddy picked me up in his arms speaking words of loving endearment as he carried me into the bedroom. He caressed and kissed my entire body until I yearned for his being. The beauty of our love was exquisite and overwhelming . . . the explosion of joy was sensuously gratifying . . . our love embodied our spirits . . . we would be one forevermore.

"I have waited most of my life to love you as I have tonight. I will always cherish you, beloved Anna. If I died tomorrow, you have made me the happiest of men. With you, I have known heaven on earth." I put my forefinger on his lips . . .

"Eddy, don't speak of dying . . . we will have a long life together and many more nights of rapture like tonight. You are my beloved."

"You're right, Anna . . . with you my love I have much to live for" . . . and with his blue eyes twinkling he went on to say "and I have so much love to give you."

Eddy wrapped his arms around me and we kissed again. I felt safe. Eddy was strong but gentle, tender but passionate and he loved me with all his heart.

"I love you Eddy . . . let me count the ways." We both smiled because of my words . . . tonight words had been followed by passionate love making that had more than adequately expressed our love for each other.

Eddy gave me a final kiss before we fell asleep curled up in each others arms. In the morning, when we both woke up, we joyfully laughed like young children . . . gleeful . . . remembering last night. I told Eddy I was certain God had smiled upon us the night before.

He agreed.

The love I had for Eddy was a wondrous surprise in my life as I was convinced I could never love anyone with such fervor after Joel. I delighted in our amorous relationship and how Eddy and I often communicated so eloquently without words. He had only to stroke my arm in passing and I felt his surge of love. Every time he looked at me, his eyes embraced me with love.

I fully appreciated that we were kindred spirits whose time had come after we had journeyed our different paths. There had been many forks in the road and yes, Eddy had always loved me and was often in my life, but I truly believe only now were we meant to love each other. Perhaps it was necessary that I love Joel, experience the pain and the agony of losing him, so that my love for Eddy would blossom as it did. Eddy loved me with every fibre in his being and the miracle was I did too. We rejoiced in our good fortune every minute of the day knowing we had entered each other's souls.

Many people that love never come nearer than to behold each other as in a mirror; they seem to know and yet never know the inward life; they never enter the other soul; and they part at last, with but the vaguest notion of the universe on the borders of which they have been hovering for years.

When I spoke to Eddy of my deep love for him, he heard me from the depth of his soul. When Eddy spoke to me of his love for me, he touched the essence of my being. We awakened in each other profound, pure love that is only possible when two souls unite.

After several glorious months in San Francisco, Eddy returned to Montreal to take care of private matters back in Canada. Eddy had proposed to me the first time we made love and I accepted. We decided our permanent home would be in San Francisco before we got married. Eddy stated "I'm not staying away too long . . . I love you too much . . . life without you is empty . . . knowing you love me and want to be with me the rest of your life is all that matters . . . we'll get married when you are ready."

I knew about the immigration process to live in the United States quite well since I went through it to marry Joel. Hopefully this would be helpful in Eddy's case.

Eddy called me every morning and every night for two weeks. "Anna, can you get on a plane and come to Montreal? I'm dying of loneliness without you."

"I thought you'd never ask. I am lonely too . . . I'm on my way."

I had not been back to Montreal since my mother's death. I was aware I had mixed feelings about going back to the city of my birth that I loved. I was dying to see Eddy but was anxious about seeing my sister, Maria. I felt she might be surprised to hear I was in love with Eddy. Deep inside I knew my concerns were not emanating from this source. Rather it involved our past issues that had never been resolved.

My reunion with Eddy was breath taking and ecstatic. A fleeting thought went through my head before Eddy scooped me off the floor, swung me around, and kissed me passionately in the airport . . . "Eddy, should we be doing this?"

"You better believe it, we should . . . I love you, love you, love you. Oh you're worried it's too strenuous . . . I just had a checkup and I'm fine . . . don't worry . . . loving is what I need . . . the doctor agrees."

I am relieved and can't wait to get to Eddy's apartment.

We decided Eddy would retain a one room apartment in Montreal so we can visit there at our leisure. Eddy had major investments in Canada but they would not require much of his time. He was confident that his transition to the United States would be easy.

"Anna, I'd live in an igloo with you if you wanted to live in one."

"Eddy, I missed you so much." It had been a long time since I had tears of happiness in my eyes instead of tears of sorrow.

"Anna, why are you crying . . . we're together."

"I'm crying because I'm so happy to see you. Eddy, these are tears of joy. Can't you tell?"

He put his arm around my shoulder, and with his other hand lifted my chin and gently brushed my tears away with his kisses until he reached my mouth with full passion.

I loved how he did that. I always looked into his deep blue eyes before my emotions carried me away.

Our days together are euphoric and a week goes by before I telephone my sister, Maria, to let her know why I am in town, along with Myrtle and Sam who can't wait to see us. I didn't want anything to ruin my time with Eddy but I knew I couldn't postpone seeing Maria anymore.

Eddy and I plan to have dinner with Maria. I hope she and I may feel less estranged if Eddy is present. When I told her he would be joining us for dinner, she was silent, then stated "I was just on my way out the door, we'll talk later on." She always liked Eddy and I am hoping she will be pleased with our good news.

The best way I can describe the evening is to suggest it was civil, courteous, and occasionally awkward. I was truly saddened by the lack of warmth between my sister and me. I inwardly acknowledged my hesitation in getting in touch with Maria came from a premonition that our reunion would not be a happy one. It felt like Maria congratulated Eddy and me somewhat reluctantly.

I was starting to feel responsible for Maria's lack of enthusiasm in that I had not conversed with her to advise her what was going on in my life. Then suddenly, my mind said stop . . . you know you are not responsible for anyone's behavior but your own. Rightly or wrongly, I knew I behaved the way I did because I didn't want anyone raining on my parade. Unfortunately, I felt Maria just might.

Eddy told Maria that he had loved me all of his life since we were young kids.

"You were married once" Maria said in a monotone voice.

"Yes, Maria I was. I convinced myself I loved her when Anna got married. It was a big mistake. I was trying to forget Anna. Even when I was married I still loved Anna . . . no wonder the marriage failed. I was responsible. That's the past . . . Anna loves me . . . we're together at last . . . that's all that matters."

We shifted the conversation to Maria's life and her daughter, Jennie. As my sister talked it was evident how different our lives were . . . how different we were. I loved my sister, Maria but internally acknowledged that there was a distance between the two of us based on ills of the past that had not been healed.

Our evening with Myrtle and Sam was just the opposite of our evening with Maria. We were all jovial and at times, I thought

Myrtle was going to jump up and down because Eddy and I were in love.

"Eddy, you know I've known Anna most of my life just as you have. This is just wonderful. I'm so happy for both of you."

Sam proposed a champagne toast to the two of us and Eddy responded by proposing a toast to the four of us.

Myrtle and I spent some time together alone.

"Myrtle I never thought I could love anyone after Joel. It is incredible, you can love again. Eddy is so loving and passionate it's unbelievable."

"Anna, he waited a long, long time to realize his dream of loving you. Both of you are glowing."

"Well, Myrtle you and Sam look like the passion lives on. I guess we all have much to be thankful for. I'm concerned about Eddy's heart but he says he's okay so I believe him. Sometimes he has more energy than I do."

"Anna, just live for the moment." We hugged and giggled like two high school girls.

Each sunrise, we celebrated the joyous harmony we knew the day would bring. There was a constant pouring of love from Eddy that I responded to in wild abandon like a young school girl. We were playful, flirtatious, gentle, tender, passionate, relishing every moment we spent together.

After an incredible night of love making, Eddy said "sometimes I love you more than life itself . . . there has never been anyone for me but you."

"Eddy, I loved Joel . . . it seems a long time ago . . . We are both who we are because of our past. I had many lessons to learn.

Eddy I love you so deeply as I have never loved anyone before." Eddy hugged me tightly then passionately kissed me from head to toe, saying over and over again, "you've made me the happiest man in the world . . . I love you dearest Anna."

We planned our wedding to include Daniel and Jackie, their sons Adam and John; Matthew, his twin sons Joseph and Michael and daughter Pamela. We would be married in a little church on the hill overlooking the ocean on a Saturday afternoon.

Daniel and Jackie were pleased that Eddy and I were so rapturously happy. They had developed a strong liking for Eddy. Matthew was courteous but did not exhibit any warm feelings towards Eddy. I felt he might still be struggling with loyalty issues towards Joel. Eddy felt that given time, he and Matthew would be friends. Matthew's children adored their new Grandpa Eddy. I was pleased Grandpa Eddy had not replaced their Grandpa Joel that they occasionally openly talked about "Grandpa Joel who went to heaven."

I asked both my sons to give me away and they agreed to do so. Matthew said it was a little strange but then added "why not if it makes you happy."

I wore an elegant long, light beige chiffon gown with a garland of flowers in my hair. The gown's simplicity was beautiful and Eddy said I took his breath away. In lieu of an engagement ring that I didn't want, Eddy gave me diamond earrings, the only jewelry I wore at our marriage.

The wedding ceremony was spiritually moving and I honestly felt there was a cluster of angels surrounding us when we took our vows. Eddy's eyes filled with tears of happiness as did mine when the minister pronounced us man and wife. A beam of light shone directly on our heads through the stained glass windows of the church and Pamela said "look daddy, there's an angel's halo over Babba and Grandpa Eddy." There was a hushed silence as we all looked up towards the light . . . Eddy and I felt my family, now his family had witnessed the intertwinement of our souls. Our spirits soared in the presence of God. We kissed shyly in the church, but with a touch of passion, then holding hands walked down the aisle.

Once I became Mrs. Edward MacLean, I decided to spend less time as a therapist and more time with my beloved husband, family and friends. I thought Eddy would burst from happiness. Every day was radiant, vividly expressing how we felt about each other. Eddy and I each wore wedding bands that pleased him no end. He was generous to a fault and would have given me the moon had it been possible and yet all I needed or wanted was Eddy. He surprised me with a beautiful diamond bracelet on my birthday and it became the only jewelry I wanted to wear.

I sent him a dozen long stemmed red roses "just because I love you" and he glowed with love. "Anna, nobody ever sent me flowers before."

Matthew told Daniel "Eddy seems to be a good man . . . mother seems awfully happy, don't you think" but he never said anything to me. I noticed the next time we all met he was much friendlier towards Eddy though still somewhat cautious. I was pleased . . . progress had been made.

Our lives were filled with bliss. Listening to music, reading, gardening, ordinary little chores . . . when done together filled us with wondrous delight.

There has always been a small fear within me when I am exceptionally happy . . . something to do with those myths and tales about not tempting the gods.

Matthew telephones me and in a quivering voice asks is Eddy there with you?

"Yes, Matthew, he's here. What's wrong?" I start to shake. Eddy is immediately at my side once he has heard my question.

"Mother, Daniel just called and asked me to call you. Jackie and Adam were killed instantly in a head-on collision with a big rig that went out of control."

"Oh my God . . . please . . . what about young John?"

"He was at home with the baby sitter. Jackie had picked up Adam after a competitive basketball game in another school . . . that's why she was on the freeway."

"Where's Daniel? Is he all right? Oh, dear Lord . . . I can't believe this."

"Daniel was at work . . . the accident happened around five o'clock."

"Matthew, thank you for calling. Eddy and I will pick up John if that is what Daniel wants. What should we do? I don't want to complicate things."

"Mother, I'll call you as soon as I talk to Daniel again."

I give Eddy an overview of Matthew's inputs, telling him Jackie and Adam are dead. There is a dead stillness within me and a pain in my chest that I recognize from past losses. I need to cry but for the moment feel immobile. Only when Eddy's stricken eyes peer into mine with the depth of his love do I finally crumble and the tears flow as if from a broken dam.

Daniel buries Jackie and Adam on top of a small mountain cemetery not very far from his log cabin. It is a simple service with only the immediate family. Young John is staying with Grandpa Eddy and Babba. No permanent arrangements have been made for his future care. John is lonely and can't fully grasp the entire situation except that he wants his mother and brother to come back, but knows full well they can't. My heart goes out to him . . . as an adult I have had similar feelings in the past when I lost Joel.

Matthew suggests that John and Daniel move in with him. He has a full time nanny, Katherine's nanny, who would be willing to take care of John along with Matthew's children.

Daniel is too distraught to think straight but knows he has to do something about John's care. He can't leave his job right now but perhaps John will be happier having children around . . . he'll be less lonely . . . and Pamela and he are close in age.

Matthew also knows Daniel is not in a financial position to pay for child care though he never mentions this part of the problem to his older brother. Daniel finally agrees it is probably better that John live at Matthew's with family until he can sort things out. Knowing John will also have easier access to his Babba and Grandpa Eddy apparently influence Daniel's decision. Initially, John is overwhelmed with his cousins' generosity and company but with time, which is what I expected, I see him missing his mother and brother and yearning for his dad.

Daniel visits every weekend, occasionally dropping in with John to visit Eddy and me. He looks ravaged by grief and I am concerned, and certain, his demons have returned. I fear he is drinking to stave off his demons that I know is a temporary way to fend them off. Grief fades so reluctantly.

Matthew has found solace in God while Daniel is very much a doubting Thomas. Eddy and I feel his anguish and pain but acknowledge there is little more we can do for Daniel at this time. I fervently pray for Daniel's soul and ask for God's help in guiding Daniel during these difficult days. I feel he is lost and often spiraling in a futile manner.

I give thanks to God for Eddy's loving presence in my life and the tremendous joy I experience in loving him in spite of the sorrow I now feel for Daniel and his son, John.

In a commemoration of a deceased child, there is an old Chinese verse that sings:

> *If I keep a green bough in my heart,*
> *The singing bird will come.*

The bird is the deceased child and the green bough loving thoughts of the child. It is further stated that every time you act in a loving, selfless manner, your deceased child will appear . . . and through memories you can keep her with you forever.

I have so many loving memories of people who have died; thus I relate to the simplicity and truth expressed in this Chinese verse. But I recognize Daniel is in a different place. I feel he is struggling with the most profound mysteries of life and death and asking himself what embodies the secret of life. I trust he will find peace in his heart before too long.

I recently wrote a poem in memory of a baby that passed away, when she entered my dreams and my heart, that I dedicated to her loving parents. I changed the names in my original poem and hope this special copy of the poem for Daniel may provide him with some comfort.

Ribbons of Light

My dream is filled with ribbons of light
I hear the birds joyously sing a lullaby
A chorus of buttercups, daisies and violets sway in happy unison
to Jackie and Adam's song
The leaves rustle in branches of trees whispering your names,
Jackie and Adam
I see you float gently in the blue heavens

You sing in my ear, caress my face
You are so near. My soul is filled with peace and love.

At first I reluctantly awake
There is warm sunlight on my face
I see ribbons of light. It is deja vu
There is a gentle brush upon my cheek
Do I hear gossamer wings fly by?
I breathe your names, beloved Jackie and Adam
My spirit soars with yours
I need not struggle to face the day knowing you are both with me always
Your purity and innocence are in the song of a humming bird,
in the flowers that bloom, in the light within us all
You are both within my heart and soul forever.

Evening reflections reaffirm I will celebrate your lives each day
knowing when the day is done, I will look upward to the sky to see your shining stars.

Chapter Eighteen

Memories and a miracle

Courage is the price that life exacts for granting peace.
The soul that knows it not, knows no release
From little things;
Knows not the livid loneliness of fear,
Nor mountain heights where bitter joy can hear
The sound of wings.
        Amelia Earhart Putnam

I have been married to Eddy for the past five years and together we have been living our lives on God's schedule, giving thanks daily for the love we have for each other and the joys of each precious day. We continue to be pleasantly surprised that our years together have only strengthened our love that seems impossible given we both love each other so much.

We enjoy the brilliant sunrises, the blooming flowers, chirping birds, children playing in the park, the magnificent sunsets and twilight hours that are my favorites at the end of a loving day. I no longer mourn those that I loved as I have learned to accept the present as my truth.

I acknowledge my sons, Daniel and Matthew have been an ongoing source of sorrow and joy in my life. I have accepted and finally forgiven myself for not always being a wise mother. Perhaps I can now state, without embarrassment, one of my strongest characteristics was my steadfast love for my children, even when I considered their actions to be unlovable.

Daniel and Matthew were strongly shaped by built-in characteristics such as gender, internal qualities such as intelligence or personality, external conditions such as their family background and the education they acquired. It sounds simple enough but the reality was far more complex. I once read "What would happen to our children if we could raise them in a world of smiles?" Would their growth and development be more wholesome?

My grandchildren continue to be true delights in my life. They inspire and encourage me to still face life as openly as they do, as has always been my bent, and to dream the impossible dream that they first heard about from Babba when they were only toddlers. In spite of their major losses, they are basically optimistic, cheerful children who share with Babba their vision that something wonderful is going to happen. Consequently together we often make it happen and share magical moments that pleasure their young souls.

Recently when I was cleaning out a closet, I came across a cardboard box, long hidden in a suitcase, that I had made as a child while playing with Jeannine who later became a Catholic nun. It was decorated with ribbons, crepe paper and a daisy flower made from various buttons. In the right-hand corner of the box, I had printed in rather awkward letters "Treasure Chest." What was in there after a lifetime of living? I opened the box with eager anticipation to behold what I deemed to be treasures from my early childhood.

Wrapped in pink tissue paper were Aurora's beads. Next was a packet of cards and letters Lily had sent me in her lifetime, including those she wrote when she was at medical school in Harvard. There was a small bracelet Billy had made in handicrafts at school . . . I remember how he nearly drove my mother mad when he kept dipping my blond pigtails in ink to see them turn green.

There was a yellowed newspaper article about Ryan O'Reilly's arrest, the young man that lent me his young sister, Kelly's skates that boosted my confidence beyond belief. There were articles I had written as the editor for our school paper. A dried up corsage that reminded me of the prom . . . I discovered colored pieces of glass, special buttons with "peace," "love" and more written on them . . . and tucked away in my high school autograph book I found a promise that I had written to myself, part of which said:

> *Live your life courageously with honesty and integrity, value the differences in others, enrich the lives of those less fortunate than you, and strive always to make a positive difference in the world. Dream your dreams knowing nothing is impossible with God's help.*

I apparently wrote these words when I was fifteen years old. They still felt right today.

I put everything back in my Treasure Chest with the realization, once again, that memories linger on . . . we may modify them with the passage of time . . . and in the telling of them . . . but they are an integral part of our lives.

In his book "A Sense of the Future," the author J. Bronowski talks about what makes up morality

> *"One is the sense that other people matter: the sense of common loyalty, of charity and tenderness, the sense of human love. The other is a clear judgment of what is at stake: a cold knowledge, without a trace of deception, of precisely what will happen to oneself and to others if one plays either the hero or the coward. This is the highest morality: to combine human love with an unflinching, a scientific judgment."*

The author was making reference to the fact that he took a different view of a scientist's duty than that which the scientist held. He eloquently went on to say:

> *"For the essence of morality is not that we should all act alike. The essence of morality is that each of us should deeply search his own conscience . . . and should then act steadfastly as it tells him to do."*

I always remain hopeful for the future when I read the works of an extraordinary teacher like Mr. Bronowski as his brilliant insights reflect the thoughts and feelings we may wish we could express. My books have continued to provide me access to outstanding noble men and women and I am truly grateful for their presence, past or present.

In the evening, I discussed with Eddy the emotional impact the articles in my Treasure Chest had on me and for some reason, how it got me thinking about Mr. Bronowski's wisdom. Eddy too was a voracious reader who enjoyed waxing philosophically about many things.

Eddy and I discussed how much people had always mattered to me and the tremendous satisfaction I felt as a therapist when I saw individuals, in some instances, overcome mammoth traumas in their lives. I knew how deeply these individuals searched their own consciences before they reconciled major issues in their lives.

Eventually, our conversation turned to Eddy's pending appointment tomorrow with his cardiologist. While this was a scheduled routine visit, I wanted to be there with Eddy to ensure there were no problems particularly since we were planning to travel to Spain and Portugal next week.

"Anna, everything is fine . . . I feel better than I ever have . . . but all right, come along and we'll go out to a romantic lunch afterwards."

The cardiologist gave us a brief report in medical jargon . . .

then looked at my face, then at Eddy, then back at me again, and said . . . "whatever you're doing to your husband sure is working . . . it's close to a miracle . . . his heart seems to be back to normal . . . I don't have a medical explanation for what has happened."

There was silence until we realized what we had heard.

"I have an explanation . . . it's our love" said Eddy as we simultaneously rose from our chairs to hug and kiss each other in front of Eddy's startled doctor.

"Well, Eddy you are a fortunate man indeed. Continue living your life as you have. It obviously works."

I felt my feet weren't touching the pavement . . . "Eddy, I believe I'm floating on a cloud . . . our special cloud."

We laughed like delighted children. "Anna, Anna . . . I'm going to tell the world I love you." He lifted his head up to the sky and shouted "I love Anna, Anna, my beloved Anna."

A young couple walking by, that witnessed Eddy's spontaneous declaration of love, burst into wide smiles and the young man turned to his young lady and said "let's be in love like they are when we grow older."

Us older . . . Eddy and I were feeling younger every day . . . especially on this precious day. On to Spain and Portugal where Eddy and I would learn to dance amorous dances under the light of the moon.

I was too happy for words so I skipped down the street as I had done when I was a very young Anuska. Eddy caught up with me . . . took my hand and together we skipped our way back to the car oblivious of bystanders close by.

Chapter Nineteen

Thoughts of life . . . hopes for the future

*First keep the peace within yourself,
then you can also bring peace to others.*
      Thomas A. Kempis

In this last chapter, I wish to share some of my most recent thoughts and feelings about serious and difficult subjects that embody and forge our values. I also wish to bring you up-to-date on my own family and others whose lives touched mine.

Perhaps we can agree with this simple, generalized statement "People experience various degrees of joy, grief, hope and love in their lifetimes." When I pause to reflect on what has been in the circle of my life so far, I realize the unknown is still out there that I can face with fear and trepidation or enthusiasm, hope and interest. I have decided to choose the latter. Life is wonderful and people matter.

Recently, I attended an art exhibit featuring various renown present-day artists. I was intrigued by a modernist mural, was trying to identify what exactly fascinated me so much and why I found it to be somewhat mysterious. I felt a familiar, strong energy emanating from the mural towards me that I did not understand. I was also flabbergasted at the price of the mural that was already sold, and was getting ready to read the artist's name when someone gently tapped me on the shoulder. I turned around and there was Steven, sculptor, artist, a former client of mine many, many years ago.

"Anna, it's been a long time. You look well. So what do you think?"

"Steven, what a surprise. Is this mural yours? I didn't get beyond the price."

"Yes, Anna, I keep expanding my horizons. Isn't it amazing what people will pay. It seems everything I do lately turns into gold. Mine you I'm not complaining."

"Steven, I could feel this energy from your mural. The more I looked at it, the more I wanted to look at it but I really didn't know why. Now I understand completely."

"You've always been honest. I always felt that someday we would meet again and here we are."

"Are you still living in San Francisco, Steven?"

"Only this past year. I lived in Italy for a couple years, then in France. I traveled around the world but now I plan on staying here for a long time."

A pretty, petite, woman holding a young boy's hand walked towards Steven and smiled at both of us.

"Anna, I want you to meet my wife, Daphne and my son, Richard."

As a professional, I would not reveal I had been Steven's therapist but Steven went on to say, "Daphne, Anna is the therapist I told you about who changed my life."

Eddy returned and new introductions were made with no further reference to my past relationship with Steven. Steven asked Eddy if he could hug his wife goodbye. When he hugged me he whispered in my ear "Thank you for saving my life."

As the three of them walked away, with their son Richard in the middle, holding his mother's and father's hand, I knew in my heart, Steven was a loving father to his son. I remembered too well how brutally Steven's father had treated him and his brothers and how fearful his mother was of her husband. I remembered how important it was to Steven when his mother secretly gave him some money wrapped up in a handkerchief when he left home.

Shortly after seeing Steven serendipity surprised me again. I received a letter from a patient that was forwarded to me from the clinic where I did my internship . . . the circumstances of this happening were very unusual. I had seen this patient, Shirley, for approximately two years, about seven years ago. The letter was prefaced by a heartfelt, sincere thank you for the work we had done together, followed by a lengthy description of her life in the past seven years. I was filled with pathos and joy as I read about her ongoing victorious struggle to live a good life free of her past drug addictions. She had written this letter to me because she felt it was important I know she had led a decent life during the last seven years . . . she was terminally ill . . . had little time left to say goodbye to the few people in her life she cared about. There is a sentence in her letter I heard her say in therapy. "You told me I mattered . . . that everyone matters. You helped me realize I wasn't just garbage like so many people said."

No matter how many patients I had, I had the ability to remember each one's history and the work we had done together. Very briefly, Shirley's parents were both drug addicts . . . her brother committed suicide when he was twelve . . . Shirley got pregnant when she was fifteen . . . had a miscarriage . . . was despondent . . . and starting using drugs.

Shirley's life mattered. Her enormous courage in writing this letter to me, during her final days, that turned out to be a documented summary of her life when she knew she wasn't garbage, was her final testament.

I was filled with deep, mixed emotions upon receiving her gift of love that she had so generously shared with me. I spent some silent time in prayer and meditation, as well as giving thanks to God that Shirley had found peace at last.

It had been some time since I had spoken to Matthew and Daniel. I was pleased when Matthew called to say he was planning to marry Maureen, a nurse, in the near future. He had been dating her for about a year. She was a compassionate person with an easy-going personality who loved children, homemaking . . . cooking, baking, sewing, gardening . . . and Matthew informed me she planned to be a full time, stay-at-home wife when they married. She came from a large family and was not overwhelmed that Matthew had three children, and Daniel's son that was permanently living there as well.

Nana, as all the grandchildren called her, who was Katherine's childhood nanny and had been with the family since Katherine's death, would be staying with them after the marriage. She was now considered part of the family and several years ago, Matthew had built a three-room unit attached to their home for her private use and more senior years. He had employed his outstanding architectural skills in building the addition that now greatly enhanced his home. Matthew told me Daniel and he had already discussed his pending engagement and marriage. Maureen had always accepted that Daniel's son, John, was part of the family.

The grandchildren informed me, their Babba, that Maureen was pretty cool. She told them she didn't want to be a stepmother . . . it might remind them as it did her of the "wicked stepmother" in fairy tales . . . but she would like to be a friend and help Nana bring them up. She told them "I love your daddy."

Nana liked her right from the start and advised the children "Maureen will help me to make sure you children watch your 'Ps and Qs' . . . I can't get around as fast as I used to."

The children had laughed happily at Nana's favorite expression.

I continued to be concerned about Daniel's life that seemed to be devoid of personal friendships. Since Jackie and Adam's deaths, apart from seeing his son, John, it looked like he was completely isolated from everyone. While he maintained regular contact with me and Eddy, there was a definite lack of substance to our conversations.

My sons and grandchildren had experienced divorce, illness and death that were major crises in their lives. I would never forget Matthew had also been sexually abused by his biological father. These traumas profoundly transformed our original family system, and my sons' respective family systems. We never returned to our former functioning as a result.

When I was a young child growing up the roles of the mother and father were usually clear cut. Simply stated the father went to work to provide the necessary money for shelter, food and clothing. The mother stayed home to raise the children and take care of the home.

There were women, in the minority, such as myself, that pursued careers due to a variety of reasons but usually because of financial necessity.

Today, the percentage of working mothers far exceeds mothers who stay at home. Current data suggests that mothers must work to provide more income to meet the family's regular living expenses. I am saddened and filled with compassion for mothers who give birth to their children and are not there to raise them. I know only too well the emotional difficulties women often experience when this is the case.

As a therapist, I constantly saw how difficult it was for many families to balance child care and work responsibilities along with their parenting responsibilities. Cultural considerations could not be ignored . . . the differences that had to be addressed when they were important to a family's welfare. Oftentimes, the child's caretaker was hampered in communicating with the child due to minimum knowledge of the family's language. In the early stages of a child's development, there was often confusion as to who was the prominent role model for the child.

Many parents also found it more difficult to develop family rituals and traditions because they are "overworked, stressed out and lack the time to do everything that needs to be done."

Over the years, I noticed that many children in California are being raised by women whose primary language isn't English, and as a consequence of their employment, their own children are often being raised by a grandmother or other family member.

What concerns me is that, in too many instances, we appear to be creating circumstances for our growing children where good language is lacking to daily communicate and teach the parent's basic moral and spiritual values. In the limited time they have, I believe the majority of working parents make the effort to nurture their children and impart their family values to them.

But the evidence of delinquency, violence and increasing divorce rate cannot be ignored and strongly suggests we need to improve the care we provide our children regardless where that care is coming from. Are we failing our children? Do our young children believe they are less important than a mother's career?

When a young child becomes an adolescent, to what extent are we as parents involved in their education and school problems?

Have we established a strong bond since their birth so our teenagers can discuss some of their sexuality issues with us . . . they know our family values and we feel confident we have done "good enough parenting" to date. When I was a young girl, sex was never openly discussed in our family. It was usually the norm in most families. I have not questioned why but have been thankful, I have always, and still enjoy a wonderful healthy sex life with my beloved Eddy. The extent of sex education with my mother was "don't get pregnant before you're married . . . it will ruin your life and shame our family."

The most dramatic contrast to my happy situation was Cynthia, a frightened patient whose religious family had instilled in her that sex was sinful. She suffered the pangs of guilt every time she tried to respond to her husband's love making and finally came to therapy when she could no longer tolerate seeing her generous, kind hearted, loving husband as an evil monster whenever he tried to make love to her.

The pendulum appears to have swung too far the other way. While we may agree sex is no longer a taboo subject, there are still too many children having children . . . we are still confronted with sexual diseases including Aids . . . and sexual deviancy, rape and violence prevail in our society.

I wish I had magical answers to the difficult problems that we as a people face today. I only know the importance of a nurturing, loving environment . . . the importance of a child bonding with its mother in the early years of its life . . . and the importance of a father's love. I applaud the many fathers who are very active in their children's lives, comfortable in expressing their love openly though many of them did not have this experience with their own fathers.

I continue to be hopeful that professionals, in cooperation with families, can envision and develop a more creative healthy working structure for families when both parents work. I would like to make available, to all families, programs that educate families about parenting skills.

As I reflected on my past experience with my own family and the families I worked with in therapy, I observed significant, positive changes took place in children when:

Parents improved their communication so their words were clear, straightforward and addressed thoughts, feelings and needs in a loving way.

Parents emphasized the positive in their children's lives thus allowing them to continue to build their self esteem.

Parents introduced alternatives in their children's lives thus strengthening their positions as role models.

When I think of Daniel and Matthew, I know it was not always easy to abide by those few stated thoughts. As an example, at a certain age children may not welcome the introduction of alternatives in their life, and as a parent, I may not always have an alternative to offer.

I believe Walter Kempler stated best what I aspire for myself and those I love:

> *"the ability for people to say who they are and what they want; the capacity to be a separate person and to accept the differences of others; and willingness and ability to stay in the here-and-now."*

I strongly believe we must teach our children to love, not hate . . . to celebrate our differences, not fear them . . . and teach them at an early age they can make a difference in the world. I have always been grateful that I grew up with a variety of ethnic families that enriched my life. I am pleased my sons did not grow up in a family environment that was conducive to hatred and discrimination and were taught they had a voice in fighting it when necessary.

There is an Irish Proverb that states "It is in the shelter of each other that people live."

In speaking of living, I will segue to two of my best friends, Jane from the book club and a professional colleague, Donna, who are valiantly battling cancer. They have positive attitudes, loving families and friends but are quick to acknowledge this is the biggest challenge they have ever faced. I pray for both of them. These great ladies have been positive influences in my life and I enjoy and treasure the friendships we have.

Am I more aware of my mortality as I age? Certainly and I readily acknowledge that I have reached the wondrous autumn years of my life. I do not fear death. Rather, I fear not living life. Thus I am pleased I continue to maintain new hopes and dreams that I expect to experience in my ongoing years.

When my friend, Helene passed away, she did so with eagerness, looking forward to the new vistas ahead of her. Though she was in much pain at times, she relished our farewell time together that was filled with endless possibilities of what might transpire in her transition from her earthly form. I am reminded of

> *Drawing near her death, she sent most pious thoughts as harbingers to heaven; and her soul saw a glimpse of happiness through the chinks of her sickness-broken body.*
>
> Thomas Fuller

. . . as well as

> *A good death does honor to a whole life by Petrarch.*

I have a zest for living that has been temporarily challenged many times . . . and yet hope always finally springs eternal in my breast.

Last week, I attended a luncheon that was held to honor me for my outstanding contribution in the community working with incest survivors. The person who presented the honorary plaque was none other than Lisa, the German model, my client so many years ago. She had recently gone public with her incest history and had resumed her modeling career. Lisa hoped her story would encourage others to be less fearful and come out of the shadows of secrecy and seek help as she did.

As for Matthew, he chose a totally different path regarding the molestation that his wife told me about. He communicated very emphatically that he would never discuss anything related to his father with me. With much work, I have forgiven myself for not knowing what was happening to my son, Matthew. I found some solace and peace remembering God knows this is the truth.

I was reading the other day how difficult it is for parents to realize their children are adults but sometimes more difficult for the children to realize that their parents are not the people they were when they were growing up.

Today I know I was attracted to the field of psychology, like many others in this profession, so I could explore the range of human experience with the hope that I could demystify some of its mysteries. If I am less nonplused in certain areas of my life, perhaps it is because I recognize my journey is a lifelong exploration. With Eddy at my side, I continue to seek new insights into our spiritual life that I believe ultimately sustains life.

How best can I describe my feelings for Eddy. I enjoy my young grand daughter, Pamela's declaration of love for her Babba. When I am feeling playful, I borrow it sometimes to tell my Eddy how I feel. "I love you Eddy oceans and oceans full . . . I love you bigger than all the highest mountains . . . I love you bigger than the universe." We both know ours is a passionate love filled with constant delight and wonder.

I am well aware that I also loved Joel whose spirit is a part of my soul. As I reflect over the years of my life, I recall that I loved Eddy as a friend since the age of sixteen. What a wonderful gift it was that after our first passionate kiss when Eddy first came to see me in San Francisco a couple of years after Joel's death, my love for Eddy blossomed into a deep love. With the passage of time, Eddy still continues to ignite my feelings as no man ever has through the touch of his hand, a simple caress, a hug, or his loving look. He responds the same way to all my acts of love.

We both believe Eddy's ongoing good health that doctors called a miracle, is one of God's blessing of our love.

Eddy and I often have discussions about eternity, our belief that spirits are eternal and that our love is eternal as well. My belief in God allows me to accept without fear that some of life's mysteries will only be revealed after my death. I know God's plan takes care of all the details in the hereafter.

It is a tranquil evening. Eddy and I have walked to the ocean to see another magnificent sunset. Tonight I am overwhelmed with the spectacular beauty around me. I lift my arms above my head reaching to the sky. I feel a light brush of the wind kiss my cheek, an angel's kiss. There is the faint flutter of wings. I remain very still so I will hear clearly the wind whispering as I remember my beloved parents, Joel, Katherine, Jackie, Adam, Uncle Mike and friends Lily and Helene. Their spirits enrich my soul and I am at peace.

Eddy is standing behind me. He embraces me with his arms and I lean against his chest. I feel our hearts beating as one.

I turn towards him in his embrace. At the same time we say "I love you." We kiss enraptured with each other.

"Let's go home, Anna." His deep blue eyes are brimming with love. He takes me by the hand and together we walk into the sunset just like in all my dreams.

The person I now am is the person I had to be.

EPILOGUE

I strongly believe that Anna will continue to celebrate her life with Eddy while remaining fully aware that her personal journey and personal evolution continue dependent on the interplay between herself and others in the world.

I also believe, as Anna would, that each one of us can only attain our fullest personal development with God's guidance and the courage to always be oneself with others.

We have the freedom to love, the predominant creative experience available to most of us. We have the ability to find more goals in our lives that may contribute to the evolution of a society that ensures all human beings experience equality, freedom and human dignity.

It is never too late to actively renounce hate and greed and to dedicate ourselves to creating a world where we may all live peacefully and joyously regardless of gender, race or religion.

I wish that every one of you may delight in the wonder of life and allow your spirit to soar all the days of your life . . . Life is a Promise.

BIBLIOGRAPHY

Abnormal Psychology: Experiences, Origins, and Interventions, Michael J. Goldstein, Bruce L. Baker, Kay R. Jamison, Little, Brown and Company, Boston; Toronto, Canada, 1986.

Adolescent Psychology: A Developmental View, Norman A. Sprinthall, W. Andrew Collins, Random House, New York 1984.

Aging Well: A Guide For Successful Seniors, James F. Fries, M.D., Addison-Wesley Publishing Company, Reading, Massachusetts, 1989. Schuster, New York, 1989.

A Sense of The Future: Essays in Natural Philosophy, J. Bronowski, The MIT Press, Cambridge, Massachusetts, and London, England, 1977.

Bartlett's Familiar Quotations: A collection of passages, phrases and proverbs traced to their sources in ancient and modern literature, John Bartlett, Little, Brown and Company, Boston; Toronto, Canada, 1968.

Beneath The Mask: An Introduction to Theories of Personality, Christopher F. Monte, Holt, Rinehart and Winston, Inc., New York, 1987.

Fantastic Worlds: Myths, Tales, and Stories, Edited by Eric S. Rabkin, Oxford University Press, Inc., New York, and Oxford, England, 1979.

Flow: The Psychology of Optimal Experience, Mihaly Csikszentmihalyi, Harper & Row, New York , 1990.

Healing Into Life and Death, Stephen Levine, Doubleday, New York, 1987.

Higher Creativity: Liberating the Unconscious for Breakthrough Insights, Willis Harman, Ph.D., Howard Rheingold, The Putnam Publishing Group, New York, 1984/

Illusion and Disillusion: The Self in Love and Marriage, John F. Crosby, Wadsworth Publishing Company, Belmont, California, 1985.

Learning Psychotherapy: Rationale and Ground Rules, Hilde Bruch, M.D., Harvard University Press, 1974.

Life's Handicap: Being Stories of Mine Own People, Rudyard Kipling, Doubleday, Page and Company, 1913

Poems from Tennyson, Browning and Wordsworth, Edited by W. J. Alexander, Ph.D., The Copp Clark Company, Ltd., 1939

Proverbs for Busy Women: Devotions to Refresh You in Your Work, Edited by Mary C. Busha, Broadman & Holman Publishers, 1995.

Our Sexuality: Robert Crooks, Karla Baur, The Benjamin/Cummings Publishing Company, Inc. Menlo Park, California, 1987.

Self and Others: Object Relations Theory in Practice, N. Gregory Hamilton, M.D., Jason Aronson Inc., Northvale, New Jersey, 1988.

Self Esteem: Its Conceptualization and Measurement, L. Edward Wells, Gerald Marwell, Sage Publications, Beverly Hills, California, 1976.

Spiritual Emergency: When Personal Transformation Becomes A Crisis, Edited by Stanislav Grof, M.D., Christina Grof, Jeremy P. Tarcher, Inc., Los Angeles,

1989.

The Golden Book of Modern English Poetry: An Anthology, Thomas Caldwell, J. M. Dent & Sons Ltd., London, England, First Published in 1922.

The Heart of Psychotherapy: A Journey into the Mind and Office of the Therapist at Work, George Weinberg, St. Martin's Press/New York, 1984.

The Inward Arc: Healing & Wholeness in Psychotherapy & Spirituality, Frances Vaughan, Shambhala Publications, Inc., 1985.

The Primitive Edge of Experience, Thomas H. Ogden, M.D., Jason Aronson Inc., Northvale, New Jersey, 1989.

The Seat of The Soul, Gary Zukav, Simon & Schuster, New York, 1990.

The Transparent Self: Sidney M. Jourard, Van Nostrand Reinhold, New York, 1971.

The Treasured Writings of Kahlil Gibran: Kahlil Gibran, Castle Books, U.S.A., 1980.

The Wheel of Life and Death: A Practical and Spiritual Guide, Philip Kapleau, Doubleday, New York, 1989.

Trauma and Its Wake: The Study and Treatment of Post-Traumatic Stress Disorder, Edited by Charles R. Figley, Ph.D., Brunner/Mazel, Publishers, New York, 1985.

Treating The Self: Elements of Clinical Self Psychology, Ernest S. Wolf, The Guilford Press, New York, 1988.